Inspector John Sanders &
Harriet Jeffries

2. Murder in Focus
3. Murder in a Good Cause
4. Sleep of the Innocent
5. Pursued by Shadows

MURDER IN FOCUS

MURDER IN FOCUS

MEDORA SALE

Charles Scribner's Sons • New York

Copyright © 1989 by Medora Sale

Charles Scribner's Sons
Macmillan Publishing Company
866 Third Avenue, New York, NY 10022

This is a work of fiction. Names, characters, places, and incidents either are the product of the author's imagination or are used fictitiously. Any resemblance to actual events or persons, living or dead, is entirely coincidental.

Libraby of Congress Cataloging-in-Publication Data
Sale, Medora.
   Murder in focus.
   I. Title.   I. Mys. +d.
PR9199.3.S165M87   1989   813'.54   89–5851
ISBN 0-684-19082-6

                    10 9 8 7 6 5 4 3 2 1

Printed in the United States of America

To Denise,
a small return for all that she has done

Police jurisdictions exerting control around the city of Ottawa:

FEDERAL

(1) The Royal Canadian Mounted Police (RCMP, or "Mounties")

- responsible for investigating crime involving the breaking of federal laws—e.g., drugs, immigration, currency, and organized crime;
- responsible for operations involving internal security. Canada's intelligence-gathering service, until recently part of the RCMP, has been separated off because of certain well-publicized abuses on the part of some intelligence officers, and has become:

(2) Canadian Security Intelligence Service or CSIS (commonly pronounced Ceesis).

PROVINCIAL

(3) Ontario Provincial Police (OPP)

LOCAL

(4) Ottawa Police Department

(5) Capital Region Police Department (operating in the broad area surrounding the city of Ottawa)

And, of course, there are:

(6) the combined military forces (army, navy, air force; now rolled into one).

MURDER IN FOCUS

CHAPTER 1

Ottawa: Thursday, April 20

Superintendent Henri Deschenes of the Royal Canadian Mounted Police (Security Service—Operations) opened his car door and paused before getting out. The pause might have been for thought, or for sentimental appreciation of the beauty of the spring day, but it wasn't. Difficult as it was for him to admit, that pause was to gather enough strength to walk across the parking lot, into the building, and over to the elevator with an appearance of normality. This was his third morning at work after almost three months flat on his back, three months lost because he had tried to spend January working eighteen-hour days while incubating a case of pneumonia. It was the first sick leave he had ever taken, and now he felt aggrieved because he was even more tired this morning than he had been yesterday. What had been the point of all that rest? He got out of the car and straightened up. The cold wind whipped his clothes, all suddenly much too loose on his thin frame, and threatened to blow him over. He bent into it and marched, grimly, into the building.

Sylvia looked up from the morning's mail as he walked into the office. "You should be home in bed," she said in greeting. "You look like hell."

"I'm fine," he said. His shoulders tightened in irritation.

"And that snotty-faced brat from External is in there already, waiting for you. Sorry. I told you to stay home today."

"Metcalfe?"

"The one and only. Do you want coffee? Or should I just go in and tell him you aren't coming in? You can hide in Charlie Higgs's office. He won't mind."

He smiled at his secretary—a thin, weary smile—and shook his head. "Coffee, yes." The smile vanished. "I have to deal with Metcalfe at some point, and it might as well be now. And for chrissake, stop fussing over me," he added with a flash of anger. "I am not ill anymore."

"And I'm the queen of Morocco," said Sylvia, not at all cowed. "The bloody trade conference will go on even if you're not here, you know. And no one is going to get assassinated. This is Ottawa, for God's sake, not Beirut. Sir." She stood up. "I'll get you your coffee. Do you suppose the Boy Wonder wants some cookies with his?"

Henri Deschenes took a deep breath, felt the familiar stab of pain under a lower right rib from the lingering effects of pleurisy, and squared his shoulders. He hadn't wasted a moment thinking about standing upright since he'd been a rookie. Until this week. He threw open his door in a parody of his old vigor, hung up his coat, and turned to face the overeducated junior would-be diplomat from External Affairs who was lounging at ease in the visitor's chair. On his knee there rested a large file ostentatiously labeled, in large white letters within a bright blue diagonal slash across its front cover, "Third International Conference on Tariffs and Trade."

Twenty rambling minutes later, the atmosphere in Deschenes's office had become very tense. "What in hell are you talking about—the tour of the countryside?" snapped Deschenes.

"They fly into Uplands, Forces Base side, direct to Hangar Eleven. Guard of honor for heads of state. Then the army picks them up and drives them to their various embassies—"

"I'm beginning to think that's not such a good idea," said Hal Metcalfe brightly. "It might have been better to whisk them off somewhere where they can be kept under guard all the time. We could still hold the conference in the Gatineau—"

"It wasn't my idea to have the delegates scattered all over hell's half acre, Metcalfe." Deschenes's words were being dragged painfully out through his tightened jaw. "Remember? Before I went on leave, this was just another international conference. That was before your boss and my deputy director general got their hands on it. At least you've put the top-level meetings into a secure area." His hands lay clasped tightly together on his desk, and his entire body remained rigidly immobile. "I come back from three months' leave and I find that twenty senior officials and their aides, from twenty countries, are going to be staying in at least twenty—no, it's more like a hundred—different places. And we have the same number of trained men we had three months ago, not twenty times as many. You might point that out to your minister now— just so he isn't surprised when some of them get blown into oblivion and come raining down all over Hull." He unclenched his hands and reached into a drawer for his own file on the trade conference, marked "Sea Gull" in discreet red lettering. "But the program's been set for weeks." He tapped the manila folder impatiently. "There's nothing here about a tour of the countryside. They're not supposed to have time to go sightseeing. This is a working conference, and don't let your minister get any crazy ideas about anything else."

"It's too late." Metcalfe's voice was flat and gloomy. "It seems when the minister was in Germany last week he got into discussions with industry and trade relations people there. They were talking about expanding facilities into Canada—opening up new auto plants and kitchen gadget factories and I don't know what all kinds of crap like that. Anyway, he came up with this wonderful idea of a tour for anyone who wanted to come along—you know, possible sites for new industry, Halifax, St. John, Sherbrooke—"

"Sherbrooke?" Deschenes's eyes appeared to glaze over as Metcalfe named his hometown.

"You know the drill; spread it around. The Maritimes, Quebec, then a couple of days in Toronto—"

"All twenty groups?"

"I don't know." Metcalfe shrugged his shoulders. "Maybe not. He wanted to take everybody out to Calgary and then Vancouver, but they don't have the time. He was disappointed." He grinned. "He had been able to see himself in the news for at least five minutes every night for two weeks."

"I see. And I am expected to supply security on that level for a tour of factories, building sites, industrial parks?" Deschenes's voice began to rise.

"They realized that might be a problem," said Metcalfe apologetically.

"Oh, good."

"And what they want you to do is organize a training seminar for local police forces in all the towns and cities where the officials might want to visit." Metcalfe produced this statement as if it were the most natural thing in the world to suggest.

"Us? I see." At moments like this Deschenes's sentences came out in clipped little bursts with significant pauses in between each. In a temper, he reverted to the speech patterns of his French father instead of his English mother. "Do you know," he snapped, "what today's date is?" He pulled a desk calendar over in front of him. "It is the twentieth day of April. And do you know when the first delegates are supposed to arrive in Ottawa? The eighteenth day of May. The goddamn conference begins on the nineteenth. And just when am I supposed to train the police from God knows how many cities in the finer points of security? And who am I supposed to use to do the training?" He took a deep breath and surreptitiously pressed his hand over his lower right rib.

"Well . . ." Metcalfe hesitated. "The deputy minister thought that you could use the Special Emergency Response Team squad for training—after all, they never have much to do—"

"Holy Mary," muttered Deschenes. "SERT? We're trying to protect the poor bastards, not massacre them ourselves. He's crazy," he said, shaking his head. "You start teaching a bunch of untrained small-town cops how to rush a group of armed and dangerous men—in five or six days, or however much time they give us—and you'll end up with a lot of trigger-happy maniacs. They'd kill everyone in sight if trouble turned up. They're better off not knowing anything."

Metcalfe paid no attention. ". . . and that each municipality would send you one representative, and that man could go back and explain what to do to everyone else. So you wouldn't need a whole lot of instructors." Metcalfe tried to look Deschenes in the eye and failed. "Great idea, eh?"

The choking silence spread through the room. "Actually, that's not so bad." Deschenes pulled thoughtfully at his mustache. "That means that we really wouldn't have to train anybody. We wouldn't use SERT, of course." He stared off into a corner, counting off points on his fingers as he spoke, but muttering so softly that Metcalfe had to strain to hear him. "We just shoot the breeze about security problems and then pray. Besides, some of these cities do their own security as well as we would. We'll send our own people into the places that don't have enough manpower." He turned back to Metcalfe, brisk and businesslike once more. "Do you think your minister would let us vet the itinerary for this tour? We might be able to eliminate some of the more difficult locations. Before I resign?"

In Toronto a week later, a senior officer in the Metropolitan Toronto Police Force stood in his office with a memo in his hand and a look of outrage on his face. "What in hell do those bloody idiots in the Mounties think they are? Teach us how to manage security? When did we last lose someone?" His secretary waited patiently for the eruption to cease. "Papal visit," he muttered, "royals, even Americans. Not a hitch." His voice died away in a series of incoherent mumbles.

"Shall I tell them we don't need to send someone?"

"Oh, for God's sake, don't do that. They'll get offended, and there'll be hell to pay. And if anything goes wrong, it'll be our fault for not going. Tell them that—uh, let's see— Tom Flanagan will be down. He has a pal in the RCMP. He won't mind. Call Flanagan, will you?"

"Inspector Flanagan has been off on sick leave recently." Her voice was sweet but inflexible. "He's back on duty, but his ulcer is still bothering him."

"Bloody hell. I'd better see how he is first. But then," he said, brightening, "a week of sweet f.a. in Ottawa will do him no end of good."

Wednesday, April 26

Superintendent Henri Deschenes was at his desk, experimenting with various postures, trying to find one that allowed him a certain air of authority—or at least dignity—without putting stress on his aching ribcage. There didn't seem to be one. His door opened and Sylvia poked her head into the room. "My God, you look as if someone starched your underwear," she said. "Are you all right?" He glared at her. "I see you are. Good. Charlie Higgs and Ian MacMillan are here. I'll send them in, shall I?" Her head disappeared before he had a chance to respond.

Two men walked into the room and Deschenes stood up. One was thin and gloomy, sunken-cheeked, and dark in hair and eyes; the other was fair and freckled, broad-shouldered, sandy-haired, and hearty in manner. Henri Deschenes was not a particularly small man, but these two filled the room on the other side of the desk. Deschenes sat down again, unperturbed. He was used to being dwarfed by his subordinates. There was a stack of files marked "Sea Gull" on one side of his desk and a single piece of paper in front of him.

"The training seminar for local police forces has been dumped back on us," he said without preamble. The two men sat down. "I tried to push it off on someone who isn't as swamped right now as we are, but no luck." He spoke without rancor. He picked up the memo from his desk. "This is my memo to the deputy director general. I thought you both ought to hear it before I send it on."

He read in a flat, expressionless tone. " 'Re: Security Seminar. Staffing in this department, as you are aware, is particularly tight at the moment and the trade conference is putting extra strain on the department, which is already below minimal strength. In addition, I have few men at my disposal whom I would choose to run an operation that is likely to become politically sensitive. Therefore I am relieving Inspector Charles Higgs of his duties as chief security officer for the conference's secure site and seconding him to this seminar. He understands the problems and will be able to communicate solutions effectively. I trust that the director general and the Department of External Affairs consider this duty to be worth the reduction in effectiveness at the site that it will cause.' That's a warning to the director and to the minister to stop buggering around with our arrangements," he said with sudden ferocity and uncharacteristic crudeness. "Sylvia wrote it. She's good at these things." He nodded and leaned back, looking from one to the other in turn.

"Politically sensitive?" said the dark man.

"When one of those delegates gets blown up in Sault Sainte Marie, ten feet away from the guy you trained, there's going to be a hell of a lot of fallout, Charlie. So be prepared."

"Wonderful," said Charlie Higgs, looking even gloomier than he had when he walked into the room.

"With luck we'll be able to blame it all on Deputy Minister bloody Gifford," said Deschenes. "I'm sorry, Charlie. I really did think we were going to be able to push this thing off onto Training and Development and get rid of it, but Benton's smarter than I took him for. He dumped it right back on us."

"It's going to take a long time to set all this up, you know," said Higgs. His tone had shifted from gloomy to hostile. "Jesus, I'm going to have to find lecture rooms and accommodations and . . ." His voice trailed away hopelessly.

"Just as long as you've got rid of them all before the conference starts. Or at least before the delegates set out for their little tour, Charlie. That's all we need. To be able to say we did it. Okay?" He straightened up again to signal the end of the interview. They both stood up. "A word with you, Ian. Thanks, Charlie. Work out some sort of agenda and let me have a look at it, eh?" Higgs nodded and left the room in silence.

"A lousy job," said Deschenes, shaking his head. "I hate giving it to anyone. But Charlie should be able to handle it. Sit down, Ian. This leaves us in something of a hole as far as the conference goes, of course."

Inspector Ian MacMillan abandoned formality and settled himself down in the more comfortable of the two chairs in front of Deschenes's desk, stretching his legs out in front of him. "You want me to take over the secure site from Charlie?" he said. "Sounds kind of interesting. I haven't even been out there yet."

Deschenes shook his head. "It's well established and running smoothly. Carpenter can look after it. Still, it doesn't hurt to shake up the director general's office a bit, even if you don't really expect trouble. Anyway, now that I'm back and fully operational, I'll be taking over the day-to-day direction of the whole operation myself."

MacMillan sat up, with a puzzled lift of his eyebrows. "Then what . . ." His voice trailed off good-naturedly into a question, but his blue eyes remained sharp and cold, as always.

"I need someone to coordinate security for the rest of the conference. Can you handle that as well as continue to monitor intelligence reports?"

"Jesus." MacMillan shook his head. "That sounds like three or four full-time jobs." He thought for a moment. "I'll need some more men. Good ones. At least three."

Deschenes shook his head doubtfully. "I'll see what I can find. I can't promise you much, though. Just about everyone available with half a brain has already been assigned.

"Dammit," said MacMillan. "I sure as hell could use Steve Collins right now. Do you think there's any way we could get him back from Intelligence on temporary assignment? There must be some sort of emergency proviso in all those new regulations."

Deschenes shook his head. "Not a chance."

"I haven't seen him around lately," added MacMillan. "He is still with those bastards at CSIS, isn't he?" His thick, pale brows creased with incredulity. "I never could figure why he decided to leave the department."

"Mmm," said Deschenes vaguely. "Restless, I think. You know Steve—he never much liked Operations. And so there wasn't much left for him to do here when we lost the Intelligence branch. I hear he's happier where he is. If no one's seen him, I suppose he's back to undercover work." Before MacMillan could answer, Deschenes was back at the files on his desk.

Wednesday, May 10

Steve Collins looked down at his dirty hands and muddy work boots and smiled grimly. He hadn't looked quite like this at the end of a working day for ten years—not since he left the farm and what he regarded then as the prison of manual labor. The situation wasn't exactly the same, of course. The end of his shift on the construction crew was nowhere near the end of his working day, and physical labor no longer felt like the imposition it had been when he was nineteen.

He paused at the little white gate in front of the boarding-house and calculated how rapidly he would have to mount the stairs to his room in order to avoid the landlady. Her hunger for small talk had already—in two days—led him to slip once or twice out of his deliberate loutishness. Once or twice he could cover easily enough, but too many evenings of cozy chat in front of the fire would be a disaster.

He tried the handle. The door was open, of course. His landlady was criminally trusting. "Evenin', Miranda," he called in the direction of the kitchen as his boots hit the stairs. "Nice night out there, eh?"

Before her reply could drift up to the second floor, he was in his room. He sat down on the bed and pulled a small black notebook out of his shirt pocket. After a moment's thought, he drafted a brief report and cast it into this week's simple code—one designed to foil nothing more sophisticated than the curiosity of telephone operators and innocent bystanders. He thrust the notebook into the pocket of his work pants, gathered up some clean clothes, and headed into the bathroom to take a shower.

Hot water gushed over his aching shoulders and then slowed to a trickle. Bloody Miranda and her ancient plumbing. As he waited for the water to reappear he found himself trying to figure out how long it would be before he could contact Betty again. The ache in his shoulders transferred itself to an ache in his loins. He leaned forward, one hand on the mildewed tiles, his head bowed under the faint *drip, drip* from the shower head, and wondered for the third time that day whether the job was worth it. Suddenly a flood of rusty water, cold this time, drenched his dull black hair. He jumped back out of range and waited. There was a thump and a clang and steam poured up from the nozzle once again.

This assignment shouldn't take that long, he thought more cheerfully: maybe he'd be back in Ottawa by next week. He picked up the soap and stepped under the shower one more time. Whoever had been hanging around the workers at the construction site last week, asking odd questions, should turn up again soon enough. And when he did, it was just a question of playing him a bit—leading him on, finding out why he was interested, snatching him, and getting who was behind him. Routine stuff. Maybe he could risk calling Betty from the restaurant after he reported in. He jumped out of the tub, winced as a blister banged against the stool, and began drying himself vigorously.

CHAPTER 2

Monday, May 15

In Toronto, Monday morning's rising sun shone in Inspector John Sanders's red and gritty eyes as he tried to make out what was happening on the top of the apartment building across the street. Twenty minutes before, he had been slithering backward across the same roof in a burst of gunfire before dropping feetfirst through an open trapdoor. Someone had already called for the Emergency Response Unit, which had been waiting, bulletproof vests on and snipers poised, for him to get the hell out of their line of fire. Pity. The stupid fool was going to try to shoot his way out of this mess, and that would be the end of him. If he had put down that goddamned arsenal of his and come out peacefully when Sanders had finally tracked him down, he would have been found unfit to stand trial. Six or eight years making leather wallets and he'd be free again. Instead of ending up with his face ground into a gravel-and-asphalt roof. Sanders turned away. He didn't want to watch. Yawning, he headed back to the car, where Ed Dubinsky, his partner, was already sitting, massive and patient, waiting for him.

"You're supposed to call in," he said. "Want some coffee?"

"Naw," said Sanders, too tired for coffee. "What the hell for?"

"Something about packing your bags and heading off to Ottawa this morning. Flanagan's sick again—it's that seminar the Mounties are running on how to catch terrorists."

"For chrissake, it'll take me all morning to do the paperwork on this thing," Sanders said, nodding in the direction of the silent apartment building.

"I'll do it," said Dubinsky, reaching forward to turn on the ignition. "I'll make like you wasn't even there, boss."

"Lay off, Dubinsky." Sanders let his head drop forward as far as it would go in an effort to ease his aching shoulder muscles. It didn't work.

"Besides, it's those guys over there that are going to have to write out the reports, anyway." Dubinsky nodded at the square yellow van parked across from them, out of which the Response Unit had poured.

"Goddammit! I don't want to go to Ottawa. I want to go home to bed. Jesus!" Sanders swore as he reached for the car radio.

Sanders shifted irritably in the driver's seat. A hot, needling pain stabbed his right knee, the long muscle running down the right side of his back was beginning to knot up, and he could feel a frozen immobility starting up in his left shoulder that presaged a stiff neck and a rotten temper. Above him the sky was a deep, impossible blue; sun poured down on the road, bleaching the gray concrete to blinding white. The car thumped monotonously over the black joints in the road surface. Trees on either side of the wide, almost empty highway afforded no relief to his burning eyes. They were at worst completely bare, at best outlined with only a faint, ragged web of pale green or reddish budding leaves. What in hell was he doing heading north in May? In Toronto you could be reasonably sure that winter was over by now. In Ottawa, with his luck, it would snow.

Up ahead a toy truck, its back end painted a hazy red, floated dreamily along the shimmering road. He fixed his heavy-lidded eyes on it and yawned. Without warning it leaped into focus, huge and solid, right in front of him. As his foot smashed down automatically on the brake pedal he jerked the wheel over and then accelerated again, lurching crazily back and forth in the left lane. A horn screamed in his ear. In his rearview mirror he saw a small Mercedes sitting right on his back bumper. No doubt it had been about to pass him when he had swung into its lane, and he could feel the righteous wrath of its driver burn through the windshield. With deliberation he flicked on his turn indicator and moved neatly back into the right lane. The Mercedes shot past with another blast of its Teutonic horn. The slow-moving truck faded into the distance behind him.

"Christ almighty," he said aloud. "This time I damned near got spread all over the road." The words sounded peculiar, echoing, isolated, in the padded interior. Where in hell was he? He glanced at his watch. He had been driving for almost three hours and couldn't remember having passed by a single landmark since he left the industrial tangle of the outskirts of Toronto. Wherever he was, though, if he didn't stop soon and get out of this damned car, he'd be driving into Ottawa in a meat wagon. At that point a road sign promised an exit for Highway 2 leading into Brockville in five hundred meters. He grabbed it before it got away on him, passed a motel with a coffee shop before he had slowed down from highway speeds, braked—but not soon enough—to make the turn, took a right through a nearby gas station, bumped over a strip of empty field, shot in and out of a parking lot, and slithered to a halt by the front door.

The coffee shop turned out to be a bar that also served food. Originally conceived by an enthusiastic architect to take advantage of its hilly, shrub-filled location on the St. Lawrence River, it soared airily above Sanders's head, all dark beams, potted plants, and shaded glass. The owners were obviously not the dark beam, shaded glass, and fern sort; the room had been cozied up with plaques and posters advertising beer, an assortment of garishly decorated video games, a pool table, and a large-screen television. There was a noisy group crowded around two tables pushed together near the bar. Construction workers, probably, to judge by their boots and coveralls. He looked at the massive collection of bottles on their table and shuddered. He hoped they weren't trying to build anything complicated.

Sanders headed for a table in the far corner and folded his long frame into a chair with its back to the room. He glanced suspiciously at the grubby menu propped on the table and ordered coffee and a club sandwich from the harried-looking waitress. His head still roared and thumped with the sound of the road, and he tried—unsuccessfully—to ignore the raucous laughter coming from behind him.

"Jesus," said a whining voice, separating itself at last from the general noise, "this country's turning into a goddamn fast, uh, fash—"

"Fascist?" said a helpful voice.

"Yeah, whatever, state, eh? First they tell us that fucking stretch of road's gotta be finished in three days—three days! Three weeks is more like it. And the other day when I go in the woods to take a leak this fucking Mountie bastard comes racing over and says he's gonna arrest me if I don't get the hell outa there."

"What's in the woods?" said the helpful voice. "Besides the RCMP?"

"Nothing, that's what." The whine was getting louder now, and belligerent. "Nothing but fucking Mounties and trilliums. Mounties guarding trilliums, that's what. We spend billions of dollars so the Mounties can keep people from pissing on trilliums." He guffawed and repeated his witticism softly. "Pissing on trilliums." The voice paused as if its owner had suddenly realized some dreadful truth. "Hey, Doreen. We're dry here. Bring us another beer, eh?"

"Look, Don, we gotta get going. It's getting late. You mind riding in the back? Joe's knee is real—" This was a new voice, reasonable and sober-sounding.

"I'm not riding in the fucking back of no truck all the way to Smiths Falls. You crazy or something? In with all that equipment and garbage in there? You tell MacDougall to go screw himself. I'm not . . ." His voice faded away as he tried to remember just where he was in his protestation.

"I'm driving up to Carleton Place," said the helpful voice. "I can drop, uh, Don off in Smiths Falls on the way. But you people sure do go a long way to eat lunch. It must be forty miles."

"We didn't come here just to eat lunch," said the new voice seriously. "We had to pick up some equipment in Brockville, and get Joe. He was seeing the doctor."

"Besides, we're not going to—" Another voice, deep and hesitant, inserted itself into the discussion.

The sober voice sliced through authoritatively. "Anyway, thanks for the offer of a lift," he said, "but we don't like to put you out."

"No trouble. I like company when I drive. You ready, Don? You'll have to tell me where to go. This really isn't my country around here." Something about the voice irritated

Sanders. It was too smooth; its lapses into the local dialect were too mannered and isolated. Slimy urban bastard trying to be one of the boys. He swiveled around in his chair to watch them leave.

From where he was sitting, he could see only backs, and they all looked pretty much the same to him. Before they got out of the room, however, one of the last two lurched and crashed into a chair, grabbed the elbow of the man beside him, and then turned around to go back to the littered table they had just left. He was a big, dirty-looking man, deeply tanned, with lank black hair, thick black brows over bright blue eyes, and a gaunt rawboned face. His eyes swept rapidly and sharply over Sanders, as if he were memorizing him for some future contingency, and then he looked, puzzled, down at his old table. He shook his head. Whatever he had forgotten would remain forgotten, and he walked unsteadily back toward the door. His companion stood in the doorway and watched the pantomime. He, too, was a tall man—almost as tall as Sanders himself—and wore his workmen's coveralls as though they had been designed by an Italian couturier. His face was arrogant and almost handsome, thin, with high cheekbones, deep-set intensely dark eyes, and a full mouth. The symmetry of his thick and arched eyebrows was spoiled by a thin white scar that ripped through his tanned face from eyelid to temple. Handsome, except for that, but not pleasant looking. As the two men started walking again, a fading but familiar whine drifted back to Sanders from the scruffy one.

"Just a minute, you guys. I gotta go to the can." So that had been Don.

Scarface stopped and allowed Don to get ahead of him before turning back toward the bar. He looked around, apparently for the waitress, then reached over and picked up the receiver of a telephone hanging in the darkness against the back wall. Whatever he had to communicate was quickly said, and he was back out in the hall long before Don could have emerged from the washroom.

Sanders turned back to his food. The sudden silence in the room was overpowering. The waitress, still frowning nervously, emerged from the kitchen and drifted by to refill his coffee cup. When he admitted he didn't want anything else, she dropped his bill on the table and disappeared.

Just as he was biting into the third quarter of his sandwich, a piercing whistle tore through the silence. Sanders whirled around in his chair. The remains of the soggy toast and cold bacon crumbled onto plate and table as his hand flew into his jacket and stopped. Nothing. He was alone in the bar. With his heart pounding, unable to catch his breath. Then the same whistle, just as loud. He peered into the dimly lit recesses at the end of the bar beside the telephone and noticed for the first time a large brass cage. He looked again and then laughed out loud. There was a mynah bird standing on a perch in the cage behind the bar, looking at him, its head cocked to one side. At least he hadn't tried to shoot it. A new set of sounds, vibrating and varied in pitch and length, but not nearly as loud, filled the empty spaces in the room. It took Sanders a few seconds to place them. "I'll be damned," he muttered. The bird was moving slowly back and forth from foot to foot while it thoughtfully imitated the sound of a push-button phone being dialed. When I was working on wiretap, Sanders thought, I could have told you what number they'd been calling when the bird was listening in by those sounds. The bird cocked his head meaningfully at Sanders and uttered his introductory whistle one more time; then he slowly and gracefully segued into the dialing sequence. This time a series of numbers crystallized out of

Sanders's tired brain, and with a self-deprecatory grin he jotted them down on the receipt portion of his bill. Neat, he thought, looking at the number that resulted, and considered asking the waitress—who had poked a resentful-looking head out of the kitchen—if she had dialed it recently. Don't be a stupid ass, he told himself, let a couple of bills flutter down onto the table, and walked slowly out.

The stranger unlocked the door on the passenger side of a dark red Toyota in the parking lot and gestured impatiently for Don to climb in. In seconds he jumped quickly into the driver's seat, started the car, and turned it rapidly onto the highway in a shower of gravel. "This the fastest way to Smiths Falls?" he asked, as he turned north onto a deserted two-lane road. By now they had left the rest of the road crew a good two or three minutes behind them.

"Huh?" Don seemed to be sinking fast into a little world of his own. "Oh, yeah. I guess so." He pulled himself upright and looked at the driver. "You never said t'other day what your name was, didja?" he said, abruptly suspicious.

"Green," said the driver laconically. Then, thinking better of it, "Rick Green. You told me yours yesterday, I think, but I forgot what it was."

"Don," said his passenger, "Don Bartholomew," and lapsed first into apathy, then somnolence.

Green drove rapidly and steadily. His eyes, constantly alert, flickered back and forth from road to rearview mirror to his sleeping passenger. When they finally reached the sign that announced their arrival in Smiths Falls, he slowed abruptly. "Where to?" he asked.

"Huh?" Don jerked upright. "We here already? Jesus! Where are the others?"

"Oh, I think we're ahead of them," said Green. "I don't suppose they drive that truck as fast as I push this little car of mine along. Where shall I drop you off?"

"Well, Jeez, I dunno." Don's eyes narrowed with cunning, and he glanced sideways at the driver. "D'ja say you're going to Carleton Place?" He pronounced it Kerlton, in the manner of the native born. " 'Cause if y'are, you can let me off there, eh. The guys are gonna drop Joe off to home here. We gotta work s'afternoon."

Green smiled. "Sure. No problem. You just tell me where to go," he said, negotiating the car out of the town traffic and back onto the highway. "Your work site right in Carleton Place?" he asked casually. "Because I'm actually going to a place on the other side of town, visting a friend out in the country. Maybe I can let you off right where you're going."

Don looked at him suspiciously. "Yeah? Well, maybe. This is one of them government secret projects like. Yeah, secret projects, you know what I mean?" He burst into a fit of laughter. "Anyway, it's a couple, three miles th'other side of Carleton Place—near Mooreton."

"No kidding!" said Green. "What a coincidence. My friend said his place is just past Mooreton."

"One of them places on the river," said Don enviously.

"I don't know. Maybe. So which way do we go when we get into town?"

"Naw, don't go into town. Turn at Highway Seven and I'll show you where to go from there. This sure beats sitting in that fucking truck," Don said, looking around with satisfaction at the shiny newness of the car.

The red Toyota sped through the sunny countryside, moving from highway to paved secondary road to narrower road, and from grassy fields to woods to thickly forested landscape.

"This really is in the middle of nowhere, isn't it?" said Green.

"Just about there," said Don. "Slow down, it's that left turn up ahead. You can just leave me off there. Keep on to the next crossroad, take a right and then a left, and you'll be in Mooreton."

Green pulled smoothly up onto the shoulder and looked across at a newly paved road that lost itself in the forest. "That's really something," he said. "Does it go anywhere?"

Don's deep-set eyes studied Green under their half-lowered lids for a few moments. "You're damned right it goes somewhere," Don said at last. "You should see the place. Used to be someone's house, all run-down, like, with a crappy road. Now they've gone and done it all up with lawns and flowers and big fences and stuff like that. And that road. The old gravel road ain't good enough for all the rich bastards coming out to use this place."

"I'd like to look at it," said Green, putting the car back into gear and beginning to turn into the road.

"Jesus! You can't do that! The fucking Mounties'll be all over you. You wanna look at it? I'll show you where to go." He gave Green a sly look. "There's this little path, see, and a place you can leave the car. I've been up to look at it lotsa times. It's a nice place," he said wistfully. "I'd like a place like that."

Green parked the red Toyota on a firm patch of ground behind some bushes and followed Don across the road. He looked back to check on the car and smiled. It had disappeared completely from view. Don was moving quickly along a small path, making no noise at all, apparently completely sobered up. Suddenly he stopped dead and gestured for silence. Then he eased himself back to where Green was standing and spoke directly into his ear. "Got to be quiet as hell. There's a big path up there where the Mounties patrol. With dogs and all. You get by them and it's a piece of cake." He slithered ahead, stopped beside a tree, listened, moved farther, and gestured toward Green to follow. Suddenly they were in front of a chain link fence looking at an enormous yellow-brick house, standing, mellow in the sunshine, in the middle of sloping lawns. "This what you wanted to see?" said Don in a whisper and stepped back.

"That's pretty nice," said Green. "I don't suppose you can get in there, though, for a closer look, can you?"

"You want a closer look?" said Bartholomew vaguely, and looked around him. "If you go up there where that stream is, the fence is broken and you can get in." The part of the garden they were beside had been left to grow wild, and they were screened from observation by flowering shrubs and small trees. "This is a good time to try it, too. Guys are all in the back of the house having coffee. No patrols right now. You can go up this way and look right in the windows if you want." Don crouched down to see under the low-lying branches, reaching casually into his jacket as if to scratch his ribs. A shout from somewhere nearby distracted him, and for one disastrous moment he turned his head toward the fence. Green reached into his pocket and extracted a neat, professional-looking cosh. Before Bartholomew had a chance to look back at the man he was leading, that man raised his arm and swiftly drove it down. Don crumpled without a noise.

Green stopped and listened for a full thirty seconds. He bent over, pressed a finger delicately into the side of the still neck, and waited another few seconds. He opened Bartholomew's grubby jacket and noted the shoulder holster and pistol without surprise. He pried the dead man's fingers off the butt and transferred the weapon into his own pocket; he picked up the body carefully and easily, and walked away at right angles to the fence. When he hit the larger path, he paused to listen again, long enough to make sure that it was not being patrolled, and then retraced his steps back to the road. He carried his burden over to a small hollow on the edge of the wood. There was a thud as Don Bartholomew landed in the flower-filled clearing, the noise covered by the sound of indignant birds chattering and chipmunks scurrying for shelter.

The sun burned through the windows onto his face and neck as Sanders followed the long line of cars into the center of the city. Chrome, glass, and water glittered hard and unpleasant around him. His head ached. He had clearly missed the turning for the parkway that would whisk him up the east side of the Rideau River and then into his motel—a turning that at least four people had assured him he couldn't miss—and was condemned to fight his way through the heavy downtown traffic. On the grass beside Dow's Lake, young women with fish-belly-white skins shivered in bikinis in the bright sun; on the pavement beside them, other young women rushed by, clutching coats and jackets around them to protect themselves from the cold. The much-vaunted tulips—pride of the city—were huddling in the dry wind, too, looking short and scraggy, their foliage thin, their blossoms small and dry-looking. The grass appeared brittle and yellow, as if it had dried up before it had begun its spring growth. But it was no drier than he was himself this bleak sun-filled afternoon. Dust and debris—pollen, dried-up tree blossoms, and scraps of old paper left over from the winter—beat on the windshield and flew in the half-open window, making his exhaustion-gummed eyes burn.

Why, in the name of God, hadn't he just yelled no into the phone when they told him to pack up at once for five days in Ottawa? He knew why, of course. If he hadn't said yes, he would be finishing off today's paperwork right now and facing a week's leave. Leave he had been postponing for months now, getting more foul-tempered and erratic by the day. Leave he would have to spend alone, watching the walls of his concrete rabbit warren of an apartment slowly close in on him until he went mad. Before Eleanor packed up the green track suit and herbal shampoo that she kept in his drawer and walked through his front door for the last time, she had pointed out with bitterness that he was incapable of sharing even a corner of his life with anyone else. Perhaps it was true. Perhaps he was doomed to live out his existence in echoing solitude. And if that were so, then there wouldn't seem to be much point to it.

That thought carried him through a bizarre series of left turns and right turns—including one that seemed to lead him in and out of a parking garage—to the street where, three lanes over on the left-hand side, he could see his motel. Of course. As he waited for a break in the traffic, he glowered sourly at it. Scruffy, standard, two-story North American, sitting, as far as he could tell, in the middle of a couple of major construction projects, surrounded by more swirling dust. The department was on one of its cyclical money-saving kicks, evidently. And he had been assured that this was the room booked for Tom Flanagan. Not bloody likely. Flanagan would have been staying with all the politicians at the Chateau Laurier at one-fifty or so a night.

When he finally stumbled into the room, he dropped his suitcase on the bed by the door, yanked the curtains shut, and began ripping off his clothes as soon as he had two free hands. He gave his surroundings one quick look, decided he had been in worse rooms, and headed for the shower. Three minutes later he stepped naked out of the bathroom, ripped the covers off the nearest bed, and collapsed on the cool sheet. The mattress billowed up around him, rocking with the motion of the road and swaying dangerously into the corners of the room. As he drifted into unconsciousness, he was troubled by the thought that he had seen, or heard, or done something that should have been noted, reported, called in, filed.

Whatever it was, it had to do with a telephone that kept on ringing and ringing and ringing. He reached into the space where it should have been and found emptiness. The ringing went on. Oh, God, he groaned, that must be a real phone, and pulled his eyes open. The room was still bright with the daylight that filtered through the motel room curtains; he finally located the phone over on the table by the door. The ringing persisted. He lurched dizzily off the bed and scooped the receiver from its cradle. "Yes," he said, his mouth thick and dry and foul-tasting.

"Inspector Sanders?" It was a cold voice, unpleasant and peremptory in tone. "Higgs. RCMP temporary liaison, civilian police forces. We were expecting you this morning." He waited, apparently for a reply. "Toronto called us yesterday when Flanagan came down sick. We understood that his replacement would be leaving before six in the morning."

Sanders stared at the receiver in his hand, stupefied. "At six this morning," he said finally, anger rising and clearing away the sleep, "I was on the roof of an apartment building, being shot at by a man wanted for the murder of three juveniles. No one thought to tell me to let him go so I could jump in my car and drive to Ottawa."

There was another pause. "The motel switchboard says that you checked in at two o'clock. Your orders were to call at once."

"I used my initiative," said Sanders. He was getting bored with this conversation. "And got some sleep first. If you object, you can go to hell—or call Toronto. Or both. I'm reporting in now—or are you people about to go home for the day?"

From the length of the pause this time, Sanders figured that he had got it in one. "The group, or most of it, is meeting for drinks and an early dinner at the Belle Mireille." Higgs pronounced the two words as if they rhymed. "It's on Albert Street, a couple of blocks west of Elgin. Albert's two blocks south off Confederation Square. We'll see you there at five-thirty." Inspector Higgs hung up the phone without waiting for a response.

"Go get yourself a bloody horse," said Sanders as he slammed the receiver down and headed back to try what another shower might do for him.

Superintendent Henri Deschenes was sitting behind three files spread out on his desk. "I've been spending a lot of time on the Sea Gull files, going back to when we first heard of the conference," he said. "There's something that doesn't feel right about them."

Inspector Ian MacMillan was wandering restlessly around Deschenes's office, fiddling with the blinds, circling the small seminar table at the far end, lining up a couple of chairs that had been left in slight disarray by the cleaning staff. He stopped and looked over. "What do you mean?"

"There's a leak, Ian," said Deschenes, looking steadily at him. "Or a blockage, which amounts to the same thing." He tapped the file marked "Reports: Canadian Security Intelligence Service" in a neat hand. "Hadn't you noticed?"

"Here?" said MacMillan.

"Yes. We're getting too much of the wrong kind of information and not enough of the kind you'd expect. As though it's all being filtered through someone who's making sure it stays distorted. Whose desk did those reports land on while I was off?"

"Sylvia's, I think," said MacMillan, nodding in the direction of the door that led to Deschenes's secretary's office. "At least, she was the one who passed them on to me. And that doesn't seem likely, sir," he added, giving his attention back to the blinds. "More likely to be those bastards over at CSIS deliberately screwing things up for us, don't you think? I mean, you can't suspect Sylvia. . . ." His voice trailed off and he shook his head. Suddenly he crossed over to the desk, sat down, and smashed the flat of his large hand down on the file. "After all, what in hell do they expect? The goddamn government takes a fully operational and functioning intelligence service and just because a few reporters start bitching over a couple of operations that go wrong and scare the hell out of some politicians they rip the whole thing apart. And then they take the most important part—the most sensitive part, intelligence gathering—and dump it into the hands of civilians? Jesus, that's where you really need the discipline and training and that sort of shit. Even if most of the bastards at CSIS trained with us originally, it can't work. There's no discipline over there, no morale. Of course they're going to screw up. And that name," he said, "that goddamn stupid name. The Canadian bloody Security Intelligence Service. Yeah. What do you expect?" He stood up again. "And where were you—or for that matter Charlie Higgs or any of us—when they were doing all this? We just lay back and let them destroy us." The indignation faded from his voice and he wandered over to the window again.

Deschenes followed him steadily with angry eyes. "For the time being, Inspector MacMillan," he said, "I am going to assume that you, like the rest of us, have been working too long and too hard and I'm going to forget that you said what you have just said." He stacked the files in front of him. "I also assume that you must have forgotten what some of your friends were doing in the old days. Remember? Planting evidence? Filing false reports? I don't know why in hell you have always believed that the fault lies somewhere up the road, Ian, and not with us. You can't run Operations if you don't accept the possibility of error— or sabotage."

MacMillan shrugged lazily. "You want me to look into it?" he asked. His tone reduced the problem to the level of a late delivery of office supplies. "Tell you what, let me get on to someone we can trust at CSIS. I'll give Steve Collins a call. No, better yet, Andy Cassidy. He'll be working downtown. Who in hell ever knows where Steve is? He's probably under cover again." He reached casually for Deschenes's telephone. "Andy'll know what they think they're doing. Let me have a word with him before we start messing around here with a full-scale inquiry. I'll do it tonight—no problem."

The telephone rang before MacMillan could dial or Deschenes could reply. Deschenes paused for a second, then nodded in agreement, picked up the receiver, and listened intently for less than a minute. "I'll be there as soon as I can," he said, and turned back to MacMillan. "Sorry. My wife, reminding me that we have dinner guests. Life goes on in spite of Sea Gull, doesn't it? Let me know tomorrow what you find out—if anything."

CHAPTER 3

Inspector John Sanders strode angry and unseeing along the broad sidewalk, daring pedestrians to get in his way. His shoulder brushed against the edge of a large kiosk that should have offered tourist information but didn't, and he looked up. "Bloody hell!" he muttered, realizing that he was still heading along Wellington instead of down Elgin as instructed. He swung quickly to his left. Where he could have sworn there should have been empty space, however, he found himself in direct contact with a sizable solid object. He felt, then heard, a dull thud and stared horror-struck down at the ground.

"For chrissake, don't you ever look where you're going?" said a voice, female, and trembling with anger.

In front of him he saw a young women, dressed in jeans, sprawled awkwardly in a half-squatting position. She had one hand on the pavement and with the other she was holding up an aluminum suitcaselike object. Sanders reached out to help her as she started to pick herself up from the concrete sidewalk. "I'm sorry," he muttered, grabbing her wrist firmly. "Can I give you a hand?" As he gave her arm a yank to bring her upright, her green knapsack, already hanging by only one strap, slipped off her shoulder and landed on the pavement.

"Don't bother," she snapped, pulling her arm back. "Just get the hell out of my way before you wreck all my equipment." By now she was back on her feet and leaning concernedly over the objects on the ground. With a slightly sick feeling, Sanders noticed that one of them was a tripod—a large, heavy-looking, and without a doubt very expensive tripod. Beside it lay the green knapsack.

"Is it damaged?" he asked.

She stared down at it for a considerable length of time. "It shouldn't be," she said finally in a grudging tone. "But no thanks to you. It's sturdy and well packed, that's all."

"Look," he said, "I'm sorry. All right?" He was turning to go when a thought suddenly occurred to him. "My God! Are you hurt? I should have asked that before worrying about the equipment."

"Why?" she said crisply. "I heal—it's equipment that has to be replaced. "Anyway, I'm fine. It takes a lot to damage me."

At that, a belated surge of conscience prompted him to grab the knapsack and drop it onto a nearby bench, and then come back for the tripod. "Let me at least help you pick up this stuff," he said.

"For chrissake," she yelped. "Will you leave it alone? It may be well packed but it's not a collection of old bricks."

"I'm just trying to get it out of the way before someone steps on it," he said stiffly, picking up the aluminum suitcase and stacking it beside the tripod.

"It'll be fine," she said emphatically. "Now if you'll get out of my way I would like to catch the five o'clock sun." With a grimace, she unzipped the knapsack and peered inside. Sanders bent his tall frame over her anxiously, trying to see what damage he had done.

She leaned back on the wood-and-concrete bench and glared at him. "I can't see a goddamned thing with you standing in my light," she said at last.

With a guilty jump, he stepped backward and smashed the back of his head against something very hard. "Watch what you're fucking well doing," yelled an aggrieved pedestrian behind him. "Jesus," the man said, and planted one large hand between Sanders's shoulder blades. With a "There, you bastard," he shoved Sanders back before disappearing into the crowd. The unexpectedness of the attack caught Sanders off guard, and he catapulted toward the girl on the bench. He grabbed the back slat, missing her shoulder by inches, and lurched awkwardly over to the side.

She bent over in a spasm of laughter.

Sanders regained his balance, clutched the back of his throbbing head, and glared furiously at the laughing woman; finally a slow grin spread across his face and he sat down quietly beside her.

"Well, then, let's see what's happened to this stuff." She peered into the knapsack once more, this time without interference. "It seems to be fine," she said. "But thank you anyway."

Sanders glanced at his watch. "You've missed the five o'clock sun," he pointed out. "It's already ten past. Why don't you let me buy you a drink? To make amends for what I did. And because I'm a stranger here."

"All lost and alone? You should work on other ways of getting to know people, I think. But what the hell." She looked at her watch and sighed. "Let bygones be bygones," she said, zipping up her knapsack. "Where would you like to go?"

Sanders followed the woman through the crowds sitting six and seven to a table on the broad sidewalk into the darkened interior of the pub. The rush hour throng of drinkers were all jammed around small metal tables in the bright sunshine and exhaust fumes of the outdoors, leaving the indoor section silent and almost empty. She took her knapsack and camera case from him and settled them on the floor in a corner before slipping into a small, damask-covered chair. "My apologies for the bordello atmosphere," she said, glancing around at the crimson walls and velvet curtains. "But it was close by and they have English beer on draft."

"Good idea," said Sanders, and ordered each of them a pint. "And since I was the one who knocked you down, I guess I should start," he said. "My name is Sanders, John Sanders. I'm from Toronto, and I'm here for a week." He stopped—not willing to commit himself any further—and looked inquiringly at her.

"Convention?" she asked casually.

"In a manner of speaking," he said evasively. "And you must be a photographer. With all that equipment."

"That's right. Harriet Jeffries."

"Harriet?"

"Right again—Harriet." She repeated it with force. "I'm sorry if you don't like the name, but it's the best I can do. I refuse to manufacture an awful nickname just to get rid of it."

"No, I like it. It suits you." He looked at her critically for the first time. She was a little older than he had thought and had dark brown hair that hung straight almost to her shoulders. Her face was long and thin and dark, but the eyes that looked directly at him were a bright shade of green. Contact lenses, he thought skeptically, but when she turned away to look at a passing waiter, they changed color again. Real. "I'm not fond of up-to-the-minute names," he added.

"Mmm," she said, "you have a point there. It would be infinitely worse to be called something from a soap opera, wouldn't it? But I *am* a photographer, mainly architectural, and I'm in Ottawa on an assignment. I've been in the city since . . . oh, around February, off and on, and hope to be back in Toronto this summer. And I'm single, thirty-two, don't smoke, and prefer living alone. There, my life history in a single breath." She moved an elbow to make room for the mugs of beer. "What do you do? Obviously if you were a surgeon or a cabinet minister you would have told me already, assuming that I would be impressed. So you must be—let's see . . ." She cocked her head to one side and looked intently at him. "Maybe a teacher—of something that makes people nervous, like math—or a dentist, and you're tired of people making bad jokes about what you do."

"You're very perceptive," he said. "But it's worse than that. I'm a policeman." He braced himself for the usual coy mock alarm, or, perhaps, chilly disappointment.

"Really?" she said, quite calmly. "You mean there's a police convention in town? How bizarre."

"Why bizarre?"

"Oh, I don't know. In Ottawa? I would have thought Calgary . . . or maybe Milwaukee."

"I don't see why," he said, somewhat nettled. "Anyway, it's not so much a convention as a meeting. There aren't very many of us. I doubt we'll be getting in your way. Anymore, I mean." As he picked up his beer another thought struck him. "At least I don't think there are very many of us. I haven't actually made it to the meeting yet, and . . ." He looked at his watch. "I'm late enough now that it doesn't look as if I'll get there tonight."

"You seem to give up very easily." Harriet's eyes narrowed with amusement, although the rest of her face remained devoid of emotion. "Obviously you're not a Mountie."

"I'm not," he said. "And I'm usually pretty persistent. But I've had a total of about six hours' sleep since Saturday, and right now I don't care whether I find my group or not. You wouldn't know some place with food that would taste good to someone half-dead from exhaustion, would you?"

"How about Turkish?" she asked. "It's within walking distance, and I'd say it's good enough to revive the corpse at a wake. You finished your beer? Let's go."

"Are you coming, too?" he asked, surprised.

"Why not? I like Turkish food."

Ian MacMillan walked into the hotel bar and looked around for a familiar face. There were several. Most of them were politicians or senior civil servants whom he knew only because at one time or another in his career he had poured over their files or wearily traced their movements. Tonight he didn't particularly care who was sharing their tables and listening to their indiscreet ramblings. Over in a far corner lounged a tall man with dark hair that stood out from his forehead at a rakish angle. He raised one hand in greeting, and MacMillan made his way over to his table.

"To what do I owe the honor of this particular summons?" asked the man at the table. "And by the way, since you made definite remarks about buying me a drink, I have been waiting here for you to turn up for a good five minutes as dry as your boss's undershirt."

"How's it going, Andy?" asked MacMillan as he pulled out a chair and settled himself into it.

"Not bad. Overworked, underpaid, nothing new—except that this had better be short. I have something interesting turning up at my place hoping for dinner later on tonight."

"Jesus, Cassidy, on a Monday? You never stop, do you?" said MacMillan.

"I should hope to hell not," said Cassidy. "Use it or lose it," he leered. "How about you? It's too bad about you and Susan—or is it? Jesus, it's been a long time since we talked, hasn't it?" He leaned over in the direction of the waiter and ordered two beers and then turned back to MacMillan. "Two, three years? How're you making out?"

"Not bad," said MacMillan. "I've got a reasonable sort of apartment—no goddamn snow to shovel, nobody whining when I've been working late, lots of broads. The only problem is, they all have that little house, yard, and snow-shoveling look in their eyes. You gotta move pretty damn fast to avoid getting caught again."

"You still got the chalet for dirty weekends?" asked Cassidy idly.

"Who has time to ski?" MacMillan poured his beer and took a large gulp. "Besides, all that expensive stuff belonged to Susan—her old man left her a bundle as well as the property."

"You seem to be doing all right," said Cassidy, reaching out and flicking the lapel of MacMillan's suit.

"Susan's got plenty to live on," MacMillan said. "And when you're not paying off a fucking house and all that crap, you can afford a new suit every once in a while. For a change. Look, Andy, there's a problem."

"Yeah? Yours? Or the division's?"

"It sure as hell isn't *my* problem. But Deschenes has been going through all the stuff you bastards have been sending over since he got sick, and he says it doesn't add up. Is that possible?"

Cassidy shrugged. "Of course it's possible. We screw up all the time. How doesn't it add up?"

"There's a blank. We aren't getting anything in connection with the conference. That true? Nobody cares about this thing but us?"

"How should I know? I don't see the reports. I just collect data and send it on. Jesus, Ian, you know how it is. Somebody up there decides how much you deserve to know and that's what you get. Nothing's changed since we were all working in the same building."

"What have you collected, then?" MacMillan asked. "Maybe if we knew that we could figure out what's happening."

Cassidy leaned back and frowned unhappily. "You know I can't pass any of that on. Besides, it doesn't mean a goddamn thing in the state I get it in." He looked at his watch. "Christ, I gotta go. Samantha'll be turning up all hot and hungry and I won't even be there if I don't hurry. Nice seeing you, Ian. Thanks for the drink."

In a pretty woodland area some twenty-odd miles from the Turkish restaurant, Superintendent Henri Deschenes was walking slowly along the broken asphalt at the edge of the narrow paved road. The ground beside the road was carpeted with trilliums in full blossom and birds were bursting their lungs in song. Deschenes seemed oblivious of the beauties of nature, however. He kept his eyes on the grassy verge until he stopped beside a group of three men and a large German shepherd. All five of them stared fixedly at an object lying in a slight hollow in the earth beside the path, the men silent, the dog whining softly.

"When did you find him?" Deschenes asked finally.

"At five-thirty-five, sir," said the man nearest to him, a corporal, tall, lanky, and redheaded, with freckles and a worried expression. "We called in as soon as we could get to a phone. We've been instructed to avoid radio communication—"

"Yes, yes, McInnis," Deschenes muttered impatiently. He turned to the man in command of the small group. "Do you know if anyone's been in contact with the local police, Sergeant?"

"Not that I know of, sir."

Deschenes grunted. "We'd better look after that pretty soon," he said finally.

"Couldn't we, uh, just move him a little farther away?"

Deschenes shook his head. "Stop and think a minute, Carpenter. Even they might notice the body's been moved." He squatted down to get a closer look. It was lying awkwardly on its right side, facedown, with both arms projecting slightly backward. Its dull black hair was matted with darkened blood that had attracted a swarm of flying insects. It was dressed in a blue work shirt and heavy jeans out of which a pair of bluish-white bony feet protruded stiffly. Deschenes reached out and touched the shoulder. Nothing happened. "Dammit," he muttered and stood up again.

"Dembrowski found his wallet in the ditch on the other side of the road. Money was gone, but his driver's license and so on was still in it," said Carpenter. His voice was controlled and wooden. "Name of Donald S. Bartholomew. Address in Brockville. His pockets have been turned out, and we figure his arms got like that when his assailant pulled off his jacket. And his boots and socks."

"Anyone recognize him?" Deschenes said.

Carpenter stopped for a moment. "It's difficult with his face hidden, sir, and we didn't like to move the body. Before someone else got here, I mean."

"Quite so," Deschenes murmured. "Beginning to get stiff already, isn't it? Just ease him over a bit so we can get a look at the face and then we'll leave him there for the regional police. Sergeant, you and Dembrowski hoist him up and turn him over. Come on, we haven't got all night."

Dembrowski was standing closest to the head. He bent down, grasped the body under its arms, and turned, his face reddening with the effort. They stared into the face; it was partially obscured by broken leaves and bits of twigs sticking to it; Deschenes reached down and gently·brushed aside a leaf clinging to the cheek.

"Goddamn," said Carpenter softly. "Jesus, it's Steve Collins. I didn't even—"

"It's Donald S. Bartholomew," said Deschenes coldly. "Put him down." The other two gratefully eased their burden back onto the ground.

"And we're supposed to think he was hit on the head by a vagrant who then stole his boots and jacket," said Deschenes. He shook his head. "Well, maybe he was. Is that possible, Sergeant? Have there been any vagrants around here?"

"No, sir," said Carpenter. "We've been keeping a careful record of all persons within a mile of the security perimeter. No one like that. Only the people in my reports, sir. And if there was a vagrant and we hadn't seen him, Horace would have," he added, giving the big dog a pat.

"And where were you and Horace when this happened?"

"I don't know, sir," said Carpenter unhappily. "Whoever he was, he came with Steve. He had to. What I mean is, Steve must have had some reason to bring the man onto the property with him. Maybe he was trying to figure out what the guy was up to. And if he was with Steve, then Horace wouldn't have raised the alarm. He remembered him too well."

"I see. Who has the wallet?"

"I do, sir," said Dembrowski.

"Good. Put it back where you found it."

"Put it back?"

"That's what I said. Put it back. If you found it, so can the Regional Police."

Dembrowski gave Deschenes a sideways look, but his expression did not alter. "Yes, sir. Anything else?"

"Now, is this the way he was lying when you stumbled across him, McInnis?"

"Yes, sir, that's the way he was lying," said the redhead.

"Good. You have just discovered him now," said Deschenes, looking at his watch. "At nineteen-oh-seven hours. That will go in your report. He is one of the workmen and he has been robbed and murdered by a vagrant. We will do our utmost to assist the Regional Police in tracking the man down. You will now inform the proper authorities."

"But we can't just leave him here like this, can we?" said the redhead. "I mean, he was—"

"You will inform the proper authorities, including, of course, headquarters. His name is Donald S. Bartholomew and he worked on the construction site. Understood? Anything else is going to attract a dangerous amount of notice to this site and destroy its effectiveness as a secure area. Thank you, gentlemen." And Henri Deschenes turned and walked, erect and unyielding, back to his car.

Sergeant Carpenter pursued him to his car. "Has anything gone wrong?" he asked abruptly, holding the door open. "Back in town?"

"Not at our end. Not yet." Deschenes shook his head. "But it's getting busy. One of the delegations got here three days early—arrived this afternoon."

"Who's that?"

"The Austrians. They're throwing a concert and a party and they wanted to be all rested up. I'll have to start bringing in more personnel from somewhere; we're stretched a bit thin right now." He sounded desperately tired. "And I'm sorry about Steve, Frank, but surely you can see that we've got to leave it this way."

"I didn't even recognize him, lying there like that. With his hair that color," Carpenter said bleakly. "I should have—I knew he was around. I'd seen him lots of times. And so had Horace. It was hard to keep Horace from jumping on him like an old friend. But they never told us what name he was using. You know what this means, don't you, sir?"

"What's that, Carpenter?"

"There really were people nosing around the site a couple of weeks ago. Just like I said. And Steve connected with them. Good-bye, sir." And he turned abruptly back into the woods.

Andrew Cassidy put down the telephone and considered what to say now. The steaks were sitting beside the frying pan, the potatoes were in the microwave, the salad was washed but undressed, and the wine was already being decanted into the girl. He didn't know her well enough to leave her alone in his apartment; he certainly didn't know her well enough to tell her why he wasn't able to stay and cook her a steak. And judging by the slightly glazed look in her eye, she was just tanked up enough to react strangely to being told it was time to go home. Perhaps he shouldn't have given her those Bloody Marys. Meet it head-on, he thought. Decisiveness was the only way.

He jumped to his feet, took two steps into the kitchen alcove, and started wrapping up the steaks in aluminum foil. "Sorry, Samantha," he said, stashing things efficiently into the refrigerator while he spoke. "That was the office. The main computer crashed and all hell is breaking loose. If I'm not there in ten minutes I'll be out of a job. The whole company'll be out of a job. Here's twenty bucks," he said briskly. "Order yourself some dinner. I'll drop you off on my way down." He removed the wineglass from her hand and draped her coat over her shoulders in the same gesture. "I'll call you tomorrow, if I can. This'll probably take all night. Come on, sweetheart, time is money." And he hustled her out the door.

Now he was sitting at his desk in the central offices of the Canadian Security Intelligence Service staring at the report on the death of Donald Bartholomew, construction worker, and cursing the blank walls around him. What in hell had gone wrong out at the secure site for the conference? According to his last few reports there hadn't been enough action out there to worry about. No recurrence of the phantom strangers the RCMP thought they had seen. One randy bastard had been sneaking off to see his girlfriend once or twice a week, but she had been a waitress at a local restaurant for the past ten years and didn't seem likely to be in the pay of some hostile intelligence service. Of course, Steve hadn't reported in for several days, but on an assignment this dull, that shouldn't have been significant. Unless . . . He paused and tried to get his mind working on something beyond the material on his desk. Was Steve still messing around with the Charbonneau killing after all this time? It was possible. No one else in the department would still be spending time and energy on the death of a lousy little informer like Maurice Charbonneau, but you couldn't tell with Steve. He had that nasty, stubborn streak in him.

A very slight smile creased Andy's lips and he shook his head. No. His death had to be . . .

His death had to be connected with the secure site. Because if you believed that some wino had managed to jump Steve Collins and kill him for the sake of his jacket and boots, and a few bucks in cash, you'd believe anything. Cassidy slammed his fist on the desk. It hurt. "Jesus, Cassidy," he said to the walls, "can't you think of something more original to do? Like look at his desk and see what he thought he was working on." He stood up and walked to the door, rubbing his throbbing hand against the rough tweed of his jacket.

A black Lincoln picked its way carefully through the quiet streets of Sandy Hill and pulled up smoothly in front of the entrance of the Austrian embassy. Karl Lang, entrepreneur, patron of the arts, scion (on the maternal side) of ancient and now outlawed nobility, slipped out, murmured a few words to his chauffeur, and headed in to the reception. He was greeted cheerfully enough by the staffers darting tensely back and forth; he was hardworking, conscientious, and affable, the sort of businessman you did a few favors for and then felt you'd helped save the national economy. For months now he had been setting up a network of independent franchise outlets for the sale of Austrian sports equipment and clothing in Canada, and the Austrian embassy staff had all become rather used to seeing him drop in for coffee, news, and gossip. This evening he entered the large reception room and paused unobtrusively to line up his targets. He noted that the ambassador's wife was firmly tied up in conversation with someone from External Affairs and abandoned her until later; instead he wandered over to the cultural attaché, a handsome, brown-haired, not particularly cultured skier with an enviable body. Herr Bleibtreu's twin obsessions were mountains and money, and he had spent many idle hours that spring with the ever-sympathetic Herr Lang, spinning out ingenious schemes that combined life above twenty-five hundred feet and getting rich. As far as he was concerned, Herr Lang could do no wrong.

Bleibtreu raised a hand in greeting, although at the moment his mind seemed to be on other things. Standing beside him was an awesomely beautiful woman, small and slightly built, with long blond hair and enormous blue eyes. Her face was high-cheeked and broad at the temple, coming down to a foxy point at the chin. The cultural attaché was leaning yearningly over her, one hand poised as if to capture her and bear her away. "Karl!" he cried. "Delighted to see you. And even more to introduce you to our guest of honor." He dropped the arm slightly and insinuated it around her waist in order to draw her slighty forward. "This is Fräulein Anna Maria Strelitsch. She is performing tomorrow night at the Arts Centre. Fräulein Strelitsch, may I present Karl Lang, a representative from Vienna for a confederation of sports equipment manufacturers. It is he who is generously giving the little supper party after your performance on Tuesday," he added in a lower voice.

"Madame," murmured Lang with a slight bow. "I have already had the great good fortune to meet Fräulein Strelitsch—and to hear her play many times. It is always a joy to find incomparable artistry matched to such unsurpassed beauty."

She laughed. "Save your flattery for your business associates, Herr Lang. It's wasted on me."

"Ah, Fräulein Strelitsch, I deal not in flattery but in truth." He looked narrowly at the simple white dress she was wearing, reached out a tentative hand, and gently touched the material of one sleeve. "And if I am not mistaken, that is one of our dresses. You inspire me."

Toni Bleibtreu neatly cut the dialogue short. "But we must let you speak to more of your admirers, Fräulein Strelitsch. Herr Andersson, of the Swedish Embassy, has been waiting far too long." When the business of introductions was over, he turned back to his friend. "Glad to see you, Karl. Isn't she extraordinary? Isn't she amazing? And she can play the violin."

"Stunning. She makes that dress look superb. Do you think we could get her to a photographer's in it before she leaves? No, I suppose not." He shook his head and scrutinized her again. She had plunged into animated conversation with Herr Andersson, apparently indicating with her hands the size of some giant structure. Her hair fell across her face as she spoke, and the Swede moved it back with the tips of his fingers. Lang frowned. "When is she leaving?" he asked, turning back to Bleibtreu.

"She's staying until after the conference this week. Seems she has a friend in the Austrian delegation. They're planning to travel around after it's over, see Niagara Falls, I suppose, and all that sort of thing." He shook his head ruefully.

"Ah, well, Toni, my boy," said Herr Lang cheerfully, "anyone that lovely is bound to have a friend. It can't be helped."

"And I have until Thursday afternoon when the delegates arrive to make an impression. Think of what can happen in seventy-two hours. Except that I shall be frantically busy every second of that time, of course." Gloom settled over Bleibtreu's features. The prospect of hard work never failed to depress him.

"You'll have more time than that," the man from External Affairs said as he drifted between them. "Because we're keeping them all locked up until it's over and they won't be our responsibility anymore. Did it just for you, Toni."

"Hal, very kind of you to come," said the attaché, switching smoothly into English. "Karl Lang, Hal Metcalfe. Mr. Metcalfe is with External Affairs. Herr Lang is a trade representative from Vienna. Have you met our musical beauty yet? And by the way, I didn't realize your grasp of the language was sufficient for eavesdropping. I must remember to be more careful when you're around."

"You forget that my first posting was in Vienna. And the prettiest girls always seemed to speak the most impenetrable dialect. I was intensely motivated to pick it up." Metcalfe winked and captured a drink from a passing tray. "Have I met the blond bombshell of the classical circuit? Indeed I have. And speaking of motivation, I am about to become intensely interested in the violin myself, I think. She's breath-taking, isn't she?"

"Are you tied up in this conference as well?" asked Lang. Hal Metcalfe nodded. "How are the preparations going for it?"

"Well, you know how these things are. Total chaos, nothing ready as planned, and yet it all manages to happen somehow. I hope." He traded in his empty glass for a full one with the dexterity of long practice.

"The ambassador's wife dreamt last night that the entire German-speaking contingent descended unexpectedly on us for dinner," said Toni glumly, "and there was nothing in the kitchen but stale bread, Canadian hot dogs, and frozen pizza. We all spent the day shopping, just in case."

"You can tell her that she needn't worry, absolutely nothing unexpected is going to be done by anyone." Metcalfe spoke with a little too much emphasis. "It won't be allowed. I have scheduled everyone and everything for every minute of the day. They won't even be able to buy a bottle of perfume for their mistresses without it going on the sheet ahead of time."

"You mean you're in charge of security for this operation?" said Lang with a low whistle. "I wouldn't like to be in your shoes right now."

"Not security, no, not at all," said Metcalfe in confusion. "Just, shall we say, logistics. Moving them around and making sure they get to the right place at the right time. Security's being done by the usual specialist types, you know. I'm not qualified for that." He grabbed another glass from the next tray going by.

"Well, I intend to stay as far away as possible from the Chateau Laurier and the Conference Centre when that thing is on." Lang smiled comfortably. "I don't want to get blown up when the crazies decide to get rid of some prime minister or other."

"The prime ministers and assorted bigwigs aren't going to be downtown, are they, Hal?" said Toni. "We heard that they will all be in the Gatineau."

"Old rumor, my boy. Very old. You're losing your touch. They're all being whisked off to a meeting room in the airport." This voice came from the group next to them, which, by the strange chemistry of parties, had suddenly opened up to include the three men.

"Don't be silly," said a tall, pretty girl. "They're not going to be at the airport."

"Aha," said the man next to her. "Here speaks one with the voice of authority. Come on, what do you know? No fair keeping secrets. Anyone in this group from the press?" They looked around at each other. "See? I thought not. Out with it."

She blushed furiously. "I don't know anything—anything at all. I just think it's a stupid place to hold a meeting, don't you? Besides, if I knew anything, do you think I'd tell you?"

Karl Lang executed a sideways shuffle and planted himself beside the blushing girl. "Here," he said, "let me get you a fresh drink." Within seconds one was in his hand.

"Hey, how did you do that?" she asked.

"The waiter's Viennese," Lang replied. "You just have to know how to signal them. Are you fond of music?"

"Oh, yes, especially violin music," she said. "I play a bit myself. I was thrilled to be invited this evening."

"Has anyone introduced you to Fräulein Strelitsch yet?" The girl shook her head. "Then come with me," he said, "and I will. She speaks excellent English and is always delighted to meet fellow musicians."

"Oh, thank you," she breathed. "I've never met anyone that famous. I wouldn't even be here, except that my boss wangled this invitation for me."

"Where do you work?" he asked as he gently steered her in the direction of the violinist.

"External Affairs," she said. "But I'm just a typist."

"Never mind about that," he said. "Anna Maria, I have a great fan of yours here," and he drew the girl into the little circle that had clustered around the violinist, almost hiding her from sight.

A significant hush descended over the crowd; something was happening. Even the drunken undersecretaries had stopped whatever they were doing and had turned toward the door. Hal Metcalfe sighed in relief. That meant that the prime minister had arrived, and with a certain amount of luck, it would be possible to get out of the place in an hour or so. That arrogant son of a bitch from the RCMP, Higgs, had suddenly materialized in the crowd close to the Austrian P.M., no doubt keeping tabs on everyone. Probably counting drinks, too. In fact, most of the revelers seemed to be bozos from Security awkwardly pretending to be partygoers. Was anyone here just to meet the man? Probably not. He looked over at the gorgeous violinist, wondering if he might carve out some time with her, but she was surrounded by the apes who were surrounding the P.M. He grabbed another glass from a passing tray and decided to get very, very drunk.

CHAPTER 4

Tuesday, May 16

John Sanders tried to keep his eyes open and fixed on the front of the room while allowing the words of the lecture to flow gently by him. Inspector Charles Higgs was standing beside a large easel with a chalkboard perched precariously on it, drawing lines and circles and indicating traffic flow with large, angry arrows. Sanders reckoned he could have written up a three-page report on what was being said without leaving his motel room, but this bastard was obviously taking attendance. So here he was. When Sanders had asked, incredulously, why they were sending him instead of someone from the Special Security Task Force, he had been told not to be a bloody fool, they needed every man on the task force this week. A flip through the roster produced the most senior person—to prove they took the RCMP's invitation seriously—with leave coming who wasn't needed. And that turned out to be John Sanders. Consigned to a week of utter boredom by a bloody computer.

Higgs snapped out a question, which was promptly answered by a kid from Halifax, sitting in the front row with that dewy-fresh air of a rookie constable. Those Maritimers didn't feel any obligation to keep the Mounties happy. Sanders mentally took off his hat to them, and then sketched an inspiring picture of a bomb-throwing anarchist with bushy hair and a huge black beard in his new notebook. What was wrong with Higgs? he wondered, carefully adding in thick eyebrows. The man appeared to be shaking with resentment as he went painstakingly through the routine operations necessary to organize the visit of a high-risk foreign delegation. Today it was advance preparations: choosing routes, sweeping an area clean and keeping it clean. Minute, dreary detail, all of it. Sanders yawned. The chalk clicked angrily across the board. But then, why shouldn't the guy be pissed off? It was probably a demotion for him to be shunted into the classroom during the week of the biggest security operation of the decade. It certainly indicated that someone thought he wasn't necessary—or maybe . . . Sanders considered the bristling mustache over tight lips, the dark eyes snapping in anger, and the penetrating, disgruntled voice. A weak, angry man? Maybe someone was trying to get him out from under foot before he screwed things up on them. For chrissake, stop trying to turn this into a cheap thriller. Higgs probably looks and sounds like that when he's making love. He's just got that kind of gloomy, weasel-like face.

Suddenly Higgs was pulling down on the edge of a screen fastened to the wall in the front of the room, and the lights went out. A slide show. Under cover of the dark, Sanders's thoughts drifted even further from the lecture. Gradually they began to cluster around the image of the slender, thin-faced woman he had eaten dinner with the night before. She had been right, the food at the Turkish restaurant was excellent, good enough to tempt him to go back another evening. If she'd consider it. He hadn't been able to figure out if she enjoyed his company or had simply let herself be picked up on impulse. She had paid her half of the check, firmly, and accepted an offer of being walked back to her car, which was parked at the Conference Centre. Even though he was reeling with exhaustion, he had made a halfhearted attempt to prolong the evening. She had laughed and sent him home to bed, but not before writing down her telephone number on a slip of paper from a notebook in her jacket.

Up on the screen ahead of him they flashed the last of a series of slides on the new and sophisticated component parts of homemade bombs. Finally, in a babble of conversation, the meeting broke up for lunch. Sanders reached into his pocket and found the piece of paper still sitting exactly where he had put it last night. He headed out of the room to look for a phone.

Peter Rennsler let his eyes slip off the page of the book he was reading and over to the window. Far off on the ground, the patchwork pattern of the fields had emerged from the cloud cover: the bright green meadows, the pale new growth, the brown plowed earth. Civilization. He looked at his watch. They would be landing soon. He closed the book and considered it for a moment. It would give him an illusion of safety, perhaps, to have it with him, but the risk involved was too great. To have his cover destroyed because he was carrying a schoolboy's historical outline on the Charlemagne period would be ridiculous. He sighed and slipped it down beside him, between the seat and the wall of the plane. He wouldn't need it anyway. No one was going to expect a graduate student to do anything but listen in modest awe should he be unlucky enough to stumble into a serious discussion.

He looked around at his fellow passengers for the first time since he had boarded the plane in Vienna. Every seat on the aircraft had been taken. He wondered if anyone else was heading for the conference he was registered at. One or two at most, he guessed. All the others crowded into the tourist section with him would be either genuine tourists or pounding toward the trade conference. There was a smell of the press about this lot.

Certainly it had been an enormous stroke of luck that the International Society of Charlemagne Scholars had decided three years ago to hold one of its infrequent meetings in Ottawa during the third week in May. Looking like an ambitious, hungry, young academic was going to be considerably easier than trying to pass himself off as a workman or a reporter. And his credentials would be less carefully scrutinized, he suspected. He found himself automatically scanning the people around him. A head snapped around, attracted by his scrutiny, and a large bullheaded man was regarding him with sharp and suspicious eyes. The man stank of Security. Damn! He had to stop looking at people. It was better to pretend not to notice anyone. He closed his eyes and forced himself to relax, starting with his scalp, which was prickling with intimations of danger as they got closer and closer to Montreal. His passport was a work of art. He shouldn't have any trouble with it, except that there had been too much publicity about forged Canadian travel documents recently, and the people at Passport Control were bound to be more suspicious than usual. He couldn't afford to emit waves of nervous energy and put them on their guard. He allowed weariness to spread out from his slowly rising chest to his arms, his neck, his legs, and he dozed lightly.

The woman seated next to him looked over and smiled. He looked so touchingly vulnerable as he slept, poor thing. Handsome, but tired and thin, his eyes sunken with fatigue.

A poor student, studying too hard, in need of a mother or a pretty girl to look after him. She shook her head at her romantic notions and returned to the last chapter of her mystery novel.

The plane was fifty minutes late. Peter Rennsler picked up his one small suitcase and forced himself to amble along after his temporary neighbor over to the control point.

"How long ya been outta the country?" The voice was bored, the question mechanical.

Rennsler's soul danced with impatience, but his response was soft-spoken and long-winded. "Actually, I'm not coming back from a trip—I mean, I'm studying in Europe right now—I live there, temporarily, anyway. In Vienna," he added. "Just here for a conference. It's at Carleton University. And to see the family, of course." He smiled and opened his suitcase. "Nothing to declare. Clothes for the five days, that's all." The suitcase was neatly packed, with a minimum of spare clothing. He closed it up and glanced at his watch. He had three minutes to catch the bus that would take him to downtown Ottawa in time for the rendezvous. He grabbed his suitcase and headed off, fast.

"Mr. Rennsler," called one of the uniformed RCMP officers who was standing by the control point. "Just a minute."

For a second he tensed, ready to make a run for it past Security and over to the bus. Poor idea. He stopped dead and turned around. "Yes?" he said, unable to control the sweat beading on his forehead and gathering between his shoulder blades.

"You left your passport." The officer shook his head. "That's how people lose them, you know. You should be more careful."

Peter nodded, his throat too dry for an answer, and slipped the document into his inside breast pocket.

* * *

At 4:55, Sanders was standing on the wide expanse of lawn in front of the Supreme Court with his legs planted on either side of an aluminum camera case, using his six feet three inches to shield the tripod and Harriet from the streams of pedestrian traffic. "Dammit," she said, as someone jostled her while she attached the camera to the tripod. "If this keeps up I'll have to wait until Sunday to get this shot. I'm going to be stuck in the bloody city until August if I can't work during the week." Sanders tried to look sympathetic. "I need a shot of the court and then the Justice Building," she had said when they arrived. "Shouldn't take too long. Just keep people from stepping on me, and don't let anyone walk off with my equipment." He hadn't realized how difficult it was going to be to fend off the curious and steer away those who walk without looking ahead of them.

"Yes, what kind of camera is it?" he asked, after the third inquisitive camera buff had asked her the same question and had received a vague stare in response.

"Mmm, what did you say?" she muttered, reaching down and picking out a lens from the collection in the aluminum case. "Oh, it's an Olympus OM-3 with a twenty-four-millimeter shift lens, wide angle. That means I can adjust the position of the lens in relation to the camera. So it remains parallel to the thing you're doing," she said, with a vague wave in the direction of the building ahead of them, "and you don't get line distortion."

"What's that?"

"Well, what it means is that these buildings aren't going to come out with wide bottoms and tiny roofs. I usually do this sort of work with a four-by-five view camera—you know, one of those big things with the photographer hunched under a viewing cloth?—but it was too cumbersome to bring along. This works on the same principle and I can carry the entire outfit by myself," she said, pointing to her modest array of equipment. "Now, why don't you just shut up and stand there while I fiddle?" She pulled a small notebook out of a pocket and checked something in it; then she made a couple of adjustments to the lens, jotted down some notes in the book, and stood back. By now an admiring crowd of five people had stopped to look. Harriet was wearing her usual jeans and a khaki jacket that came down to her knees. The jacket had at least seven pockets that Sanders could count from where he was, most of them bulging. Out of one she extracted a cable release that, frowning in concentration, she affixed to the camera. "There," she said, "that was quick, wasn't it?"

"Not when you were expecting someone just to point the camera and take a few pictures," said Sanders.

"Don't be silly," she murmured. "No one does that. What do you think I am? Nancy Newshound, girl photographer?" Suddenly she stepped back and looked up at the western sky. "Shit! The sun's gone."

"Isn't it bright enough to take a picture?"

"It's not that. The whole purpose of waiting until five and putting up with all this pedestrian traffic is to get the contrast in the details. And you need sun at the proper angle for that. I want to get all that carving and stuff." She looked back up. "All is not lost. There's a break coming in the cloud mass—I'll get it then."

Then, with her eye more on the suddenly cloud-filled sky than on her building, she waited until the sun had broken through. She smiled, looked once more through the viewfinder, and squeezed the shutter release. There was a gentle whir as the film advanced automatically. "There," she said happily.

"Now where?" asked Sanders, his natural impatience overcoming his curiosity to see her work.

"Nowhere," she said. "Not for a minute. I just have to stop down a bit. I always bracket my shots." She bent over the lens once more, made an adjustment, checked the viewfinder, and stepped back.

"What do you mean?" asked Sanders.

"Mean about what?"

"Whatever that was you said."

"Just a minute." She glanced up at the sky and squeezed the shutter release. "Just one more," she said, "and it's on to the Department of Justice." She repeated the same procedure, straightened up again, and looked at the sky. The sun had ducked once more behind a scrap of cloud.

"I still don't see . . ." said Sanders, bending over her to look down at the camera.

"What?" said Harriet, and jumped. There was a click and a whir as the film moved forward once again. "Christ! There's a wasted shot. That's the last time I bring you along," she said. "You rattle me." She looked up. Cloud had taken over the western quadrant of the sky completely. "I wonder if it's worth waiting."

"A friend of yours?" asked Sanders curiously, pointing at a slender figure, probably male, who seemed to be rushing across the lawn in their direction.

"Hmm? That guy? Don't think so," she said, still looking skyward. "What the hell. Let's go get a beer. Any one of those shots ought to do."

Superintendent Deschenes parked his car in front of a small grocery store and headed for the grubby-looking restaurant next door. It seemed to be as good a place as any for a clandestine meeting; a dog dozing on the porch of the house next door to the restaurant was the only sign of life in the village. Frank Carpenter was sitting in a booth, almost unrecognizable in jeans and a sweatshirt, chatting up the waitress. He waved cheerfully at Deschenes as he walked in. "Over here."

When his coffee had been slapped down in front of him, Deschenes turned to his sergeant. "You blend in well. Any luck?"

"Well, you said you didn't want me to look as if I'd just come off parade," he said. "And yes, no problems. They were pretty easygoing about letting us have everything. We have—or they have—several descriptions of him. And they're remarkably uniform. He's between five-eleven and six-one, medium to slender build, has black straight hair, deep tan, dark brown eyes, and a scar that runs from his eyelid—or maybe his eyebrow—all the way to his upper temple. A man fitting that description rented the Toyota from Avis Rent-a-Car at ten o'clock Monday morning. Paid in cash in advance for a twenty-four-hour rental, identified himself with an Ontario driver's license issued to Richard Jarvis of Toronto—I have the number here; it's being checked at the moment—and dropped the car off again outside the agency, forfeiting his deposit. By the time Ottawa police got there, the car had been efficiently polished up, no prints. Same guy in the same car turned up in Brockville dressed as a construction worker at the office of the company working on the secure area, flashed identification as some sort of inspector to the woman on the desk. She wasn't sure what kind, just that he was 'real polite and knew what he was talking about, and they're always being harassed by government inspectors so how was she to know.'" He paused and Deschenes nodded. "And she sent him to the motel because she knew that was where they'd be having lunch. Apparently he got there just as the two crews were going in, and behaved as if he belonged to one of the crews. Anyway, they're easygoing guys, and probably would have asked him to join them even if he'd walked in by himself. They said he seemed to be a great guy, quiet, bought a couple of rounds, and took Steve, uh, Bartholomew off their hands. The guys on his crew said they were grateful, because he was getting plastered."

"Was he?"

Carpenter shook his head, worried-looking. "It doesn't seem possible. I can't imagine him getting drunk, not under the circumstances."

"And what do you make of the rest of it?"

"The description? Except for the height and weight, maybe, it could have been faked. Hair, scar, even eye color." Carpenter shrugged. "But we'll keep an eye on the case. It's going to leave me pretty shorthanded out there, though, if I divert anyone over to it," he said, worried.

"Administration is giving us extra people," said Deschenes. "In the meantime, do what you can."

The pub was, if anything, even darker than it had been the day before. Sanders rushed over to grab a table close to one of the dim wall lights and almost crashed into their waitress from yesterday and her full tray of drinks. She paused, recognized them, and grinned with excessive cheer. "Hey, guys. Welcome back," she cried, as though they were her oldest and most valued customers. "You want the same? Two pints of Smith's?"

"Sure," said Sanders. Harriet was too busy stowing her equipment safely into the corner to concern herself with such questions.

"What a phenomenal memory," said Sanders, "Do you think she knows what everyone has, or are we particularly memorable?"

"It's good for tips," said Harriet, her head in her knapsack and her voice muffled. "And she has bloody little else to think about. You ever work as a waiter?"

He waited until her back began to straighten, and shook his head. "I have one question about all this," said Sanders when her head emerged up above table level once again.

"All right. What is it?" asked Harriet, smiling politely at the waitress as she swept their beer down in front of them with a flourish.

"Who carries your equipment and guards the camera case when you haven't managed to pick up a footloose police officer?"

"Ah," Harriet said. "That's a very sad story." And she took a healthy mouthful of beer. "I had an assistant, wonderful girl, named Jane, good eye, tall, strong, very clever. Gesture hysterically and she knew exactly what you wanted. She was getting pretty good in the darkroom, too." Harriet looked up mournfully, her dark hair hanging down over one green eye.

"What happened to her?" asked Sanders.

"She fell in love with a painter, a bad painter, and went all broody on me. Then she discovered she was pregnant and moved to Montreal to be with the infant's father. And thus was one of the world's best photographic assistants destroyed." She flipped the hair back out of her eye. "I sometimes even hope that she'll become fed up with his horrible paintings and come back to me, infant and all."

"Did she live with you?" asked Sanders casually.

Harriet raised an eyebrow at him and then shook her head. "No, that isn't the reason why I yearn for her to come back. She's more a work object than a love object as far as I'm concerned. Although, of course, one grows fond of a good assistant—the way you grow fond of a good camera." She sighed. "Then, since my life was totally disrupted anyway, I decided to come back to Ottawa. I'd had this project in mind for a while, and I scurried around and found a few paying assignments in the city to keep me going until the book is finished. So here I am. Sublet my Toronto apartment, rented out my studio space, and drove up in February. I was thinking of settling here permanently— this is where I grew up, and I like it—but I'm not sure there's enough of my kind of work to keep me going here full-time."

"So you've decided to move back to Toronto?"

"Well, *decided* is too strong a word. I'll probably go back. Sometime." She shook her head. "Who can predict what anybody's going to be doing in six months' time? Or six minutes' time? Look at that guy over there—not literally, my friend the inquisitive police officer—he'll think I'm talking about him."

"But you are."

"Of course I am. You know what I mean." Amusement crinkled the corners of her eyes. "He's sitting in a bar, surrounded by noise and jollification, and what's he doing? Flipping through a trashy novel, pretending to read it. Did he anticipate at lunchtime that he was going to be sitting here—"

"How do you know it's trashy?" interrupted Sanders.

"Did you know you were a very irritating person? Let us assume for the sake of discussion that it is trashy. Why sit in a bar drinking overpriced draft beer in order to read trash? Or not read it? He seems to have trouble concentrating. I'll bet that pint cost him more than the book."

"He's probably meeting someone," said Sanders. "And experience has taught him that she's always late."

"Then why does he never glance at the door in passionate anticipation? The only direction he's been looking in so far is over here, at us."

"Well, try this one. He's one of your devoted admirers," said Sanders. "And he's hoping you'll get rid of me so he can pick you up."

"Idiot," said Harriet. "He doesn't have much of a chance, anyway. I can't stand pale, weedy redheads. You want to go with me while I drop the film off at the lab? That's something else Jane would have done."

"Don't you develop it yourself? I'm disillusioned," said Sanders. "What about those movies with photographers up to their elbows in chemicals in the darkroom? While sinister portraits of gruesome murders being committed gradually emerge from the blank paper. You know the kind."

"Not Ektachrome," she said. "Color," she added when she saw his blank look. "Positive color—you know, slides. Labs just throw it in a machine and it's ready in three hours. I'm not a big enough outfit to run my own color lab. If you like, I'll take you to my darkroom one of these days and show you some black-and-white developing, though, just to prove that I'm genuine."

"That's an intriguing possibility," said Sanders cautiously.

"Actually," she said, drawing out the word and then hesitating. "I have a more intriguing possibility. Do you like music?"

"Is this a test question?"

"No, of course not." She paused. "Well, I suppose it is. Before you answer, I'll give you a clue to what you're getting into. Anna Maria Strelitsch, the violinist, is playing at the Arts Centre tonight—Mozart and some moderns, I think—and I have two tickets. Good tickets. But I'm not going to take you if you're going to hate it. I refuse to have my evening spoiled by someone squirming in agony—or falling asleep—beside me."

"Hey, what makes you assume I'd squirm?" he said defensively. "I like music. It sounds wonderful. And I only fall asleep if I've been up all night. What about you? Are you going in those disreputable jeans and that peculiar jacket?"

"No call to throw rocks at my working clothes. I wouldn't be much use scrambling around the landscape in a tight skirt and high heels with no place to store my bits and pieces. But don't worry, I'll get dressed up. You won't recognize me."

"Fine," he said. "How about dinner first?" he asked casually.

She picked up her beer and put it down again. "It would be wasted on me," she said at last. "I hate eating in a rush. It puts me in such a foul mood I can't even taste what I'm eating. I'll go and get dressed and meet you in front of the Arts Centre at twenty to eight. We can eat later. That way you're sure not to fall asleep."

"Well, all right," he said. "Don't you want me to pick you up?"

"No need," she said. Her voice was cold. "I'm a big girl. I can find my way around the city by myself." A slight smile failed to remove the sting in voice and words.

"Right," he said abruptly. He stood up, irritated, grabbed his raincoat, and then waited with heavy politeness while she rescued all her bits and pieces from the floor. "I'll see you in front of the Arts Centre at twenty to eight."

"If you insist on being gallant," she said, "you can carry the tripod and camera case back to the car." This time the smile was close to looking real. "And I thought you were coming with me to drop the film off."

Sanders scooped up the two items and followed Harriet out of the pub. As they were leaving, the man with the novel snapped it shut, losing his place, slipped it into his pocket, picked up his own coat, and followed them out.

He paused in the door to look around, then strolled nonchalantly after them in the direction of the parking garage where Harriet had left her car. Just as he was about to cross the road a tour bus pulled up to the curb and forty-four camera-carrying tourists spewed onto the pavement around him. By sheer numerical force they carried him back a good ten feet in the direction he had come from. By the time he fought his way out from the center of the throng, Harriet and Sanders were nowhere in sight.

Andrew Cassidy looked at his watch and began restoring the material on his desk to the folders he had taken it from. 6:05. He should be able to work his way through the rest of Steve Collins's files now without the irritating necessity of explaining his presence to every clerk and junior word-processing assistant in the entire intelligence service. Not that what he was doing was any of their business, of course, but that didn't seem to stop anyone.

He walked down the empty corridor until he reached Steve's office, pulled the key out of his pocket, and walked boldly in. Last night he had stayed late enough to inventory file names. Tonight he was going to have to see if they contained anything of interest.

At 7:15 he heard a noise in the corridor and looked up, yawning and unworried. Right now, he would have welcomed an armed robbery to relieve the tedium of reading through these files. The noises stopped. Probably the cleaning staff, thought Cassidy, and turned back to his reading. Just as he began to work up a new sense of speed, however, the door was flung open. "What in hell are you doing in Steve's office?" said a hostile voice. It was Betty Ferris, who spent most of her days in the duplicating room.

"Hi, Betty," he said. "Sorry about this. I'm just clearing things up in here. We've got to check out what he'd been working on recently. In case there are things that haven't been finished up." He shook his head impatiently. "For God's sake, don't look at me like that. I was asked. I'm not just snooping. And what are you doing here this late?"

"I often work late," she said. Her voice had little expression. "I got in the habit. It sort of makes up for the mornings I can't get in on time because of Stacy. Anyway, I saw a light on in here, and I wondered who was pawing around in Steve's stuff."

A new light on Steve presented itself to Cassidy. And quickly formed itself into a comprehensible picture. He leaned back and examined the woman more closely. Maybe not everyone's ideal, but now that he looked, palely beautiful and certainly intelligent. Underemployed at the moment, running errands, making coffee, and doing everyone's photocopying. Mother of a small child, as well, he remembered. Losing Steve must have been a blow. "Sorry," he murmured. "I'm trying not to paw, as you put it, but it's the only way we'll find out what in hell is going on—why someone killed him. And why might tell us who." She still stood where she was, looking angry and suspicious. "Look, Betty, an awful lot of this seems to be out-of-date reports and stupid memos. You wouldn't know where he kept his current files, would you?"

Betty shrugged. "In with the rest of the stuff in there, I suppose," she said. "I don't know where else they'd be. You want some coffee? I've got it ready in my office." He shook his head and watched her as she slipped quietly out of the room.

The last note of the Mozart Violin Concerto died slowly away, and the violinist lowered her hands to her sides, bow and violin forming a delicate frame around her. She bowed, head down, and a river of blond hair cascaded over the front of her white dress. Applause surged up through the hall. She straightened up, flipped her hair off her face with her bow hand, and smiled broadly. She raised both arms high above her head, gestured to draw her accompanist into the general enthusiasm, and skipped off the stage to a startled burst of laughter.

"Extraordinary, isn't she?" asked Harriet as she stood up. "Do you like to mingle, go outside, or stay perched during intermission?"

"Let's go outside and catch pneumonia. There isn't anyone here to mingle with, as far as I'm concerned. I don't know Ottawa's cultural elite."

She grabbed his hand and made a break for an exit door. "Come on, there's a path through here," she hissed. Suddenly his hand tightened on hers and he stopped dead, bringing her headlong rush to a jerky halt. "What the hell?" she muttered, and looked up. Someone tall and dark-haired, with a thin face like an anxious weasel, was blocking their path.

"Good evening, Inspector. I didn't expect to see you here."

"Ah . . . Inspector Higgs. Miss Jeffries. We came to see the violinist. I suppose you came to see the bigwigs."

An amused smile crossed Higgs's face, and Sanders realized that the man might even be relatively pleasant some of the time. "Something like that," Higgs admitted. "At least, I'm not here for pleasure. Or not *just* for pleasure, at any rate. Not my favorite sort of assignment, either. Any potential bomb throwers in this crowd, do you think?" he asked suddenly.

"I'd go for one of the Austrians," said Harriet, and both men turned to look at her, surprised.

"The Austrians? Which ones are they?" asked Sanders.

"Judging by the voices around us, I'd say that the hometown contingent is pretty strong. Place seems to be stiff with Viennese."

"How can you tell?" asked Higgs.

"It's the funny-sounding German. You can't mistake it." Harriet smiled pleasantly at Higgs and started across the lobby. "Happy hunting," she whispered as she went by him.

Sanders stood for a moment where he was and watched her make her way toward the door, before heading after her into the cold spring air.

There was still a hint of twilight in the sky to the west beyond Parliament Hill, and in the soft light Harriet Jeffries looked startlingly lovely. She had traded her jeans for a dress of gray, loose-waisted, full-skirted, and cut high to the neck. It had the paradoxical effect of making her look more desirable than the acres of semiexposed bosoms in the lobby. Sanders sat down on the edge of a concrete planter to look at her. She walked back and forth restlessly in front of him, talking ceaselessly and with earnest intensity about the music, until she leaned over him to point out something on the program, which he still held in his hand. Her faintly perfumed hair fell down over his cheek, and her breast brushed against his shoulder. He looked irritably at the crowds of people who had poured out of the lobby with them and tried to keep his mind on talk of music.

Karl Lang was making his way slowly across the lobby in the general direction of the crowd from the Austrian embassy who were circling the prime minister like a flock of tugboats, nudging him toward the room set aside for his intermission refreshment. He bumped into the tall and pretty girl from External Affairs and changed course abruptly. "Miss Henderson," he said with pleasure in his voice, "so delighted to see you."

"Hello, Herr Lang." Her cheeks were pink with excitement, making her eyes look brighter and livelier than ever. "Isn't it a magnificent concert? I've never been to anything so wonderful."

Herr Lang smiled indulgently. He wouldn't have placed it quite at that level—in fact, he thought Anna Maria was a little off her stride tonight—but the child was young, no doubt, and unused to live performances. "Where are you sitting?" he asked. "I hope you have a good view."

"It's not bad," she said. "Up there." And she waved vaguely in the direction of the doors that led to farthest corners in the hall. "I can hear really well."

"Are you by yourself?" She nodded. "Look, I have two tickets. They're splendid seats, center front. I was supposed to be bringing a business acquaintance, but he developed some sort of late-blooming spring cold. Actually, I suspect that he couldn't face an entire evening of unrelieved good music. But I would be charmed if you would take the other seat. If you don't mind sitting beside a sentimental Viennese," he added disarmingly.

She hesitated a moment and blushed slightly. "Oh, thank you, Mr. Lang," she said at last. "I'd love to. Everyone's being so nice to me."

"Anyone likes to see these things go to someone who really enjoys them," he said, a trifle sententiously. "Shall we go and investigate the seating?"

"I must run and get my coat," she said. "I left it up there."

"Well, well," said Toni Bleibtreu to his friend Hal Metcalfe. "Look at that devious fox." They were standing indecisively in front of the room where the prime minister had just been berthed.

"Who?" said Hal. "Oh, him. And, Toni, foxes are wily, not devious. If you're going to be colorful and colloquial, try to get it right."

"This one is devious."

"Why do you call him that?" said a third voice from the doorway. "It is not the term I would have thought to apply to him." The English was accented, but careful.

"Oh, good evening," said Bleibtreu, drawing the speaker invisibly into the group. "Hal Metcalfe. Carlo Hoffel, our . . ." He looked over and caught the slight frown. "One of our early-arriving delegates. And it's very obvious. Karl Lang, everybody's pal, the kind you trust with your wife or your mistress. He has captured Sarah Henderson, that pretty creature from External who was at last night's party, and seems to be carrying her off to the empty seat beside him. Do you suppose he always buys two tickets so he can seduce pretty girls in the cheap seats?" Hoffel smiled gently and shifted position enough to follow their progress through the lobby.

"Perhaps." Hal stared at her in turn, trying to remember what was significant about her besides her long legs and sweet face, but last night's alcoholic haze dropped a curtain down on whatever it was. Probably nothing. "Are you both going to the reception after the concert?"

"*Natürlich*. And so are you, I hope."

"I shouldn't. My boss would like me to be in and functioning by six A.M. tomorrow. But I shall. Has Lang invited that little creature?"

Toni shook his head. "I don't know. But if he can lure her down in amongst the snoring contingent from the diplomatic, he can certainly lure her to a free booze-up. And if he can't, I will. She's almost as delicious as the *artiste*."

"Booze-up! Delicious! My God, Toni, where are you picking these things up?"

Bleibtreu winked and headed in the direction of a pretty redhead who was standing, looking mildly bewildered, in the middle of the lobby.

"Are you here on business?" said a voice behind him. "Or on a cultural mission?"

Metcalfe whirled around, startled, and found himself looking up at the gloomy visage of Inspector Charles Higgs. "A little of both, actually," Metcalfe said. "I mean, I had no choice, but on the other hand, I would have come anyway." He frowned. These goddamn security people always afflicted him with a need to maintain a constant line of foolish chatter. "Not much doing, though," he added. "The Austrian P.M. looks to be pretty thoroughly walled in there. And none of the other big shots seems to be here yet."

"Mmm," said Higgs noncommittedly. "Arriving Thursday, most of them."

"I wonder what the Austrians are gearing up for, though," added Metcalfe brightly.

"Gearing up? What in hell do you mean by that?" said Higgs.

"Well, they seem to have brought Hoffel along," he said, nodding in the direction of the broad shoulders and stocky frame of the Austrian delegate they had been talking to. "You know, their deputy security head. Rather large cannon for a conference like this, I would say." Metcalfe glanced around him with a somewhat desperate look on his face. "Jesus," he said with relief, "there's my boss over there glaring viciously at me. If I don't move I'll be on the Pago Pago desk tomorrow."

Higgs looked long and intently over at the burly Austrian. At last he took out his notebook and scribbled down a few words as the lowered lights began to chase patrons back to their seats.

"Where would you like to eat?" asked Harriet. They had broken away from the crowds milling about in front of the Arts Centre and had started walking slowly down Elgin. "But that's not really fair, is it? Not when you don't know what there is. What kind of food do you feel like?"

"Oddly enough," said Sanders, looking down at her in the light of a street lamp, and feeling another sort of emptiness, "I am not particularly hungry."

They were walking down from the Arts Centre, roughly following the path of the canal. "Look at that," said Harriet, grabbing his arm and pointing over to the left. "Isn't it gorgeous? It's my favorite building in the entire city, though I wouldn't want you to tell the architect who hired me that, and it isn't even made of stone, so I can't include it in my book."

"What is it?" asked Sanders.

"It's the old Drill Hall." She dropped his arm and walked slowly on. "It's funny, but I'm not hungry either. How about a drink somewhere?"

"Sure," he said. "Good idea. Anywhere in particular?" he asked lightly.

She stopped, frowning. "What about there?" she said, with a wave in the direction of any one of a number of establishments across the street.

Without waiting for a reply she stepped out onto the road. Almost at once Sanders grabbed her by the arm and yanked her back. She stumbled and fell against his chest; he encircled her with his other arm to steady her. "Hey!" she snapped, shaking herself free. "What in hell do you think you're doing?"

"Just trying to keep you alive long enough to get that drink" he said calmly. "There was a bus coming."

"Oh," she said, her voice trembling. She stood absolutely still, staring after the retreating bus until he took her by the arm again and steered her firmly through the traffic.

"What do you do when the sun isn't just at the right angle?" asked Sanders, after they had settled into a corner of the first bar they came to, in that pause before their drinks arrived.

"Oh, this and that," she said vaguely. "I do a fair amount of darkroom work—it can be time-consuming when you're using a lot of black-and-white film. But otherwise I walk around and look at things. And take pictures. Just for me, sometimes. I like it—it's a marvelous way to spend your time," she said defensively. "Although I have to admit it's even better when you get paid for it."

"That's it? You walk around and take pictures? Don't you ever talk to people?"

"Sometimes. A friend of mine was supposed to be coming up yesterday and staying for a week, but she couldn't make it. That's why I had two tickets to the concert tonight. In case you were wondering." She twirled the cocktail napkin in meaningless patterns around the small surface of the table.

"I was," he said, putting a fingertip on the napkin close to her hand to stop its gyrations. "But I was beginning to hope you had picked them up recently, like maybe today." He moved his arm onto the back of the bench until it brushed lightly against her shoulder; he bent his head closer, drawn by her perfume, the light playing on her hair, and the soft movement of the material of her dress. She stiffened at his touch and pulled her hand away, then edged farther down along the padded bench.

"Here come our drinks at last," she said, smiling brightly at him.

He moved back, puzzled, and started to talk about the odd collection of people at his seminar: the brash rookie from Halifax, two depressed French-speaking constables from Sherbrooke who probably found Higgs's clipped speech incomprehensible, and, of course, Higgs himself. Sanders heard himself speaking without having any clear idea of what he was saying; he was too busy watching her gazing at him as if every nonsensical word were desperately important. What in hell was she thinking about behind that facade of rapt attention? When the waitress tried to get her another drink, she jumped, startled, shook her head, and began to gather herself together.

"Thank you for the drink," she said, heading for the door and looking suddenly miserable. "I'm parked just over there. You can find your own way home, can't you?"

"Oh, yes," he said. "I, too, have been looking after myself for some time now." He turned north and began walking back toward his motel.

Hal Metcalfe pulled up in front of a brightly lit Georgian house on Echo Drive. "Are you sure this is it?" he asked. "Didn't you say he lived by himself? That looks as though it has a helluva lot of bedrooms for one guy."

Toni Bleibtreu leaned forward into the front seat. "Well, I suppose he has some faithful slaves in there, too. The man is sickeningly rich."

Sarah Henderson turned from contemplation of the house and stared past Metcalfe down at the canal, rippling in the dim half-light cast up by the city. "What I wouldn't give to have a place like this," she said. Her voice was flat. "You should see my apartment."

Bleibtreu dropped a hand on her shoulder. "Who knows, someday you might—no, someday you will."

"Sure, and I'm the Princess of Wales," she said. "But I really don't think I should come. I'll get a cab. I wasn't invited, and it's supper—"

"Of course you were invited," said Bleibtreu. "Lang expects you. We promised to bring you along. Anyway, he's not going to have to add water to the soup and run out for another loaf of bread because you're there. The place will be drowning in food and drink. Come on, and after the party we'll go for a stroll along the canal."

"And just who are those two guys in uniform at the door?" said Miss Henderson suspiciously. "They look like Mounties to me. Guess whose name isn't on the guest list. Or shouldn't be."

"Well, if they won't let you in, we'll sacrifice this intensely exciting evening and not go in ourselves. Right, Toni?"

"Right."

"And then we'll all go for a walk along the canal."

CHAPTER 5

Wednesday, May 17

Superintendent Deschenes walked into the restaurant and looked around. That erect back in the booth on his right he recognized as Charlie Higgs; Deschenes dodged the hostess and headed straight for him. "Good morning," he murmured. "And I appreciate your coming out this early. Were you late last night?"

Higgs shook his head and stifled a yawn. "Not very. I think the prime minister has jet lag. He was crumbling by eleven o'clock and left before midnight." Higgs dropped his voice suddenly and began speaking rapidly. "He brought top-level security with him. A man named Hoffel, Carlo Hoffel. Metcalfe from External seems to know him."

"Not surprising," said Deschenes. "He was posted in Vienna."

"Anyway, I don't like it when they bring someone that big. It means the Austrians are expecting something to happen. Listen," Higgs said earnestly, "they're bloody nervous about this visit. And whatever they've heard isn't filtering through to us. Maybe our surveillance on the Austrian contingent ought to be upped to a more adequate level."

Ian MacMillan slipped onto the seat next to Charlie Higgs and dropped his folded newspaper between them on the table. "What's this about adequate surveillance? When does anyone ever have adequate surveillance, I'd like to know?" He stopped speaking as the waitress leaned over the booth to take their orders.

Higgs ordered bacon and eggs and stared patiently out the window while the others were deciding. "They seem to be expecting something close to home," he said as soon as they had ordered.

"Close to home?" asked Deschenes.

"Hoffel's edgy. And he has his eye on that violinist. Strelitsch. He spent all his time at the reception trying to monitor all her conversations."

"Maybe he has a letch for her," said MacMillan. "I hear she's pretty spectacular."

"I didn't know you followed the world of classical music, Ian," said Deschenes.

Higgs paid no attention to Deschenes. "Could be, but he's also suspicious as hell of her—there's a difference. He wasn't behaving like a jealous boyfriend, he was behaving like a security man on a live trail. Of course, I could be wrong. I didn't talk to the guy, I was just watching him." Apparently offended, Higgs opened up his newspaper as he waited for his breakfast to arrive. Almost immediately he put it down again, pushed aside the coffee cups, and spread it out on the table. "Look," he said in a quiet voice.

He had placed the paper so his superior officer could read it; Deschenes pulled his reading glasses out of his breast pocket and bent over the first page. There, in the bottom right-hand corner, was a picture of "Don Bartholomew," accompanying what appeared to be a lengthy story on the murder.

Henri Deschenes shoved the paper away, leaving MacMillan

to pick it up and read the text. "Where did they get the picture?" Deschenes asked.

Charlie Higgs shook his head. "Not from us," he said. "And I don't suppose he passed around snapshots of himself to all the boys on the crew."

"Driver's license?" said MacMillan. "Some helpful bastard at Regional must have passed it on."

"So much for keeping the whole thing low-profile," said Higgs. "Somebody's always got to be the clever bastard and screw everything up."

"I wonder," said Deschenes. "That's a pretty high-grade picture of him to be from his driver's license, wouldn't you say?" Higgs leaned over and looked again. He nodded. "CSIS has to be investigating. Maybe it's their file picture of him. Charlie, see what in hell they think they're doing right now, will you? Send that class of yours off to a spy movie or something and have a look. And, Ian, find out what the Regional Police have picked up. See if they gave the picture to the papers. I had better talk to Austrian security." He ran his hand over his forehead. "As my father used to say, *'Il ne me manque que ça.'"**

"To you?" asked Higgs.

"No," said Deschenes. "To my mother."

"And what did she say?"

"She pretended she couldn't understand him."

Wednesday morning's lecture was on interpretation of intelligence reports—not something, thought Sanders, that anyone in this room was likely to have to do. So Higgs had either run out of useful things to say or he was showing off.

---

*"That's all I needed right now."

Or, most likely, both. But Sanders flipped through his scribbled-on notebook looking for a clean page and waited for the man to say something worth committing to paper. He had begun to feel sorry for Higgs. He knew he was not the only person in the room who failed to find the lectures riveting, and his sketches were a mild protest compared to some of the ways people had chosen to pass the time. So this morning he was going to take some notes—real notes—and try to look at least vaguely interested.

At the mid-morning break it was evident that the instructor had noticed Sanders's newly awakened interest.

The enforced camaraderie of occasions like this brought out all of Sanders's latent misanthropy, and he had found himself a corner table where he was unlikely to be disturbed. He had barely had time to pull a book out of his pocket as insulation against the world when he felt someone looming over him. "May I join you?" The voice was sharp, unpleasant, and familiar.

"Certainly, Inspector Higgs," said Sanders, putting aside the paperback with a scarcely audible sigh.

"Sanders, isn't it?" Higgs asked. "Toronto. We were surprised Toronto would send someone of your rank. We expected a retired sergeant when we heard Flanagan couldn't come."

No, thought Sanders, it took Maritimers to have the guts to do something like that. "We are always ready to improve our techniques," he said. "And it's an interesting subject."

"You seem to find intelligence work more interesting than most of the people here. The response is rather disappointing," Higgs said bitterly.

"I take it that intelligence is your specialty," said Sanders, and then wished he hadn't.

"I've been in intelligence for twenty-two years, one way or another," Higgs said. "Here and in the army. Not that

there's much use for an intelligence officer here these days."
He stared bleakly into his coffee, as if he had reliable
information that it contained cyanide but he was going to
drink it anyway.

"I'm surprised you didn't move over to Intelligence at
CSIS, then. When it split off. So you could continue on in the
same area."

"Surprised, eh?" Higgs gave Sanders a speculative look.
"Can't desert the old service," he said. "Not after all these
years. Let the younger men start off there. Good training for
them, off on their own." He pushed his half-full cup away.
"No offense, but I was sorry not to see Flanagan come up
from Toronto."

"Oh, do you know Flanagan?" said Sanders, who was
also pretty sorry that Flanagan hadn't come.

"Flanagan and I go way back," said Higgs, staring at the
concrete block walls of the cafeteria as though the lost
years were floating behind them somewhere. "We were in
the Mediterranean together. Then he went off to Toronto,
and I ended up here. Why did they send you? Do you do
intelligence work?"

Sanders shook his head. "Homicide. I once tried going
under cover but, you know, no matter how you dress, if
you're my size people take one look at you and say 'cop'
and that's it. I walk into a poolroom and in five minutes
there's no one there but me and the cockroaches. Not even
the owner. So I went into Homicide, where people expect
cops to look like cops."

Inspector Higgs appeared not to be listening. "Then why
send you?"

Sanders shrugged. "Beats me," he said. "Maybe they were
expecting a few bodies to float up."

"You're joking," Higgs said. "Aren't you? Nobody's really

expecting any trouble this week, are they?" His look of pop-eyed nervous anger had altered in some way in the last few minutes, and if Sanders hadn't known that they were sitting in one of the most secure places in the civilized world, he would have said that it had been replaced by fear.

"I wouldn't know," Sanders said casually. "You're the specialist."

Sylvia looked up as Ian MacMillan walked into the office escorting a dark-browed, fierce-looking man whose eyes were hollow with fatigue. In spite of his relative lack of height, he made MacMillan look pallid and effete. Sylvia smiled briskly, pushed a button on her telephone, and stood up. "He's waiting for you," she said. "Coffee?"

"Please," said the stranger. The voice arising from that broad chest was unexpectedly muted.

Deschenes appeared in the doorway to his office. "I would like to thank you for coming all the way out here on such short notice." He held out his hand. "It is *Mr.* Hoffel, is it not?"

"Mister will do, Superintendent," he said. "And Inspector MacMillan was a most efficient chauffeur. It was no trouble." As they were speaking, MacMillan herded them unobtrusively into the office, sat down behind them, and took his notebook from his pocket. Hoffel glanced rapidly back and frowned.

"What we're interested in, Mr. Hoffel—" Sylvia's entrance with the coffee interrupted Deschenes. He sat back and waited for her to pass cups around.

MacMillan's voice cut through the rattle of china. "What we're interested in, *Mr.* Hoffel, is finding out what in hell you're doing here—why your government decided to send you instead of the usual bodyguard types. I mean, why the whole bloody Austrian secret service, or whatever you call it, here in Ottawa?" MacMillan waved Sylvia out of his way with an angry gesture.

Hoffel pivoted slowly around in his chair and looked at MacMillan before turning to speak to Deschenes. "We had hoped to make my arrival appear unobtrusive," he said. "I had not really expected to be recognized."

"Our Mr. Metcalfe from External Affairs was posted in Vienna last year," said Deschenes.

"Ah. I see. Well, why am I here? Just as a precaution, of course. Our prime minister has become—what can I call it?—a target recently of some unpleasant attacks, most of them merely verbal. But there have been threats of violence. You know what these things are. One must pay attention to them even though it is very rare that anything happens as a result of them." He smiled and spooned sugar into his coffee.

"Why would your prime minister be subject to threats?" asked Deschenes.

"Why? All politicians, all famous people, receive threats," said Hoffel. His face had arranged itself into an expression of great sweetness.

"Indeed," said Deschenes. "But people like you are not sent out to hold their hands, are they?"

"Perhaps not." Hoffel paused, his head to one side, appearing to weigh Deschenes's usefulness and reliability. "We have a particular group of rightist fanatics who are convinced that our government is swinging dangerously to the left once more." His dark eyes danced with amusement. "I am sure that you Canadians think that we are all disturbingly right-wing, but on the whole we are really quite centrist, although we have our share of people on both sides of the political sea. This particular group seems to feel that a little destabilization would help to bring them to power. They are probably wrong, but we do not care to have them try."

"Especially if their destabilization techniques consist of killing off the members of your government?"

"If they tried that, it would be most unfortunate, yes," said Hoffel. "It is, of course, a remote threat, but one that must be taken into account."

"Why over here?" said MacMillan suddenly.

"Why not?" said Hoffel. "But we are investigating every area that the prime minister and other members of the government must visit. We are not more suspicious of your peaceful and well-guarded country than of any other place." He smiled again and put down his coffee cup. "I must return to the embassy, I'm afraid. I have a meeting there in a few minutes. If I could prevail upon you to—"

"Of course," said Deschenes. "Inspector MacMillan will arrange for you to be taken back downtown."

MacMillan followed Hoffel in the direction of Sylvia's office, stopped at the door, and then walked back to Deschenes's desk. "A helluva lot of good that did us," he hissed. "I've had more information out of the Mafia on a bad day. 'Ve are not bloody vell suspicious of your country,' " he mimicked in a harsh, badly rendered German accent. "The hell they aren't. They know something—and I'm going to find out what it is."

"Thank you, Ian," said Deschenes coldly, and picked up his telephone receiver.

"What I don't understand," said Harriet Jeffries, "is why you're here. Aren't you supposed to be communing with your fellows all day? What's happened to your meeting?"

"What meeting?" asked Sanders lazily. He drained off his beer and looked over at Harriet. "Our leader, the inestimable Higgs himself, declared that he had other duties and ordered us to go sightseeing. That's what I'm doing, obeying orders. An excellent quality in a police officer, the ability to obey orders." He pushed aside his glass. "But what is more important now," he said, "is lunch. Do we take risks and eat here—I think I smell something that might be food—or do we go elsewhere?"

"Elsewhere," said Harriet. "Where's your car?"

"At the motel. Why?"

"Excellent." She leaned back and raised her hands expansively in the air. "We will go in mine, which has a cooler in the backseat filled with things to eat and drink. When you called, I decided that I was in the mood for a picnic. I can find you a place both quiet and pleasantly sheltered from the wind. How does that sound?"

"Terrific," said Sanders. As they stood up to go, the person at the back table slipped his book into his pocket and set out after them.

"This is terrific," said Sanders. He was lying on his back on the grass, staring up at a small tree that had grown green and luxuriant in the protected environment of the city, and trying to figure out what kind of bird was darting around in it, singing furiously. "I do believe that some of my fellow officers have joined a tour of the city, poor suckers. They don't know the half of it."

"What do you mean?" asked Harriet from her perch on a large granite boulder. She had attached another lens to her camera and was focusing on a seaplane moored downstream from them in the river. "Do you like seaplanes?"

"The essence of pure enjoyment," he said. "That's in answer to your first question. And I've never thought much about them. That's in answer to the second."

"Well, I've taken a picture of it anyway," said Harriet. "Whether you like them or not. Can you reach the beer?"

"Certainly," said Sanders. He rolled over and extracted a bottle of beer from a small orange cooler. "How did you find out about this place?" he asked, propping himself up on his elbow to open the bottle and look around him. He was lying on the grass inside a circle of rocks that looked as if it had been built by Stone Age men of modest aspirations. He had placed himself strategically within reaching distance of Harriet and the cooler, which contained the remains of a picnic lunch, several rolls of film, and beer. To the east the river flowed away from them, swirling around the point; to the west thick shrubbery and trees hid them from the noise and smell of heavy traffic on the bridge to Hull. The worn grass and flattened beer cans testified that many others knew about this retreat, but on this sunny Wednesday they had it to themselves.

"Isn't it nice?" she said. "I found it when I was a kid. We used to have a house near the canal, and I'd set off every day in summer with a lunch and just go and look at things. Deserted corners were my specialty. I know lots more of them, too." Sanders rolled over on his side to look at her, but by now she had twisted herself around and was contemplating the shoreline across the river through the viewfinder of her camera. "Hey, I didn't realize it was that late," she said, pointing at a distant clock face.

"What about it?"

"If we leave now, we'll just make it out to the lab to pick up the Ektachrome and get back to my place before rush hour starts. Don't you want to see those pictures you helped take?" She glanced sideways at him and started picking up the empty bottles.

"Of course," said Sanders, propping himself up on his elbow and watching the sun glint on her dark hair as she moved.

Andrew Cassidy was back in his own office at CSIS, with piles of material stealthily transferred from Steve Collins's filing cabinet stuffed into his hitherto empty bottom drawer. As he finished reading one document, he would drop it into a cardboard box beside his chair and pick up another. He reckoned he had enough here to occupy him until the end of the day, with plenty left in Steve's office to keep him busy until noon tomorrow. And then he was going to have to start thinking, because the pages of careful notes he had compiled so far wouldn't lead a cat to a mousehole. The squeak of the door opening made him close the folder in front of him and look up.

"Oh. Hi, Betty. What's up?"

"It's Charlie Higgs. He's in my office and he wants to see you."

"Damn," said Cassidy. "What for?"

"About Steve, I expect," she answered. "What will I tell him?"

"Anything. Tell him I've gone to Kenora for my sister's wedding and I won't be back for a week; tell him I got hit on the head and I'm still in a coma. Look, Betty, I haven't got anything to say to Charlie Higgs. He'll ask me what we're doing and I'll say everything we can and he'll know that means nothing at all and he'll get mad as hell. And I don't blame him."

"I'll tell him you're out, shall I? Even though he knows you haven't checked out with downstairs?"

"Sure. He'd expect nothing less from me. He always thought I was an insubordinate son of a bitch. Thanks, love. I'll do the same for you someday." And he blew her a kiss. "Oh—and Betty?" She turned back. "Is this all Steve had around? Because most of it isn't worth a pinch of shit. What about at home?"

She looked thoughtfully at him. "Well, as far as I know, that's it. But why would he tell me where his stuff was kept? You know."

Her tone was dismissive, almost contemptous, but she remained standing in the doorway with her head tilted slightly to one side and her hair falling carelessly across one half of her face, hiding her expression. Cassidy waited, afraid to move and break the mood, for her to say something else. But after a moment more, she flicked the hair off her face, nodded abruptly, and left. Maybe that meant he had kept things at home. It wouldn't hurt to check, even if it meant putting off the lovely Samantha one more time.

"Where are you staying in Ottawa?" Sanders asked as Harriet jumped into the car, dumped the envelope from the lab on his lap, and headed into the steadily thickening traffic.

"In the Glebe," she said. "Near the canal. One of those miraculously lucky six-month sublets. Actually, I'm only a few blocks from Dow's Lake, practically in the country. It's nice." As she was speaking, she made a right turn through a red light without bothering to stop, screeched into the oncoming traffic, and bucketed along the potholed road. "Bronson," she said. "It's a little faster than Bank, I think. You know, this is where I learned to drive when I was seventeen. Around here."

"They should have tried teaching you a little harder. Don't traffic laws impress you at all?" asked Sanders as she ran her second red light.

"Not at all," she said. "Does my driving bother you? I've never had an accident. I'm probably much more careful than you are, friend."

"No doubt," he said, yawning and lapsing into semicomatose silence until the car stopped on a shaded street in front of a big, dark red house.

"Hey," she said, touching him lightly on the arm. "We're here. These are my temporary quarters, or at least the top half of it is. Or are. Like it?"

Sanders yawned again. "Not bad. It's not quite what I expected, though," he said as he got out of the car. "Not nearly arty enough."

"Come around to the back. We use the tradesman's entrance." She pushed open a wooden gate that led into a large garden, and pointed with a flourish at a set of wooden stairs going up to the second floor. "Private entrance."

The stairs led directly into the kitchen, and it was clear from one look at that room that no one had done anything to the house since it was built sixty or seventy years before. It had a huge old porcelain sink; an ancient, yellowed stove; and an antique refrigerator. The floor was wooden, dark, and stained with years of cooking spills. Sanders looked at it and laughed. "This reminds me of home," he said. "Except that it's bigger and seems to have a better class of neighbors. And my ma isn't standing in front of the stove yelling at me."

"Isn't it great?" she said. "Come in here." She led him impatiently into a room off the kitchen that was being used as a study, walked over to an enormous wooden desk, and took the envelope from him. She ripped it open, extracted a small box, and began laying the slides that she took out of it onto a large rectangular structure with a milky glass top.

"What's that?" he asked.

"A light box," she said. "Don't cops ever take pictures?"

"Of course we do. But we have these people called photographers, and that's what they're paid to do. Then the rest of us don't have to know anything."

"Philistines," she said cheerfully, and flipped on the switch. There was a long silence as she bent over the slides and examined each one. Just as Sanders had begun to think that there was something seriously wrong with them, she looked up and said, "Perfect. I am bloody good, you know. Look at that one—the one we did with all those people charging by me—it's awe-inspiring, that's what it is." She pointed at the slide of the Supreme Court building.

"Where did those two come from?" asked Sanders. "I didn't see them standing there."

"They came along between the time I was setting up and when I actually took the shot. See how far over they are? The camera was pointed in that direction," she said, indicating the center of the building, "and yet it picked up those two guys. That Olympus twenty-four-millimeter shift is a beautiful lens. See how straight those lines are? You know, they probably didn't even realize that they were in the picture. I mean, if they saw us. Remember where we were standing? They would assume that anyone set up like that was taking a shot of the door."

"Does that matter?" asked Sanders, curious now. "I mean, do you have to get someone's permission to take a picture of him? Of course, they're so small you wouldn't be able to recognize them anyway."

"What do you mean? There's enough detail in that slide to blow it up to four by six feet and turn it into a mural.

Here, let me show you." She handed him a small object like a jeweler's glass. "Look at it through the magnifier. You'll see."

Sanders clutched the magnifier to his eye and obediently looked at the slide. The two men, dressed in dark suits and clutching newspapers under their arms, were looking in the direction of the camera, as if they were trying to decide what to do about it. He looked at the hollowed cheekbones and wide mouth of the one on the right with a sense that he should know the man. But then, he was probably a politician and had his picture plastered over the papers two or three times a week. "You're right," he said. "You can see their faces."

"Most of the book is going to be done in black and white, of course," she said. "But I wanted one really spectacular wide-angle shot in color for the dust jacket. Or the editor does, I should say. What do you think? Splashy enough? Yet filled with Canadian restraint?"

"I'm impressed," he said. "Maybe you really are a photographer. In spite of the lab."

"Thanks," she said casually, and switched off the light box, leaving the slides where they were. "Come into the living room and sit down. Can I get you a beer? Of course. Just a minute." She led him into a large room with high ceilings and long windows and pointed him at an armchair. "There," she said, "sit." She handed him a newspaper. "Amuse yourself while I get the beer."

Sanders looked idly down at the copy of the Ottawa *Citizen* lying in his lap. The news of the world seemed far away and insignificant right now. The headline told him that the latest provincial budget was going to hit smokers again, which meant nothing to him. He didn't smoke. Then, unfolding the paper so that the entire front page would be visible, he stared. There, beside a feature story on safety in the workplace, was a picture of someone he knew, someone he had seen recently. And that someone, whose name was apparently Don Bartholomew, was now dead. Murdered. Don. And he saw it all again in his mind in the bright colors of exhaustion. The drunken construction worker, the mynah bird, the man who took him away.

The man who took him away. High cheekbones, sunken cheeks, that mouth, those mean, son-of-a-bitch eyes. And the scar. "Hey," he said to Harriet as she brought in a couple of bottles of Henninger beer. "Do you have a better magnifier? Can you make those slides bigger?"

"The detail is there," she said. "I don't have a stronger magnifier, but I can throw the slide into the enlarger and we'll make it as big as you want. Which slide did you want to see?" She looked mildly curious, but not sufficiently so to ask why.

"The one with the two men in front of the court. I think I've seen one of them before."

"I'll get it." She was heading through the kitchen with the slide before he got to his feet. "Come through here," she called, pointing to a door he hadn't noticed before that led out of the kitchen beside the back entrance. "It was the scullery," she said. "It's small, but it makes a pretty workable darkroom." She reached up and clicked on a light, and then took the plastic cover off an enlarger. "This ought to give you what you want. It's a secondhand Beseler I picked up here in Ottawa. It's a sweetheart. Almost as good as my new one at home," she added. "These lenses are just about as sharp as the one I took the picture with. If it's in the slide, we should be able to see it." She slipped the slide into the film carrier and turned on the light. The picture appeared, pale and distorted, on the easel below. She loosened a nut on the top of the enlarger and pushed the entire head gently back until it clicked solidly into place, now in a horizontal position. The picture gleamed on the freshly painted wall. "Okay. Flip off that light, will you? And I'll get this into focus."

He leaned over her in the dark, distracted by the scent of her hair and her skin, but trying to concentrate on the image in front of them. Slowly the lines sharpened and straightened, the shadows gathered into themselves, and the highlights leaped up between them. And there, over on the left, was the man with the deep-set eyes, the hollowed cheeks, and those thick and sensuous lips. He was staring right at Sanders, daring him to take that picture. Beside him stood a fair-haired, tanned man, whose eyes were directed at his companion. "Which one is it?" asked Harriet.

"The dark one," said Sanders.

"Who is he? Besides a mean-looking son of a bitch."

"A murderer, I think," said Sanders.

"I was wrong about one thing," said Harriet finally, after they had looked in silence at the image for a long, long time.

"What's that?"

"About them not knowing they were in the picture. That one's looking straight at the lens and he doesn't seem very happy." She fell silent again. "What do we do now?"

"Well," said Sanders, "I suppose we can take this slide in to the locals. The Ottawa police'll be able to deal with it. After all—"

"The hell we do! This is my slide, John Sanders, and it's not going to spend the next three years kicking around some courthouse waiting for trials and appeals and God knows what and then finally come back to me in tatters years after the book is published."

"I think they're actually looked after a little better than that," he said mildly. "And I understand what you're saying, but this picture may be their best chance of finding out who he is. You can't just ignore that, Harriet." He was trying to sound as calm and reasonable as he could. "Can you?"

"Oh, I can, without any difficulty. The problem is, will you let me?" She frowned. "There are the other slides—let's have a look at them."

"The other slides?"

"Sure. Whenever I'm taking slides for anything important I always bracket my shots—do a couple more at a slightly different exposure. Actually I often do at least two at each exposure. It's cheaper to expose another few inches of film than to have copies made. You get better results, too. But not when there's someone dancing around breathing down my neck, trying to get me to hurry," she said pointedly.

"I don't see how you manage to get an exact copy if you take two pictures at different times."

"I do buildings, remember? They don't have any trouble holding a pose. Just a minute." She left him in the darkroom, staring over at the pair of men on the Supreme Court lawn, trying to figure out exactly what he should do now. "Here it is," she said, and switched slides.

The shot was flatter, the colors less brilliant. "That was the one where we'd lost the sun again," she said, frowning at it. "The filtration is wrong. And the men have gone, so it's no good to you. Let's try the second shot." The same deep color and rich contrasts jumped up at them again. "That's good," she said. "But dammit, look at those bastards. I told you they'd seen me." Where in the first slide there had been two people staring into the camera, now there was a pair of slightly fuzzy backs. "They're getting the hell out of there."

"Can't you use one of the others for your cover and give the police the one with their faces showing?" asked Sanders.

"Are you kidding? The other two are disasters. I couldn't give them to a printer." She turned off the enlarger, flicked on the light, and stood in the middle of the room, chewing her lip. "But I'll tell you what I'll do. We can zip back to the lab now and get copies made of the good slide, and we'll take them to the police tomorrow." She picked up the three slides carefully. "I don't suppose they'll pay me to have it copied. It costs."

"They're going to want the original, you know."

"Well, they're not getting it. There probably isn't anyone there who could tell the difference anyway. The printer gets the original, the police get what they think is the original. Okay? That far I go, and no farther."

The way out to the lab seemed even farther this time, and the scenery no more gripping than it had been the first time around. Sanders sat impatiently in the car waiting for Harriet to emerge. Just as he had decided that she had walked out the back or been kidnapped, the door opened and she came bouncing out, looking completely unrepentant.

"What took you so long?" he asked, his voice developing that nasty edge he used on his partner.

"It's all your fault," she said blithely. "I knew you wanted the slide in a hurry, and so I told them it was a rush, absolutely urgent job. But they have an old client who's coming in tonight with another huge rush job and they wouldn't budge for us."

He noted the "us" and filed it silently away. "So how long is it going to take? Two weeks?"

"Oh, no. I was trying for tomorrow noon. But it looks like Friday morning, realistically. He made some vague promises about tomorrow at six if they could, but these vague promises never pan out. Is that impossibly long?"

"If that's the best they can do, then it can't be, can it?" He smiled. "I don't know why I'm worrying. It's not my goddamn case."

"Right. Now where to? Aren't you getting hungry after all that?"

"A police station."

"A what? What's the matter with you? Feeling like eating in a familiar environment?"

He gave her a look of long-suffering patience. "I have to let someone know that I saw the man they're looking for both in the coffee shop with the victim and in front of the Supreme Court. At which point he no longer had a scar. I'll tell them there are pictures, too, but they're in being developed."

"Now you're making me sound like Mummy with her sixty-nine-dollar camera special. I don't like it." She leaned back against the car door, looking mulish.

"What do you want me to say? That I know this photographer with a magnificent picture of the man you're looking for and one of his pals, only she won't give it to us? You don't want that, really."

"Why? Do the Ottawa police go in for torture?" She sat up straight again. "Oh, forget it." With a vicious grating of the starter, she got the engine going. "Any particular police station you want to go to?"

"I think there's one off Rideau Street. That'll do nicely. It doesn't matter a pinch who gets the report at this point. The

Ottawa police aren't handling the case, anyway. They'll send it on and maybe someday someone will ask to see me. Or they may have caught him already, in which case they won't need me or you *or* the picture. Okay? The station, then dinner."

Harriet sat in the car this time, and watched Sanders striding up to the front door of the police station. She opened up the glove compartment and took out a book—she always kept one ready in case she drove out to a location and had to wait. For a client, for the sun, for people to get out of the way. She was always having to wait. Thirty pages later he opened the car door and slid in. She closed the book with a snap and tossed it back into the glove compartment.

"What took so long? And are they coming out to arrest me?"

"Why do people always make jokes about getting arrested when they meet police officers?" asked Sanders irritably. "It really isn't very funny."

"*People* do it, I assume, because they're nervous. I have never made a joke about you arresting anybody, especially me, so far in our brief acquaintance. What I said was referring to the very real possibility that they might take umbrage at what I have done with that slide."

"Sorry, sorry," he said, holding up his hands. "I take it back. And they probably won't, because they don't seem to care very much. They took down my name and particulars, as we say, and then passed them on to the relevant authority. That's what took so long. Passing it on to the Regional Police. Because they, in turn, felt some compulsion to pass it on to the RCMP, and that took forever. Do you think you can wait another hour or two for dinner?"

"Wait? Can you give me a reason why I should?" Before he had a chance to answer, she shook her head gloomily. "I hope you realize what you're asking me to do. I don't survive very well without food."

"Because my presence is requested back at the goddamn RCMP building. Whatever we saw seems to have excited the bloody Mounties no end." He stretched and then turned and gave her a gloomy look. "I should have just waited and told them tomorrow morning."

"Leave me out of it if you can, please. I'd rather not spend the evening being grilled by a couple of horsemen. I'll drive you out there and hide in the car."

Harriet dropped Sanders off outside the grounds to avoid having to pass through any inspections, formal or informal, and offered to wait.

He shook his head. "I'd rather walk," he said.

"Walk? From here? You're crazy. This is the middle of the goddamn suburbs. Nobody walks around here. You'll get hit by a car."

He looked mulishly at her. "I'll go up the path by the river," he said. "I'm restless and it's a nice evening. Why shouldn't I walk? You go ahead and eat somewhere. I'll join you later."

"You want to walk by the river, be my guest. Only I will be downstream sitting in the car next to a little park—it's about a half, maybe three-quarters of a mile away—and you can ride with me from there."

He felt a surge of annoyance and immediately felt petty and foolish. "Sorry. Okay. The little park. But I have no idea how long I'll be."

"I brought a book," she said as she slipped the car into gear and drove off. A worried frown creased her brow as she pulled over again at River Road and made for a parking

spot as near the river as she could get. But the pale blue
Ford Escort that had been in her rearview mirror since they
left the point, no matter how hard she tried to shake it,
apparently hadn't wanted to look at scenery. Maybe it hadn't
been that same one, after all. How many blue Fords are
there in a good-size city, anyway? she thought. Thousands,
probably. And so the chances of one being behind her at any
particular time were excellent, weren't they? She got slowly
out of the car and looked around; she reached into the
backseat and unwrapped a brown towel tucked in a corner.
Out of it she took the tiny camera she always kept handy,
and headed down to the river to indulge in some shots of
the water. As she walked back to the car, it occurred to her
that perhaps the blue Ford was following John, and was still
kicking around outside RCMP headquarters. She hoped so.
It was going to have a devil of a time following him
along that bicycle path without attracting some unwanted
attention. She smiled in relief and got back in the car,
pulled her book out of the glove compartment, and opened
it to page thirty.

Sanders sat in the waiting room and began building himself
up to a full-size fury. He had redescribed the scene in the
bar until his mind was soggy from the repetition. He had
gone over the photography session again and again, each
time with extreme caution, a fact that was evidently not lost
on Superintendent Deschenes. And now he had been parked
out here like a piece of inconvenient and outmoded furniture
and told to wait. And that was what he had been doing for
the past hour. He jumped to his feet and was headed for
Deschenes's secretary's office just as she poked her head
wearily in the door. "Sorry to keep you waiting so long,

Inspector," she murmured. "The superintendent would appreciate another word with you if you don't mind."

"What the hell do you think—" he started, looked at the smudges of fatigue under her eyes, and stopped. "Sure," he said, and followed her into the office.

Inspector Higgs was sitting there when Sanders came in. Higgs was studying a pile of material sitting on the edge of Deschenes's desk. "Sorry for that delay, Inspector Sanders," said Deschenes. "But, as you can no doubt appreciate, we had to check on a few things before letting you out of our grasp. Do sit down."

Sanders took the other chair, which was directly across from the superintendent's desk blotter. On the blotter sat a pile of computer printouts, topped by a picture that he recognized instantly. Trusting bastards. They must have been on to Toronto all this time, pulling his personnel files and identification photos. He hoped they were pleased with the result. On the whole, he thought they were not. No doubt they had been hoping for an imposter, who would give them a nice, juicy, and easy lead into something. He grinned. "I never thought it did me justice," he said, nodding at the mug shot.

"These things seldom do," said Deschenes. "However, it is unmistakably you. And that was all that we really had to ascertain. Now it only remains for me to repeat my apologies." There was a noise at the half-closed door and another man walked in, someone brutally big and sandy-haired. "Hello, Ian. This is Inspector Sanders, Toronto. Ian MacMillan. To repeat my apologies, as I was saying, and to let you go."

"Why so much interest in a construction worker?" asked Sanders abruptly.

"Well, we're not really that interested," said Deschenes. "He may have been involved in an organization we've been looking at. He himself isn't really that significant, I think. Wouldn't you say, Charlie?" And without waiting for Higgs to answer he went on. "Regional Police weren't really quite accurate in implying that this was our case. We made a simple inquiry and they jumped to some complicated conclusions. You know how it is." He smiled and got to his feet. "You say you'll be able to get that picture later in the week. Do you know exactly how much later? It might, after all, be rather useful."

Sanders shrugged. "Two or three days, I imagine. I think it's off being processed right now. You know these places. They mail them off to God knows where and pray that they get back sometime. I'll call you when I hear. I wouldn't have thought you really needed it that much. You probably have a good description, don't you? Just take off the scar and there he is." He stood up as well. "If you don't need me, I'll be off then."

"Would you like a ride anywhere?" said MacMillan. "I'm heading back into town in a minute or two."

Sanders shook his head. "Thanks, but I have a ride. Good night, gentlemen."

Sanders strode rapidly down the pathway by the river. The briskness of the pace was beginning to purge his residual irritation, and he felt buoyed up with new energy. At every bend in the path he glanced around, expecting to see the park that Harriet had promised; that half mile was becoming a very long one. At last it occurred to him that even if he found the park, no one in her right mind would have waited, dinnerless, this long for him to turn up. The river concurred with a melancholy roar, and once more his old bleak loneliness enveloped him. He plunged his hands into his pockets, slowed down to a depressed saunter, and stared gloomily at the ground beneath his feet while he followed the curve of the path.

The voice came out of nowhere and hit him in the belly with a shock of pleasure. "You bloody well took your time, didn't you? Don't you ever get hungry?" Harriet was sitting on the iron railings, wedged against a concrete pillar, focusing her little camera in the direction of a particularly interesting swirl in the rough and tumble of the water. He stopped in front of her. A sudden desperation made him reach out his arms. She jumped down, allowing his hands to encircle her waist briefly and smiling demurely. "Why, thank you, sir," she said. "But I do believe I could have managed that on my own. What happened at the Bastille over there? Or have you been dodging around trying to prevent them from finding me?"

He shrugged his shoulders and turned away. He was convinced that his violent and irrational mood swings of the last five minutes were stamped across his face, and he tried to avoid her quizzical eye. "Nothing much. Anything these bastards touch turns into a ridiculously time-consuming exercise, even when it means nothing. They had to check out everyone's story, that's all. Including mine. It takes forever. Most of the time I was just sitting there reading old issues of *Maclean's*." He glanced back to where she was standing looking gravely at him. "Where's the car?" he asked.

"Up the path—or actually it's down the path, isn't it?—a piece. I got bored and started walking up to meet you."

"Good," he said. "I feel like walking." He started, paused to let her catch up, and then shortened his stride somewhat to match hers. "Tell me," he said, and his voice came out more fiercely than he had intended, "how did you end up as a photographer?"

"Oh, that. That's simple. I did German in university and went off after I graduated to study in Germany."

"That seems logical," said Sanders. "But I don't see how—"

"Well, that's obvious, isn't it?" said Harriet. "I met a man. A student. He was learning photography, and I decided that there was no point in an English-speaking Canadian trying to compete with a lot of German-speaking students in studying German literature. And so I decided to learn photography along with Martin. As he went along in his course, so to speak, so did I." She looked dreamily off across the river. "He was thin, dark, and poetic-looking."

"What happened to him?"

"My visa ran out and I began to get serious about being a photographer. That meant I had to go somewhere where I could work legally." She flashed a small, rueful smile at him. "I came back here. Anyway, his father ran a nice little business in Hamburg and I think Martin wanted to go back home and live the good life after all."

"In spite of being poetic-looking?"

"In spite of being poetic-looking. Art was not enough, apparently. But he taught me a lot. I'm grateful to him. Ah," she said, "the car. It's late and I'm famished. Aren't you?"

CHAPTER 6

Cassidy stood in the middle of the living room in Steve Collins's apartment and stared, depressed, at the wall of books. He had been through the bedroom, inch by careful inch, and more rapidly through the small, neat kitchen. All he had discovered so far was that Steve was an obsessively tidy person with—apparently—no great fondness for mementos of the past. Except for a thin bundle of letters from Betty, written while he was on vacation last year, hidden in the back of his sock drawer. Those letters were still bothering Cassidy. First, he supposed, because they were witness to the fact that the affair had been going on for at least a year without anyone knowing about it, and that irritated his professional pride. Then, because he had read them purely in the line of duty, so to speak, and hated himself because he realized he had enjoyed reading them. They were literate, witty, amusing, and filled with passionate longing. Christ! They made poor Samantha seem as exciting as yesterday's porridge, he had thought as he slipped them into his jacket pocket. He had found himself envying Steve the possession of all that intelligence and good humor. And passion, he had to admit. They also almost made him forget why he was here, pawing through Steve's things. There was nothing in those letters that could have anything to do with Steve's death—Cassidy was sure of that—but maybe he would keep them a while, just in case, and return them to Betty quietly. Or was that really why he was keeping them? Was there any possible reason why he shouldn't either leave them here or return them right away? If he left them here, of course, someone else would find them, some slimy, snickering bastard who would probably read out the juicy parts to anyone who would sit and listen. He was surprised his colleagues at CSIS hadn't searched the apartment already. Or perhaps they had, and had laughed over the letters before leaving them behind as unimportant. With a slight start, he realized he was beginning to think of the letters as his, and was jealous of them; he couldn't cope with this. He turned his mind back to the question of the books.

If there was anything hidden here, it would be somewhere in all those books, of course. He pulled up a stool and took one off the shelf. It was a thin volume of poetry. He looked at the title page in surprise, riffled the pages for enclosures, and found himself reading one of the poems, then another. His view of Steve—the shy country boy who liked hiking and hockey games—was being violently wrenched askew. Of course, Steve's ready ability to take on and shed accents and personalities never had fitted his image as a bumbling rustic, but that had been accepted as a peculiar, but useful, aberration. Cassidy was having real trouble envisaging his colleague as the ardent and—if the letters were accurate—inventive lover, the collector of recently published poetry. What else was Steve up to that the boys in Intelligence were unaware of? After all, if Cassidy knew that little about him, then maybe . . . "For chrissake, Andrew," he said aloud. "You are going off the edge." His voice echoed in the empty apartment, and he reached for another book.

The answering voice hit him with a thrust of pure terror. "I thought I'd find you here, but I didn't expect you to be talking to yourself."

Cassidy dropped the book in his hand and whirled around on the stool. "How in hell did you get in?" he snapped.

Betty Ferris was standing in the doorway, her face an unreadable mask. She had changed into a pair of jeans and a large sweater, and the effect of the casually heavy clothing was to make her appear even more fragile. She stared at him as if she needed an enormous amount of time to decide what to say. When it did come, it was not particularly remarkable. "I have a key," she said mildly. "I have some right to be here. How did you get in?"

"I signed out his keys. This is, uh, sort of official," said Cassidy. There didn't seem to be anything to add that wouldn't sound offensive. "Did you want—" he started and couldn't finish. "Was there anything—" Unfortunately he thought of the letters in his pocket and reddened. "Why are you here?" he said at last.

"We shared this apartment on weekends," she said simply. "That's when Stacy is with her father. Or if she was with me, she came, too. They got on together." She paused and drew in a ragged breath. "I cleared out all my stuff as soon as I heard about . . . when they told me he was dead. I tried to leave everything tidy. I knew you bastards would be in here. But I just realized I left some things behind and I was hoping to get here before you did. I guess I didn't quite make it."

"So that's why the place looked like it did," said Cassidy in relief. "I couldn't believe that Steve was that fussy about how he lived. And these must be your books, then." He ran his finger along the spines of the books in front of him, as if happy to clear his old comrade of the charge of reading literature.

"How in hell do you know what Steve was like?" she said. Her voice was low and vehement, and her cheeks were scarlet with anger. "As a matter of fact, they are his books. I hadn't even heard of a lot of them until I met him. But not a single one of you arrogant, stupid, illiterate sons of bitches would ever have taken five minutes to find out what he was interested in, to talk to him about anything except what you wanted to talk about. He used to think you guys were funny, but I never did. That's why no one knew about us, no one. Except my five-year-old daughter, and she'd had to learn the hard way to be careful about what you say to people." Tears began to pour down her cheeks, and she brushed them away with nervous, contemptuous fingers. "He knew what you guys would say. He said that he wouldn't mind, except that you'd be saying it about me, really, not him. And he couldn't stand that. He still used to like you bastards, too."

"Listen, Betty, I don't know what you're talking about—"

"You wouldn't," she interrupted bitterly.

"—but we all liked Steve. Everyone did. Jesus, can't you see how upset everyone is? Everyone who worked with him. For chrissake, what can I say?" He whirled around on the stool, away from those accusing eyes, and reached into his pocket. "I think this must be what you came for," he said, holding out the packet of letters.

"You read them, didn't you?" she said dully, taking them and putting them in the pocket of her sweater. "Of course you did."

"Hey, Betty. Don't be unreasonable. He would have read them, too, if my girlfriend had written them to me and he found them after I'd been killed while working on something.

Just in case there was something in them that told him what was going on. That's what he did for a living. That's what we all do for a living."

She held out her hand again and he stared down at her thin wrist. It emerged from the sagging, folded-over cuff of the sweater, a cuff that had been stretched by arms much sturdier than hers, and he realized what was bothering him. He remembered that sweater; he could see Steve disappearing off into the bush wearing it one Thanksgiving weekend they had all spent at Ian MacMillan's chalet. Back in the good old days, before politics and policies had split them apart. "The diary," said Betty, her hand still outstretched.

"Diary?" The shock of the sudden memory made his eyes prickle with sorrow, and he turned away, embarrassed and angry. "What diary?"

"Steve's diary. The letters were tucked inside it. Come off it, Andy. If you found the letters, you found the goddamn diary. There's nothing in it for ghouls like you. It was personal and I want it." Her hand trembled. "Did you take all of them, you bastard?" She walked over to the other end of the wall unit that held his books and knelt down in front of a pair of doors in the bottom section. She peered closely at the small lock, shook her head, took a key out of her pocket, and opened the doors. "Goddamn you!" she shrieked and went very still. "You took them all. All of them." She slammed the door shut and knelt there, her hands over her face, her shoulders heaving with sobs.

"Betty." He knelt beside her. "Betty." He touched her shoulder. "I swear I didn't take any diaries. I didn't even know he kept a diary. Someone else—" He got up resolutely and went over to the phone, dialed, spoke, and waited. And waited. He murmured again, too softly for Betty to hear, and waited again. At last he said, "Well, thanks anyway," and hung up. "Look, Betty," he said, walking back over to where she knelt on the floor, "we haven't got them. Are you sure they were here?" She nodded. "Can I see that lock?'

"It's been forced," she said hoarsely. "But you can look at it if you want." She got up and moved away.

He stared at the pattern of scratch marks on the shiny white finish. Someone had been messing around recently with the lock. He opened the doors. Faint dust marks showed him the shape and size of what was missing from the cabinet. He stood up at last and walked over to Betty, awkward and miserable in the face of her misery. He patted her mechanically on the shoulder, and then in a wave of some indefinable emotion, gathered her into his arms and held her tightly. For an instant she fell into his embrace, then she stiffened and tore herself loose.

"Let go of me," she hissed. "He hasn't bloody well been dead that long, Andy Cassidy. I don't need any of your comforting. What in hell do you think I am? Who in hell do you think you are? Trying to jump into his bed as soon as it's empty. Let me tell you, you'd never make it. Never!" She turned and began running for the door.

"Betty, I'm sorry," he called after her. "Betty! Goddammit! Come back here. You've got to tell me what—" The footsteps slowed, and he followed her into the hall.

"Tell you what?" She was standing with her hand on the door, looking back at him.

"What he was working on. I have to know what else he was working on. Just in case."

"Does it matter?" she asked. "Does any of this whole stupid business matter?"

"If it's what got him killed it does. At least to me it does," he answered softly.

Betty stared at him for a long time. At last she shook her head. "You ask a lot," she said. "Wanting me to get mixed up in this. I have Stacy to think of. She counts on me. And anyway, I don't really *know* anything. Not facts, not names, just what little he told me." She paused, rubbed her foot over a dirty mark on the floor, and stared intently at the effect. "I suppose if you want that, you can have it," she said, raising her head again.

Andy Cassidy looked at her, puzzled, and nodded.

Betty walked back into the living room and looked around. "Is this room clean?" she asked suddenly.

"As far as I know," said Cassidy. "You want me to check?"

Betty shook her head. "Let's go get some coffee. Just in case."

"How about a drink?"

"I'm not ready for that yet," she said. "I need to keep my wits about me."

Betty Ferris stirred the whipped cream into her cup of cappuccino with an intensity that seemed to preclude speech. When she broke the silence, Andy Cassidy jumped slightly, startled. "I take it you already know about this last official thing he was doing," she said. "I mean, that was assigned, standard stuff, I guess." Cassidy nodded. "So you want to know what else he was up to."

"If he was up to anything else."

"Well, he was, of course. Something he brought with him from the RCMP." Cassidy opened his mouth to interrupt and she held up a hand for silence. "I know what I'm talking about. It had to do with an incident from when he was on the organized crime unit in Montreal. One of his old pals was shot. Someone he had put away once, a guy who turned informer for him a couple of times after he got out. It wasn't the shooting that he was working on—his guy was shot by a drug dealer whose territory he moved into—"

"Maurice Charbonneau," said Cassidy. "His snitch. I remember."

"Was that his name? I don't think he ever said. Probably. Anyway, Maurice—we'll call him that for now—Maurice told Steve when he was dying that someone—a cop—had taken fifty thou to let a shipment get by nice and quietly. Anyway, not only had the cop hung on to the fifty thou, but he'd also stolen the shipment. Half a million worth of heroin. Anyway, Steve's been—was"—she amended hastily—"chasing whoever it was. I did a lot of searching through files for him. That was how we got to know each other. Working late on this thing."

"Did he ever find out?" asked Cassidy casually.

Betty looked across the table and then shook her head. "I don't think so. He was close, though. He'd eliminated a hell of a lot of people."

"Like who?"

"Anyone on the Montreal police. Or the Quebec provincial police."

"And that leaves . . ."

"You guys. After all, he called it Royal Twist. That was his kind of joke." Her eyes filled with tears suddenly. "He must have known he was looking for someone who had been in the RCMP."

"And still is?"

She shook her head again. "I don't know. For all I know, Andy Cassidy, it could be you, couldn't it? You were RCMP before you went to CSIS."

He laughed uneasily. "If I had half a million bucks, would I still be working for the goddamn government?"

"I don't know," said Betty. "I really don't know."

Harriet stood in front of the Italian restaurant and shook her head. "For God's sake, it's not bad, but it's expensive. Fair-to-mediocre food for spectacular prices. So unless you're absolutely made of money, because I'm not paying for a meal here, we'd be better off at the deli on the corner."

"No," Sanders said. "I'm sick to the teeth of eating in delis. We'll eat here if we can get in. Otherwise we'll find someplace else with tablecloths. Even if you have to go home and change."

"My God," said Harriet. "It's amazing. You must be the first man I ever ran into who was so blind, stupid keen to throw away his money like that. On me. What's wrong with you?"

"Maybe you have me permanently at a disadvantage," he said. "After throwing you on the concrete and manhandling you I feel I should be making amends."

"Well, you can make them tomorrow night," she said. "Besides, I want to get my equipment put together again, not spend the entire evening over a second-rate dinner."

"Shut up and walk in there," he replied, "before I knock you on the pavement again."

"Now," she said, as they handed their menus back to the waiter and started in on their bottle of wine, "what the hell was all that about? Do you realize that you were at RCMP headquarters for two hours? That is assuming that it took you no more than fifteen minutes to walk down to the car.

And don't try to fob me off with that line about the Mounties being slow-moving again."

"I would guess," said Sanders, "that we have stumbled into the middle of something they would rather we were out of."

"What does *that* mean?"

"It means that Bartholomew is involved—was involved—in something that the RCMP worries about. You know—terrorism, drugs, forgery, whatever. And since they're being so goddamned cute about him, I would guess that he was an informer. Poor bastard. And maybe they have other informers in place around the operation, or they're about to make a big pinch on his information. Anyway, they would just as soon we would keep our noses out of the whole mess."

"Did they tell you this?"

"Hell no."

"Then how can you tell?"

"Because they're lying their socks off, that's how."

"John," she said, very slowly, twirling her glass around. "Would they follow us—or you, I guess—because they were worried about what happened? Do they do things like that to other police forces?"

"I wouldn't put it past them," said Sanders easily. "But I really don't see the point. Unless they have so much manpower around here no one has enough to do. Why? Are you seeing Mounties around every corner?"

She laughed. "Of course not. Ah, here comes the soup. It had better be edible, John Sanders, or I'll make you suffer for it."

It was almost two hours later when the waiter arrived to clear away the remains of dinner and suggest dessert and coffee. Sanders looked speculatively across the table at Harriet.

The wine had brought a slight flush to her cheeks and had softened her normally clipped and somewhat sarcastic tones. He was no longer paying attention to her words, just listening to the excitement in her voice as she tried to tell him about something terribly important. He picked up her hand from where it had dropped to rest for a second on the table and looked at it carefully. "Do you *want* coffee?" he asked, looking directly at the hand caught in his own.

"I beg your pardon?" she asked, startled.

"That's what the waiter wanted to know before he gave up in despair. Do you want coffee?"

"I'm sorry." Her cheeks reddened even more in confusion. "I don't know what got into me. I don't usually go on like that. It must have been the wine." She looked up, leaving her hand where it was. "Do you want some?"

"I could do with some. Although it's getting hot and noisy in here." The crowd had changed perceptibly in nature as the hour advanced. "So I could do just as easily without it."

Harriet looked steadily at him for a moment or two, and then turned her head and stared in fascination at a poster of the Italian Alps, framed, hanging on the wall beside her. "You could," she said, her voice almost lost in the Alpine scene, "come back to my place for coffee. I think I must have some."

"Really?" he said. "Are you sure . . ." His words trailed off into nothing.

"Sure," she said, almost nonchalantly. "Come on, before it gets too late."

Sanders followed her up the stairs, still baffled. On the way back in the car, she had chattered ceaselessly about the essential differences between restaurants in Toronto and

Ottawa. It had formed a wall between them—amusing, but impenetrable. Now he balanced on the second step, cautious about moving too close, while she struggled with her door key. "Goddamn," she muttered. "I can't get this thing to turn. This is the last straw."

"Here, let me," said Sanders, reaching around her to try the key. It wouldn't budge.

"See?" she said bitterly. "It's not just because I'm a weak little woman. Don't break it. It's a new deadlock. I just had it put in."

He didn't bother answering, but pushed her slightly to one side to look more closely at the mechanism. Then he grasped the door handle, gave it a turn, and pushed the door open an inch or two. "It's open. You forgot to lock it when we went out," he said gently.

"The hell I did," she said. "It's never unlocked."

"Really?" he asked. "You're sure?" She nodded. He stood very still for a moment, then gestured for silence and pushed her firmly behind him. "Stay there," he whispered. He flattened himself against the door, his right shoulder pressed close to the partially open side, and reached into his jacket. When he withdrew his hand, it contained a pistol. He eased the door farther and farther open, listening intently as he went, his eyes flickering over the shadowy kitchen. Light streaming in the window from the house behind them played on the green knapsack, lying empty in the doorway into the study; otherwise, as far as he could see, the room appeared normal. He held up a hand to forestall Harriet, and gave the door a steady shove until it rested against the wall. Nothing behind it. With his back against the wall, he moved sideways to the right until he came to the darkroom. He pushed that door open gradually with the toe of his shoe. By now his eyes had adjusted to the darkness, and in the light of the open door he could just make out all the spaces in the room large enough to hold a man. It looked odd but empty. He drifted silently over to the open back door.

"Do you have a flashlight?" he asked softly.

Harriet moved into the kitchen, opened a drawer, and put a flashlight into his hand. He nodded and moved like a stalking cat over to the study. The light picked out a litter of empty boxes on the floor. Every drawer in the room had been pulled open, and the contents of some were spilled on the floor; otherwise the room was empty. He stepped sideways and shone the beam over the living room. It seemed untouched.

"What in hell is going on?" whispered Harriet.

"For chrissake, stay out of here," he hissed back. "Whoever made that mess might not have left, and I don't care to have you run into him as he does. He might still be upstairs. There is an upstairs, isn't there?"

She nodded at a closed door in the corner, sitting on a broad, raised step. "Up there. Two bedrooms and a bath, but nothing to steal."

"I don't think he's after the family silver," said Sanders as he moved over to the door. "Does that other door lead to the front?" She nodded. "Then get out of the apartment. In fact, get right out of the house, in front, across the street by the canal, where there's lots of light and people," he snapped. "I don't want to have to worry about you." He eased the door open very quietly and peered up the narrow staircase. The hot, dusty smell of a thousand old attic rooms rushed down to greet him, but no noise. If there was anyone up there, he was remarkably silent. Sanders moved up the stairs, stepping close to the wall, one at a time. He paused at the landing and looked up. The flashlight picked out gray paint, wooden railings, sloping ceilings, dust, and silence. He ran swiftly up the last flight and glanced into each bedroom. One was empty, except for an old iron cot neatly made up; the other contained Harriet's carelessly made bed. No people, unless they were hiding in the closets. The bathroom echoed with solitude. He walked back into Harriet's bedroom, leaned out a window, and looked down. There in the light of a street lamp he could see her, beside a maple tree, looking up at the house with a frown on her face. But unmolested. He returned to his search. In each room and in the hall there were low, wide doors that gave onto the space beneath the eaves. He went from one to another, checking with the flashlight. In each one there was a riot of overturned boxes but no human inhabitant. He sighed, got up from his crouching position, and went back to the window. "Come on up," he said.

Harriet stood in the door of the study with her hands on her hips, and stared. She moved a few paces in and picked up an empty box from the floor. She found its cover, put them together again, and set them on the desk. She moved back and forth, picking up more boxes, closing them, and piling them neatly with the first.

"What was in those boxes?" asked Sanders.

"Slides." She looked around her. "I had three boxes of slides. Gone. And the bigger boxes held black-and-white negatives. That's even worse. All the material for the book. And everything for Wheeler and Shogatu except for what I've already sent them."

"Wheeler and Shogatu?"

"The architects for that complex I'm doing." Her voice was flat and expressionless. "It means that if they want copies of anything I just can't do it. You don't understand,

John," she said, and pushed her hair off her forehead. "That's six or seven weeks' work—hard work. And I lined up some smaller projects as well when I knew I was going to be up here."

"Did they damage any of your equipment?"

She shook her head. "I don't know. The camera case was lying open; the OM-3 body had been taken out of its foam nest and its back was not fastened down. She picked it up, looked at it, and closed it again. "I don't think so. They were looking for film in the camera, I suppose. Just a minute." She walked across the room, shut the top drawer of a built-in cabinet in the wall, and pulled the second drawer out even farther. She took another camera body out of it, clicked its open back shut, and tried the rewinding mechanism. "No, they just opened it up. It's all right. This is my Canon F-1. I've had it since I first started. It was my first real working camera." Tears began to pour silently down her cheeks as she stood staring at it.

Sanders walked across the room and looked helplessly down at her. He took the camera and set it back into its drawer, then gathered her awkwardly in his arms. It was like trying to comfort a store mannequin. She stood stiffly in his embrace, her arms at her sides. Tears splashed down on the lapels of his jacket. "Harriet," he murmured in distress. "Please, Harriet, don't just cry like that. It's not that bad. It could have been worse."

She pushed herself violently away. "How? Just tell me. How could it have been worse?" Her words erupted in strangled bursts, interrupted by hiccups of grief.

"You've lost a few weeks' work, okay. And you're upset. But they didn't break anything, at least not in here."

"Oh, Jesus," she muttered. "The darkroom. What's happened to it?"

"Wait," he said. "Nothing, I think. They just pushed stuff around. It looked pretty much the same to me. There's nothing broken. Come here," he said, pulling her back and holding her very tightly this time. "Don't be so damned difficult."

She drew a deep breath and relaxed her taut shoulders slightly. "Why in hell shouldn't I?" she said angrily. "You haven't just had a whole project ruined."

"Listen, you could have been here when they arrived," he said. "Or you could have walked in on them without me right behind you." He put his hand behind her head and drew it protectively toward his shoulder again. "You're more important than a few yards of film. Believe me, they were probably not very nice people." She shuddered.

An hour later two detectives from the break-and-enter squad of the Ottawa police had come and gone. They had shaken their heads politely over the mess, and then congratulated Harriet on having escaped so lightly. The sergeant had declared it was difficult to believe that a few boxes of slides and some negatives had more than sentimental value, but he shrugged his shoulders and wrote down the figure she had given him. Hysterical citizens who had just been robbed tended to place an inflated worth on their missing possessions. He was used to it. His partner pointed out the futility of dusting for fingerprints in the apartment, since every ten-year-old apprentice hood in the city knew enough to wear gloves. Not to speak of the futility of installing a fancy new lock on the back door, when the front door could be opened with the equivalent of a paper clip. They both scoffed cheerfully at the possibility of the thieves returning, and prepared to leave. Besides, the sergeant had remarked with a leer as he headed out the door, with Inspector Sanders on the premises she should be pretty safe.

"One more comment like that," said Sanders, listening to the two men clattering down the stairs, "and I would have smashed his ugly nose in for him. Stupid, incompetent sonuvabitch."

"What's wrong with you?" asked Harriet as she walked back into the study. "It's not your apartment. They didn't just tell you how terribly considerate the bastards were."

"I don't appreciate some goddamn sergeant looking at me like a john caught in a whorehouse." He stalked back into the kitchen, then shook his head and ran his fingers through his hair. "I suppose I'm not used to being treated like a citizen," he said ruefully.

"You mean you're used to people bowing and scraping to you," she said, bending over and picking up more boxes from the floor.

"You're damned right I am." He looked around him reflectively. "You'd better go upstairs and pack something," he said. "Do you want to take your cameras and stuff as well?"

"What in hell are you talking about?" She spun around and looked at him.

"You're not sleeping in this apartment," he said. "You can stay in my motel room where you'll be safe. Don't worry," he added, "There are two beds. I'm not in the habit of attacking women. Especially unwilling ones. Besides, my car isn't here, remember? That way you can drive me back."

In the silence of the room he could hear her ragged breathing. "And if I don't want to?" she asked at last. "Maybe I'd rather stay here. Maybe I like sleeping alone." A shrill tone was creeping into her voice. "In case you hadn't noticed, I don't appreciate being pushed around. I assure you I am quite capable of looking after myself."

"Don't be stupid," he said flatly. "Believe me, no one's capable of looking after himself. Not me, not you, not anybody. Not in this world. But if you're going to be stubborn, I'll stay here instead. Although, frankly, I'd rather spend the night somewhere where we'd both be safe. I'm not especially crazy about sitting up all night waiting to be clobbered. Unnecessarily." His voice was cold.

They stood on either side of the doorway into the study, glaring at each other. At last Harriet's eyes dropped. She rubbed her cheek in weariness. "I don't know," she said. "I just don't know. I guess you're right. Give me a minute or two to pack some stuff."

Harriet trudged slowly along the outdoor corridor into Sanders's second-floor motel room, knapsack on her back, camera case and tripod in her hands. "Right there," he said quietly. She stopped and waited silently for him. He put her overnight bag down on the concrete flooring, unlocked the door, cautiously pushed it open, and listened. With a slightly embarrassed grin, he extracted Harriet's flashlight from his pocket, shone it quickly in all the corners, walked over to the window, and pulled the curtains shut. He turned on the small lamp on the table between the beds, went back to get her luggage, and gestured with an attempt at gallantry for her to precede him. The room looked pleasant and inviting, its minor defects hidden in the softness of the light. She paused in the doorway for a second or two, and then headed for the back corner, where a large niche provided closet and storage space. She lowered her equipment carefully to the floor and stowed it neatly in as small a space as possible.

Sanders dropped her small bag on the bed nearest the bathroom. "You'd better take this one," he said.

"It doesn't matter," she said dully. "I don't care." She stood beside her camera case, rooted to the spot.

"Goddammit, Harriet," snapped Sanders. "Will you get the hell out of the closet? And stop looking like a sacrificial virgin? I'm not going to rape you, I'm just offering you a bed in a safe place."

"It isn't a closet," she said, with considerably more spirit in her voice. "I only wanted to put my equipment where you couldn't trip over it."

He sat down on his bed, too tired to care.

"And I'm not a virgin, sacrificial or otherwise." She took off her long, many-pocketed jacket and laid it carefully at the foot of the bed. Then she pulled off the red sweatshirt she was wearing under it and dropped it on top of her jacket. She hunched over, with her hands clamped between her knees and her eyes on him. In the lamplight they glowed as yellow as a cat's, and as yellow as her little T-shirt.

"Now what is that supposed to mean?" he said, looking warily at her. "That you tried it once and didn't care for it?"

"Is that what you think about me?" She jerked upright in astonishment. "Good God. I never realized."

"What in hell else am I supposed to think?" he said, explosive with sudden fury. "You go drinking with me, you talk to me, you drag me along with you to watch you work, you eat dinner with me, you drape yourself all over me, and then you project a wall of solid ice around you at least six feet thick. So either you find me disgusting, but you're lonesome enough to talk to anybody, or you have some sort of powerful hang-up where men are concerned. And I guess

I find the last explanation a little less damaging to my pride."

"You expect a lot, don't you?" she said, drawling her words contemptuously. "What are you used to? Women who take one look at you and fall panting into the nearest bed with their legs spread?"

"For chrissake, you're the most unreasonable bloody bitch I've met in a long time. I don't expect anything!" He smashed his fist down on the bed beside him. "You're the one who expects it all. For God's sake, you have to admit that. I don't expect a thirty-year-old—"

"Thirty-two-year-old," she corrected, her deep voice icily precise.

"That's worse. A thirty-two-year-old woman to hang all over me and then look absolutely terrified if I accidentally touch her. You should have outgrown that at sixteen." He shook his head. "I'm going to bed. This could take all night." He began unbuttoning his shirt.

She paid no attention. "Well, I wouldn't want you to think I found you disgusting, anyway," she said wearily, and then laughed. "Not nearly as disgusting as the Ottawa police. Obviously Toronto produces a better class of cop. Anyway, if it were true, I don't suppose I'd actually be here. I could have checked into a hotel."

Sanders stood up and walked toward the bathroom, dropping his shirt on the television set as he went. "Listen," he said, turning to look at her. "I don't mind being dragged all over hell's half acre, I don't mind being frozen out by an iceberg, I don't even mind sleeping in my goddamn underwear so I won't offend your sensibilities, but don't try to get funny at my expense at twelve-thirty in the morning. I lost my sense of humor a few hours ago."

"I'm sorry," said Harriet almost inaudibly. She stopped

abruptly and took an enormous breath before going on. "And I'm sorry you got saddled with someone as screwed up and goddamned miserable as I am. It's not your fault. But if I don't make a joke of things, I'll start crying all over your chest again." She turned away from him and began pulling clumsily at her watch strap.

"Dammit," he muttered. "Now you're making me feel like a flat-footed louse." He sat down beside her. "I'm sorry. I'm not very good at noticing when there's something wrong." She kept her head turned away, staring down at her recalcitrant watch strap. "Look, don't pay any attention to me. Think of me as a brother you've gone camping with. And maybe tomorrow you can tell me all about it. You wouldn't know it from looking at me, but for an arrogant bastard I'm a very good listener." He reached out and gently ruffled her hair. Then he dropped his arm and ran his fingers softly and, he hoped, comfortingly along her shoulders. She shivered convulsively and half turned toward him. The taut lines in her face had softened; her eyes were half-shut. Without thinking, he bent down and kissed her lightly. With a sudden violent motion she twisted her body and pressed up against him, opening her mouth under his and delicately forcing her tongue between his lips. She caught him around the neck and fell back onto the bed, dragging him down with her. When he pulled away to catch his breath he realized that she was pushing up her T-shirt to reveal her bare breasts, and he began to fumble hastily at the fastenings of her jeans.

"No," she murmured, "please . . . don't."

"Don't what?" he said, pulling back and looking at her. He stroked her face, pushing her damp hair back onto the pillow, and then bent down and kissed her. "Don't what?"

"Nothing. Pay no attention." Her voice was hoarse and faint.

"Here," he said, pulling her to her feet and yanking the covers back, "there's no hurry. Let's do this properly." She sat down on the edge of the bed again, toed viciously at the backs of her running shoes and socks, and then stood up and let her jeans fall to a heap on the floor. In one rapid movement she had discarded her underwear, letting it join his clothes in a pile between the beds. Sanders leaned over and pulled the little yellow shirt above her head before pushing her back down on the pillow and easing himself gently down beside her. He ran his hands all over her now. All the hard and awkward angles she had made out of her body before—except for her small, erect breasts—felt infinitely warm and yielding under his exploring fingers. He stopped to look at her for a moment, oddly detached, like the spectator at a special performance. Her skin was gleaming with sweat; one hand was pressed frantically under her left breast, the other was thrown across her mouth. The lids were fluttering over her unfocused eyes. He forgot whatever reason he had had for waiting any longer. He kissed her fiercely until her long legs wrapped themselves around him and he fell dizzily into her. She reached up and clutched at his neck and shoulders like a fighting cat and thrust herself upward. In three or four fierce movements he felt her muscles contract in an enormous spasm, and she screamed, a low-pitched, sobbing scream.

"How long have you been separated?" asked Sanders. He was lying comfortably propped up on pillows, with Harriet's head on his chest.

"Let me see," she said thoughtfully, twisting the luxuriant

hair on his chest with her fingers. "November to May. Six months."

"Married?" he asked.

She shook her head, and her hair flipped lightly over his shoulder. "Living together. How did you know?"

"I'm a detective, remember, sweetheart?" He kissed her on the nose. "After all, that was a breathtaking reaction to a simple kiss. Which says to me," he said, stroking her breast, "that you're a passionate woman who has been living a celibate existence for a while. Elementary, my dear Jeffries."

"Smug bastard that you are," said Harriet.

"And why not? What I haven't figured out is your reason for that ice maiden act."

"Come on," she said. "That's not fair. It wasn't an act. You were getting to me. For some peculiar reason I found you disturbingly attractive. And I had bloody good reasons not to get myself involved. With anyone." She turned her head and muttered something into his chest.

"What did you say?" he asked, half sitting up to look at her.

"I said, it wasn't much of an act, anyway. We only met on Monday."

"Don't worry about it," he said cheerfully. "I don't mind. Why are you so worried about getting involved? You strike me as having enough independence for six women."

"You want me to tell you why?" she asked bitterly.

"If you insist," said Sanders, stretching lazily, then propping himself up on one elbow and looking at her. "Go ahead."

"Remember my assistant who ran off to Montreal to join her boyfriend?"

"The bad painter?"

"Well, he was *my* bad painter. And I knew he was a lousy painter and an even lousier boyfriend. He was an arrogant, conniving leech, and half the time—no, most of the time lately—I hated him, and I was the one who threw him out. But still, when Jane told me about the baby . . . that was pretty bloody humiliating."

"Is that why you threw him out?"

"Uh-uh." She shook her head vehemently. "Jane told me the happy news after he had moved on. It was about then I decided I couldn't afford a sex life."

Sanders snorted with laughter. "I'm sorry," he said, raising his hand contritely. "I'm not laughing because your boyfriend got your assistant pregnant. Just that I knew damn well there was sex under there somewhere, but I assumed it was your assistant who had dumped you. Which seems pretty funny right now. I apologize."

"Don't bother," she said coolly, and sat up. "And don't be so damned smug. I don't regard it as an insult. If I'd been someone different, it could have been true." She watched him silently for a moment. "Anyway, you've had plenty of time to cross-examine me." She was looking at him steadily, her head slightly to one side in an attitude of detached, scientific curiosity. "It's my turn. There's something I need to know about you before I spend any more time in this bed."

"Ah," he said cautiously. "This is where we get into wives and kiddies, right?"

"Not at all. It's something much more important." She dropped back down onto the pillow again "Tell me, do you always carry a gun when you're taking people out to dinner?"

"Does it bother you?"

"Of course it bothers me. I wouldn't have said anything if it didn't bother me."

He sat up, dislodging the hand she had draped over his belly. "Hell, what do you want me to say? It's part of the job. And there have been moments when it's come in handy. I don't care much for the damned things, and they're not much bloody use, let me tell you. Inaccurate as hell." Harriet sat up, pulling the sheet around her, and rested her chin on her knees. "I suppose if I'd thought about it I wouldn't have brought it with me, but I'd been working all night when the word came down to leave for Ottawa—at once and double quick. I threw some shirts and underwear into a suitcase and jumped in the car." Her silence was unnerving. "So here I am in Ottawa and I've got the damned thing with me. What do you want me to do with it?" he asked accusingly. "Leave it in the motel room drawer? A very bad idea, Harriet. The things are dangerous. At least I don't wear it to bed," he added with a sly smile. She didn't react. "Look, Harriet, I don't go around killing people. We have a whole squad of people who specialize in firing at human beings, and when things are really desperate, we call them in."

"You whipped it out pretty handily in my apartment."

"Slight overreaction."

She shivered and retreated back under the covers. "Have you ever killed anyone? No, wait. Don't tell me, not right now." She rolled over on her belly and leaned her head on his thigh. "I have to think about this. Are you going back to your own bed, or are you spending the night in mine?"

"I'm spending the night in yours," he said. "I want to make sure you're still in the room when I wake up again." He moved the extra pillow over to Harriet's side of the bed, slid down, and reached out for her. She threw a leg over his and in a second had them entangled again.

"This time," she murmured, "you can turn out the light."

CHAPTER 7

Thursday, May 18

"How do you feel?" asked Sanders. He was sitting across from Harriet at a table by the window in the coffee shop attached to the motel. With his index finger he traced the pattern of bones and ligaments in her hand as it lay on the table between them.

"Aside from starving?" she asked. "Strange. And empty." She smiled. "Something to do with lack of sleep, I think, as well as everything else. I ordered bacon and eggs with extra toast for both of us. Where were you?"

"In the office, telling them my wife had arrived from Toronto for a few days. Just so you don't feel you have to duck around avoiding the management."

"Your wife? Me? How quaint. Did they believe you?"

"I don't suppose they cared, one way or another. Do you mind?"

"Being called your wife? I don't know. Ask me when my head has cleared a bit." She waved energetically at the waitress, who wandered over to pour them some coffee. "How do *you* feel?"

"Fine," he said automatically.

"That's it? You feel fine?"

"Sorry," he said. "Habit. I suppose if I really tried to

figure out how I felt I'd say I was dizzy. Or light-headed, however you want to describe it." He picked up her hand. "And somewhat pleased with myself. You can't imagine how much you've inflated my male ego," he said with a grin.

She looked around the room and laughed. "I think we'd better change the topic. All that food," she said, nodding in the direction of the waitress, "must be ours, and half the people in the place are eavesdropping like mad. That guy over there is about to faint in ecstasy. Pervert," she hissed distinctly in the man's direction, and giggled again. Sanders winced.

"What are you going to do today?" he asked when they had finished the last of their toast.

"I don't know," said Harriet. "I haven't really decided. But I want my pictures back. Every time I think about them I get absolutely furious. Where should I start? With the police? That's thousands of dollars' worth of work they walked off with, you know. I've got to get them back." She stopped to give him an intensely concentrated look. "Should I get the insurance company to offer a bribe? They have contacts in the criminal cases, don't they? They always seem to in movies."

Sanders shook his head. "I'm not sure that would do much good. If you'd lost some diamonds, sure, the insurance company has contacts and it could use them, but whoever walked off with your stuff wasn't just some break-and-enter artist. He wanted those particular pictures. So either we're looking for the two men who were in them, assuming that they're shy and don't like their pictures taken, or somebody else wanted to know what they looked like. My guess would be the RCMP—or CSIS."

"The RCMP? But why in hell *break into* my apartment?

They could have—no, don't answer that. I know already.
What makes you think it might have been them?"

"Those bastards from the local police," said Sanders,
yawning. "That's been bothering me ever since they walked
through the door of your apartment."

"What has?"

"Their attitude, I suppose. They were just a little *too*
casual and uninterested in your break-in. Okay," he said,
raising one hand as if she had been contradicting him
ferociously, "they're busy, it was a sort of weird thing, and
they probably felt that not much of value had been taken, but
still. Pretty casual. Too casual. And maybe that was because
they'd been told to keep their hands off the case. And why
would someone tell them that? Because the Mounties had been
doing the searching." He shook his head. "And that's where
we stand. The Mounties have the pictures, which means we
haven't a hope in hell of getting them back, or those two guys
have them. And they're not much better from our point of
view. They didn't look to me like small-time B and E artists."

"Damn!" said Harriet, and nibbled her lower lip. "There
must be some way to find them. I wish you didn't sound so
bloody plausible." She yawned and stretched and then smiled
at him. "Well, if you're right about that, then it's all not
much use, is it? I think I'll go back and straighten up the
mess in the apartment—"

"No!" He interrupted her with such force that everyone
in the little coffee shop turned and looked. "Look, Harriet,
don't go back there alone." She opened her mouth to protest.
"Think of it as humoring my paranoia if you want. Maybe
it's safe—if they've decided that what they're looking for
isn't there—but still . . ."

"And I used to think I was twitchy," she said. "That
poses a problem. I didn't really pack much in the way of

clothes. In that case—I don't know—maybe I'll go shopping. And buy a skirt. After all, wouldn't the wife of an inspector wear a skirt once in a while?" She gave him a look of impassive innocence and then winked.

"My God," he said. He could feel himself sinking into deep water. "I don't know. I suppose she would."

"Are you trying to imply by that remark," said Harriet sternly, "I mean, are you really trying to convince me that you have reached the age of—"

"Thirty-eight," he said.

"Thirty-eight, and you're not married? And not gay?"

"You should certainly know I'm not gay," he protested, "if anyone does."

"Not necessarily. You could be a passionate and oversexed bisexual." She gave him a calculating look, biting her lip as she considered the question. "No," she shook her head. "You're right. Not on the police force."

"Not very likely, anyway. I'd have had a rough time." He started building little walls with the napkin dispenser, the salt and pepper, and the ashtray. "I used to be married. Does that matter?"

"It depends. How used is used? Last week?"

He laughed. "No, a couple of years ago. And I have two almost-grown-up children who haven't really noticed that I moved out. My abandoned wife has married a nice guy—well, truthfully, he's a sleazy bastard—who owns a store in our old neighborhood. He seems to suit her better than I ever did."

"So you're off the hook. How nice for you."

"Yes, it is. And you're sitting there thinking that I'm a heartless son of a bitch. Well, maybe I am. Sort of."

"How could I think that?" said Harriet, widening her eyes in mock amazement. "You're sweet. A real pussycat.

All six foot ten of you. And you're bloody late for that meeting."

He looked at his watch at last. "Christ," he breathed. "So I am. Look, stay away from the apartment and I'll see you around four-thirty. I got an extra key to the motel room for you"—he threw it down on the table as he got up—"and here's a twenty. Do you mind paying for breakfast?" He bent down to whisper in her ear. "Watch out for yourself, please? And it's really only six foot three. You should see Ed Dubinsky, my partner."

She looked up and caught his hand, a worried frown on her face. "Then I'll meet you at four-thirty this afternoon. With the change. I'll wait around right where you knocked me down, all right? Just to give you another chance."

"Great." He brushed her forehead with his hand and then threw open the door, fumbling in his pocket for his keys. One of the men eating alone turned with deliberation to watch him leave; as Sanders drove out of the parking area the man picked up his coffee cup once again and settled into his newspaper.

Once Sanders had worked his way past the islands of construction onto the relative breadth of space on the parkway, he accelerated and allowed his attention to wander. How in hell was he going to set about finding those damned pictures? Because it was obvious that he had been silently elected to the job. Otherwise Harriet was going to start charging all over the city looking for them and God knows what was going to happen to her. There was something very clear and simple he could do, he was sure of that. But he couldn't remember what it was. He slowed down for the light and put on his right turn indicator. There, on the broad grounds belonging to RCMP headquarters, a man was walking with a briefcase tucked under his arm. A briefcase. That was it. The briefcase, with something written on it. What? He pulled into a parking spot. It was the name of a conference. A conference on ... maybe Harriet would remember. After all, she *took* the goddamn picture. As soon as he got in the door he turned to the nearest pay phone and dialed the motel.

"Of course," she said. "I thought you knew that. It's a conference on Charlemagne. I'll call around and see if I can find out exactly what it's called and where it is. And then we can wander out there and see if we recognize anyone."

By the time Sanders put down the phone and looked at his watch, the first session was about to end. He bypassed the lecture room and headed straight for the cafeteria; their little group was crowding around the counter, picking up coffee. As he reached for his change, the constable from Halifax thumped him on the back. "Hey, fellas, look what just turned up. Shit, do you look rough!" The constable guffawed and hit him again. Sanders stiffened angrily. "Jesus, you should see yourself. What have you been up to? When he said go sightseeing you really took him up on it, didn't you? Whaddya find, eh?" The constable leered.

Sanders grabbed his coffee and glowered repressively at the man. It had no discernible effect.

The constable showed serious signs of following him to a table. "Just kidding," he said, with another snort of laughter. "When we got here this morning we had a little bet on, trying to guess who wouldn't make it in. Never figured it'd be the big in-spec-tor from Toronto, though" he said, drawing out the term. "But you're not the only one," he added, lowering his voice confidentially, as he walked along beside Sanders. "You know that bastard Higgs didn't show this morning. Sent some prick in with a stupid movie. Oh, Jesus, there he is," the constable muttered. "I wonder if he heard me."

Higgs was stalking across the room, coming straight for them. "Inspector Sanders," he said. "I wonder if I might have a word with you?"

"Well lah-di-dah," whispered the young man. "Pardon us."

"Would you excuse us, Constable?" Higgs said stiffly.

"Certainly, sir," said that rising diplomat, all politeness and deference, and headed for a more congenial group.

"About that picture we were discussing yesterday," said Higgs quietly as he sat down at an empty table. "The one with the man who is wanted for questioning, whom you say you also saw in a bar in Brockville—"

"Coffee shop outside Brockville," said Sanders. He sat down, his interest aroused at least temporarily, and leaned back.

"Whatever," Higgs said impatiently. "'Do you have it yet?"

"I said it was going to take a few days, didn't I?" asked Sanders.

"You also made it very clear that you hadn't actually taken it or delivered it for processing. We were concerned that it be delivered directly to the superintendent's office. Not to the local police. Do the Ottawa police have that picture?"

"Why?" asked Sanders, yawning. "Does it matter who gets it? Anyway, I thought you said, or someone said, that it wasn't your case."

Higgs dropped his voice slightly. "We have a strong interest in assuring discretion where that investigation is concerned."

"Why?" asked Sanders again, idly balancing his spoon on the salt shaker. He didn't feel particularly helpful anymore, and he wished Higgs would get the hell out of there. He was too distracted to be interested in someone else's little games for long. He touched his bruised lips with his tongue. Was it that obvious what he had been doing? Or had that brat just made a lucky guess? Probably. At that age you think of sex twenty hours a day and assume that everyone else does, too. He made an effort to pull himself back to his surroundings. Higgs was taking his question seriously.

". . . found in the secure area around the perimeter of a site being used for the conference. This is highly classified information, of course. We are trying to pursue our own investigation without alerting local police or the press. I was asked to get the photograph from you as quickly and as unobtrusively as possible. Do you have it on you?"

"What's that?" Sanders said. His attention had slipped again. "Do I have the picture? No, I don't. Sorry."

"Did you hand it over to some other police jurisdiction?" asked Higgs, with slow emphasis. "This is important," he said. "We need to know where it is. Who has it affects how we proceed from now on."

"As far as I know, no other jurisdiction has it at the moment," said Sanders cautiously.

"Oh," said Higgs, and paused. "Have you discussed the existence of the picture with anyone else?" he asked casually. "Besides the person who took it."

"Me? No." Sanders didn't care for what was going on. Cautious bastards like Higgs don't just drop classified information into your lap—not without some reason, at least. And he couldn't quite imagine what innocent reason he would have for doing it.

"I assume the woman—Harriet Jeffries, the photographer, isn't that who she is? anyway, the woman who was waiting for you in the car—I assume she's the one who actually took the picture," Higgs added. He looked at his watch. "Excuse me," he said. "Just one small thing to attend to before the session begins." He stood up, his face frozen into its usual blankly hostile expression, and walked out of the room. Sanders watched Higgs's rigid back as it progressed. His euphoria was rapidly being chased out by a sense of restless uneasiness.

Harriet walked slowly out of the offices of the Ottawa *Citizen* and paused on the sidewalk before heading toward her car. She looked at her watch and began nibbling her lower lip. One o'clock. If she forgot about lunch she would have plenty of time to get out to Carleton University and nose around before meeting John. Except that she was going to have to go back to the motel and change into something slightly more respectable than her working jeans. There'd still be time, though, to do that and get out to the Charlemagne conference before the two o'clock sessions. If she hurried. She snatched her car keys out of her pocket and dodged her way through the passing pedestrians and over to the curb.

She pulled into the almost empty parking lot and parked in front of the door leading to the second floor of the motel. As soon as she stepped out of the car, the wind tossed a handful of dust into her face and she sneezed. The area was deserted except for one laundry cart, overflowing with dirty linen, left unattended beside the door. A stale smell of sweat and vomit hit her as she walked past it, and she was momentarily consumed with loathing—for herself, for mankind, for the drunken, incontinent oafs who made themselves at home in godforsaken heaps of concrete rubble like this one. Oafs she felt at one with as she walked down the windy passageway to John Sanders's room.

The chambermaid had drawn back the curtains; the hard spring sunshine poured into the room, lighting up all the corners. Harriet stood in the open doorway and stared. Every square inch of floor, bed, and countertop was covered with a jumble of things, tumbled, confused, unidentifiable things. The drawers had been yanked out and overturned, the suitcases were open and spread-eagled upside down on the beds. There was underwear—male and female— tossed on the pillows and draped over the mirror, where it had apparently caught when it was flung in the direction of the wall. She pushed aside two drawers with her foot and stepped into the room, closing the door after her.

The view from inside was even more devastating. The lock on her aluminum camera case had been smashed or wrenched open; the floor on the far side of the beds was littered with bits of camera equipment. Several thousand dollars' worth of lenses lay, smashed, at her feet, and in the middle of them was her OM-3. It looked as if someone had taken a heavy mallet to it. She reached down and picked it up. It had resisted destruction as best it could, but that twisted body told her that it was beyond repair. She glanced into the bathroom; nothing had been left untouched, not even the toothpaste. She dropped her mutilated camera on the bed and turned toward the telephone. Her finger was poised to enter the last digit in the emergency number when she paused, put down the receiver, and walked out of the room, closing the door carefully behind her.

Once in the car she plunged through downtown traffic, pushed by a feverish, reckless sense of haste over to the west of the canal, where she had grown up and learned to drive, the area where she knew the crazy-quilt pattern of one-way streets the way she knew her own darkroom. As she moved, she kept one eye on the road and one eye on her rearview mirror. She darted back and forth, zigzagging across

Bank Street, making sudden and unheralded left-hand turns. Finally, she decided that no one could possibly be following her, pulled back to the drive along the canal, and moved sedately downtown. She headed slowly in the direction of the motel once again, saw no familiar car behind her, made a sudden right turn, and was in the huge downtown parking garage. She pulled into an empty space and waited. Nothing. If anyone had followed her here, he evidently knew what she was going to do even before she herself decided to do it. Perhaps he did. Perhaps when she pulled open the door leading into the huge downtown mall he would be waiting for her. Whoever he was. "For chrissake, Harriet, don't be an ass," she said aloud, and felt even more foolish. She got out of the car, set out across the gray concrete floor, and headed calmly and deliberately in the direction of Ogilvy's department store.

An hour later she pushed her way into the crowded ladies' room with an armload of paper bags. She walked up to the vanity counter in front of the mirror, smiled sweetly but firmly at the three people who were standing there fiddling with their hair and makeup, and piled up her things on the counter. "Well! Ex*cuse* me," said the one nearest Harriet as she snatched her purse, compact, and mascara out of range. Harriet paid no attention. Out of the largest of her bags she pulled a soft nylon carryall, which she unzipped, detagged, and began to fill. Two bags of new underwear went in first, as they were; next she tilted a bag filled with panty hose in, extracting one pair as she went and clutching it firmly between her knees. She crumpled up the bag and pitched it in the direction of the wastepaper disposal. She missed. Another woman glared at her. From a larger bag she extracted a full beige skirt, a matching blouse, and a bright pink jacket. She draped these over her arm, pitched the bag away—successfully this time—stuffed the remaining bags into the carryall, and marched into a cubicle. A few minutes later she emerged, in her stocking feet, dressed in the skirt, blouse, and jacket and clutching her jeans, sweatshirt, and running shoes.

"Not much room to change in there," she remarked to the girl who was still trying to get her mascara on, and thumped her bag back on the counter beside her. The wand jumped and a blob of black goo landed under the woman's eyebrow in the middle of her elaborately drawn eye shadow. Harriet dropped her running shoes on the floor, slipped her feet into them, and stuffed her remaining clothes in the bag. " 'Bye," she said to the young woman, who was now engaged in stripping mascara and three shades of eye shadow from her lids with a combination of tissues and tears. Once out of the room, Harriet bent down to tie up her laces and set herself to finding suitable shoes.

Harriet was standing in the bright afternoon sun, her old Canon F-1 dangling from a strap wrapped tightly around her left wrist, her tiny Olympus grasped possessively in her right hand. The nylon holdall was sitting at her feet, which were now encased in elegant little shoes that matched the new blue purse hanging from her left shoulder. It was exactly 4:30. She had been pacing restlessly through the shops for the last thirty minutes, unable to wait at the corner and too nervous and distracted to do anything useful. Now she stood looking at the information kiosk, memorizing the dates and times of events and exhibitions of absolutely no interest to her.

Suddenly an arm encircled her shoulders and a voice said in her ear, "You made it."

"I thought I might as well show up," she said casually, and felt herself turning pink.

"Good," he said simply, but he tightened his grip on her shoulder. "Anyway, let's get a drink before I collapse from dehydration." He gave her a sharp look. "Is anything wrong?"' he added.

She shook her head. "A drink sounds fine."

"Then why are you carrying luggage around with you?" he asked, pointing at the bag. "And two cameras?"

"I bought some new things, since you wouldn't let me go back to my apartment," she said accusingly, "and I needed something to carry them in."

"My God," he said. "When you shop, you really shop." He took the bag from her, stepped back, and looked at her again. "Hey, pretty nice." His tone was judicial. "I like pink." He looked at her critically. "Good color," he added. "Is that all new? But I'm afraid you've gone overboard."

"What do you mean by that?" she asked, annoyed.

"An inspector's wife would never be that extravagant." She aimed a blow at his ear. He put his arm up to protect himself, grabbed her wrist, and started pulling her down the street. "Let me put the bag in the car so you don't have to cart it around with you."

"No," she said firmly. "Afterward. Right now I have a few things to tell you. In there," she added, pointing at the pub.

"I'm waiting," said Sanders, after they had ordered. "What's all this mystery?"

"Well, first, I got the dope on the conference. I have a friend from the old days who's working as a news photographer on the *Citizen*, and this morning I camped on his doorstep while he tracked everything down for me. I've got it here," she said, patting her handbag. "It's at Carleton University, and we have plenty of time after this beer to get to the cocktail hour. Apparently the Charlemagne conference—can you believe that? What do you suppose they talk about for three days? Anyway, apparently it created all sorts of problems because it had been booked a year before the trade conference was even thought of and the organizers refused to give up their time. I gather the security types don't like having too much going on at once in one city. Scott—that's the photographer, Scott O'Reilly—says he might come over as well and take a few jolly old human interest shots." Her voice oozed sarcasm for a second before returning to normal.

"Did you tell him why we wanted the information?" asked Sanders. He felt a stab of possessive pain thinking about this anonymous lout—who probably used to sleep with her—to whom she would confide her troubles, and then a sharper pain when he remembered he had no right even to inquire about things like that.

Harriet had a faint smile on her face. "How stupid do you think I am? Of course I didn't tell him why. I mean, I gave him a reason he'd be likely to believe, but not the real why. And don't look at me like that. He isn't interested in girls, but he takes a kindly interest in the love lives of his friends. I'll explain all that later," she added hastily. "Anyway, I decided that instead of going shopping, I'd nip over to Carleton and see if I could lay eyes on one or other of those two guys."

"Jesus, I thought we'd agreed you'd lie low—"

"Would you let me finish for once?" she interrupted. "I went back to the motel to change and someone had torn the room apart." Her voice was flat and expressionless. "Clothes, everything, scattered everywhere, and my equipment all smashed. Everything but these cameras," she said, and patted the Canon F-1 on the table. "They were in the car. I didn't want to leave them there," she added defensively.

"What did you do?"

"I looked at it all very carefully, backed out of the room, got the hell out of the place, and went shopping to buy some clothes to go out to Carleton in. I didn't want to stay there, and I didn't feel like going back to the apartment, either. I started to call the police and didn't, because I wasn't sure what was going on. I figured you'd have some bright ideas about what to do. Oh, and I drove around for a while to see if anyone was following me, but I'm pretty sure that no one was. Or if they were, I lost them."

Sanders didn't comment. In silence he traced a complex pattern in a few drops of spilled liquid on the table. "What's wrong?" asked Harriet, frowning. "Pretty stupid to react the way I did, I suppose."

He looked up at her. "Nothing's wrong," he said. "Well, it is, of course, but probably not the way you mean." He took her hand. "Except that I'm not very pleased about what just happened."

"Well, of course not,," she said. "But you looked, I don't know, unhappy about something."

"I did? Nothing could be further from the truth. Worried, but not unhappy. Not now. I was thinking about something odd, that's all."

"Besides the motel room?" He nodded. "What?"

"Well, that useless, tight-assed, unimaginative bastard Higgs—who would be the last candidate on my list for a job that needed brains or discretion—was asking me questions about your picture, and, incidentally, about you. I don't like it. If he's in Security, what's he doing running this idiotic seminar? This week, when the city is stiff with top-level foreigners, with more about to arrive. And if he's what he looks like—a nobody—why does he know you're a photographer? And why should he care? Look, Harriet, I know this sounds like a stupid question, but are you famous?"

"Famous?" she said, putting down her beer and spluttering slightly.

"Yeah, famous. Has your picture been in the papers and magazines, only I'm a slob and never noticed it? Would a hell of a lot of people take one look at you and say, 'Oh, look, Mabel, there's Harriet Jeffries, the photographer, let's get her autograph'?"

"You mean like, let me see, Anthony Armstrong-Jones?"

"Who's he?" said Sanders, and ducked in mock terror. "No, I know who you mean. Yes. Like that, or him."

"No," she said. "Definitely not. I am well known—thank God, because otherwise I'd starve—among a small, very small, group of people who hire me. I've had pictures printed in architectural and photo magazines, so a few more people might recognize my name but not my face. I am not famous. Sorry."

"Then . . ." He picked up her hand and held it tightly. "Harriet, have you been in . . . Goddammit." He searched for a tactful way to put it. There wasn't one. "Is the RCMP running a current active file on you?" he asked bluntly. "So that someone in Administration would recognize you just like that?"

"Are you asking me if I have a criminal record?" she said coldly as she tried to pull her hand away.

"No, dammit!" he snapped. "Be reasonable. Of course I'm not asking you if you have a record. You're from

Toronto, for God's sake. If you were that well known to the police, I'd bloody well have recognized you. Remember where I work? For chrissake, I am not asking you if you go around robbing banks. It would have to be something the RCMP were interested in—political demonstrations, God knows what. They're all bloody paranoid," he added in disgust. "Have you taken pictures of Mounties beating up Indians or bashing strikers? They'd sure as hell keep a file on you for something like that."

She stared at him for a moment, and then slowly shook her head. "I don't do news photography," she said. "I've never published a picture of people doing anything, except occasionally standing somewhere to show the scale of a building. I don't think I've ever taken a politically sensitive picture in my life, and I've certainly never had one printed."

"Then why in hell would someone who does PR work for the Mounties—because that's all this goddamn seminar is—see you across a parking lot, through a car window, and know who you are?"

"Maybe he made it his business to find out who I was because he saw me with you. Some people are just nosy. Couldn't he get my name from looking up my license plate number?"

Sanders shook his head. "That goes beyond common nosiness. Let's get out of here."

"To the conference?"

"Is that what you want to do?" She nodded. "We really ought to call the local cops, you know. That break-in has to be reported. Even if they did it. But come on. We'll call them later. Let's go."

CHAPTER 8

"Was it the RCMP who wrecked the motel room?" asked Harriet abruptly.

Sanders felt his hands tightening on the steering wheel; he made a concentrated effort to unknot his shoulders and keep his gaze calmly on the road. "Don't know," he said, his voice devoid of anger. "They could have, I suppose. If they were the ones who turned over your apartment."

"Would they have done that? Really? John, whoever went in there smashed up several thousand dollars worth of equipment. Doesn't that come in the category of criminal behavior?"

He made a noncommittal noise. "More convincing, though, isn't it?" he said. "You'd never believe that a government agency would do something like that, would you?"

"Oh, wouldn't I," she growled. "But why would they do it?"

"If it was the RCMP," said Sanders, "and I'm not saying it was, they're looking for evidence. The wrecking was just distraction."

"Evidence of what?" Her voice crackled with impatience.

"Oh, they want the pictures, that's clear. It's possible they need them for identification—or maybe they're trying to destroy them."

"Why? Why destroy a picture of someone who apparently goes around killing people? I realize I'm just a stupid and naive woman, but I thought the idea would have been to use the picture to help catch him."

Sanders accelerated around a truck and a van and found himself speeding past RCMP headquarters. "That's easy. Either they want to find out who killed this Bartholomew or they already know and they want his identity suppressed. There's nothing much in between. And if it's the second option, then probably they're up against something they consider to be much bigger than murder. Or at least than Bartholomew's murder." He glanced down at the speedometer and eased up on the accelerator. This was no time to get picked up for speeding. "Of course, they could have had nothing to do with your apartment—or my motel room. I could be suffering from a conspiracy obsession. It happens to you after you've been around these security types for more than a day or two." Harriet coughed, a cough of disbelief. "And while we're asking questions, lady. Would you mind telling me why we're racing out to Carleton— where we probably won't find any nests of Mounties conspiring about anything—when you seem to be convinced that they're the ones responsible for what happened?"

"Because I'm not convinced," said Harriet. "I'm just confused. And besides, can you think of anything more useful to do? The camera equipment is insured, and so there's nothing else I can do there, but the pictures are gone somewhere, our only lead is that damn conference, and the final banquet is tonight. So," she said in tones of weary patience, "if the guys are at the conference and if they have the pictures, maybe we can get a line on them. And if they don't, well, what the hell. What have we missed out on?"

"I suppose I follow you," said Sanders. "Are you sure we can get in for free drinks?"

"Scott said there'd be no problem. They're dying for press coverage and he said we could slip in with him if worse comes to worst." She stared out the window. Her anger and irritation had given way; she was tired and felt now that she was being foolish. "I hope I'm not dragging you out there on a wild-goose chase," she said at last in a forlorn voice.

"It'd be nothing new," said Sanders, feeling suddenly cheerful. "That's what I spend most of my life doing. Fifty wild geese for every tame one." He reached over and took hold of the back of her neck, massaging it affectionately. "Besides, it's your gas."

Harriet sighed and dropped her head back, wriggling her shoulders in a gesture of pleasure and relief. "Where'd you leave your car?" she murmured.

"In the parking garage," he said, withdrawing his hand and returning it to the wheel. "I'm thinking of renting a space for it on a permanent basis." He flicked on the left turn indicator and pulled into the wide and barren grounds on the perimeter of the university.

It was only a few minutes after five when they located the room where the reception was being held. As they looked through the packed mass of humanity, Harriet spotted a small, elfish man fighting his way over to meet them. "Is that him?" asked Sanders incredulously. Harriet nodded, and they both watched his progress through the delegates. The crowd dividing them was large and ill assorted. Men in grubby tweeds rubbed elbows with other men in black tie and dinner jacket; the women were clad in every possible variation of dress, from jeans to floor-length brocade.

"I didn't need to go shopping," said Harriet, looking around. "You could wear anything in this crowd. Or nothing. Although I suppose we might have stood out if we'd arrived with nothing on."

"I doubt that, Harriet darling," said a voice beside her. "They would have assumed you were part of the entertainment."

"Oh, hi, Scott. What entertainment?"

"A play, I think, on the Seven Deadly Sins or something equally juicy. You'd be Lechery, of course, slithering about in the nude." He smiled seraphically. "A sort of medieval dinner theater."

"Scott, this is John Sanders. A friend of Kevin's. He's looking for him as well. Scott O'Reilly."

Scott took Sanders's hand for a brief and firm shake. "And you'd be Wrath, I expect—or maybe Pride."

Sanders looked down at him, assailed by sudden anger and an urge to grab him by the shoulders and shake him. Who in hell did he think he was? Clever, snotty little bastard, counting on his malice and brilliance to protect him from physical injury. Not to speak of Harriet, who would be appalled if he hit him, no doubt. "Stop being so damned clever, Scott," she said, as if she could read Sanders's thoughts, "and let me look for Kevin. Can you see him, John? You're taller than we are."

Sanders bent down with his mouth close to her ear. "What in hell have you been telling this guy?"

"We're looking for my depressed, beautiful, drunken, and cocaine-soaked cousin, Kevin. I thought it would intrigue him. Especially the beautiful part," she whispered. "Omigod, John, there he is. Don't look. He's standing by the tall plant near the door to my left. Damn, he's looking over this way. He'll see you." Her voice took on a slighty desperate note.

"What's wrong?" said Scott, scenting trouble and looking as bright-eyed as a beagle after a rabbit.

"He's over there," said Harriet. "By that plant. I hadn't realized how painfully obvious John is in a crowd. As soon as he sees John, he's going to bolt, and we'll never find him."

"In that case, my love," said Scott, "we'll just have to ditch your tall friend here and tail him ourselves. He certainly won't recognize me, and anything that gorgeous is pretty easy to spot. Stay behind me; we'll follow him when he leaves and find out where he's staying."

"What do you think?" asked Harriet, turning to Sanders.

"I think it's a lousy idea," said Sanders forcefully.

"Temper, temper," said O'Reilly irritatingly. "Don't worry, love. We won't stop to talk to him. We'll just get his address and hurry right back. I promise." He winked at Sanders.

"I have to talk to you," said Sanders, his voice grim. He caught Harriet by the arm and dragged her away from the little photographer.

"Go ahead," said Scott. "I'll keep an eye on the beautiful Kevin for you."

"You're crazy. If that's the guy who trashed the motel room and ripped apart your apartment you're not going to want to meet him in a dark alley somewhere. If anyone's following anybody, it'll be me."

"He'd spot you in two minutes, John. Have you any idea how much you stand out?"

"For chrissake, I've been doing this sort of thing for a living for almost twenty years. Give me credit for some sense, at least."

"How much time do you spend following people? Without them seeing you? Listen, John. We'll be in a car. We aren't going to follow him into dark alleys or even goddamn parking garages. Give *me* credit for some sense, as well. And

Scott isn't nearly as flitty as he looks—most of that's protective cover. He just got back from two years in Beirut. Alive. As you can see." Her cheeks flared red with anger.

Sanders gave up. "Can you go in his car? Just in case?"

"Hurry," said O'Reilly, who had materialized out of nowhere. "He's decided to leave. Of course we can take my car. This is such fun, Harriet, my dear."

"See you back at the motel," breathed Harriet at John, and melted into the crowd after the photographer.

Sanders watched uneasily as the three of them left. It was the second man in the picture who had come to the reception, not Scarface, and he was moving away as though he had nothing more pressing on his mind than dinner. A pro, thought Sanders. Or an innocent. He frowned. Harriet wasn't bad at tailing, he concluded, watching her weave her way through the assorted medievalists, apparently absorbed in Scott's chatter with wide-eyed girlish enthusiasm. With a little luck, Mr. O'Reilly would be able to shield her from doing anything disastrous. This also left him free to work things out. Because it was time to stop reacting to events and start using brainpower. When the three of them had had enough time to clear out of the corridors, he left the room and headed for the nearest telephone. He could use a little help from his partner at this point. Sanders glanced at his watch. Not yet 5:30. Ed Dubinsky might still be at his desk in Toronto. He reached into his pocket and fished out a quarter.

"Goddammit, I know you're about to go home. The miracle is that you haven't made it out the door already," snarled Sanders into the phone. "But I need some information and I'm in no position to get it myself. Not from here. Christ, all I'm asking you to do is make a simple little phone call to the Capital Region Police Department."

"And what am I supposed to want to know?" asked Dubinsky.

"What they have on a corpse called Don Bartholomew."

"And what goddamned reason do I have for wanting to know about their fucking corpse?"

"I'm sure you'll think of something. Your sister-in-law was in love with him, the chief of detectives was in love with him . . . something."

"Thanks. Where do I call you when I've found all this out?"

"Back at my motel. In an hour. And, Ed, thanks a lot."

When he pulled into the motel parking lot, he did what he should have been done hours ago. He parked at the entrance and went in the scruffy door marked "Management." Management raised its head from a page of figures on the desk in a hopeful manner, recognized someone who was already staying there, and sank back again. "Can I help you? Inspector Sanders, isn't it?"

Sanders grunted. "Just wondered if anyone dropped in today looking for me. I was expecting a friend."

Management leaned back in its chair reflectively. "Sanders . . . today. Yes. Someone did, I think. Wanted to know if you were still staying here, I think. No message that I can remember."

"Was he tall?" asked Sanders. "Sort of thin face with high cheekbones and dark eyes?" He ran a set of fingers in front of his face, indicating the striking configuration of Scarface's features.

Management paused and thought. "No. Nothing like that."

"Blond and good-looking, then?" asked Sanders, thinking of the young man Harriet was pursuing and hoping that he wasn't the one who had smashed the room apart.

Management shook its head. "Don't think so. Just sort of sandy hair and ordinary-looking, I think. You know anyone like that?"

"Thanks," said Sanders, and walked over to have a look at the room.

"Jesus, they really did a job this time, didn't they?" said the loud-mouthed sergeant from the break-and-enter squad.

"Yeah, and this time they destroyed a lot of equipment," said Sanders. "Expensive equipment. About ten thousand dollars' worth. So you might at least pretend you're trying to do something about it. Like looking for prints, or something. Or don't you know how?"

"Back off, eh?" said the first man's partner. "We'll check, but I'll lay you five to one the whole damn place has been polished up like a new car. What'd they take?"

Sanders shook his head. "Can't tell. Nothing, as far as I know. Maybe when Miss Jeffries gets back, she'll know if anything's missing. It looks to me as if they didn't find what they were looking for and got mad."

"Maybe," said the sergeant, and sighed. "We'd better get a list of what's wrecked. Come on, Bert, might as well start back here."

The telephone rang while they were still picking up each small piece of equipment on the floor and trying to put a name to it. Sanders grabbed for it and snapped into the receiver.

"It's me." His partner sounded tired and bored. But Dubinsky usually sounded tired and bored, so that meant nothing. "About Bartholomew, your corpse. I've got his address. It's a rooming house at Fifty-nine Main Street, Stittsville. Got that? He was bludgeoned to death, no weapon found. He was in good physical condition."

"And drunk," said Sanders.

"Don't think so," said Dubinsky. "Just a minute." There was a pause. "Cold sober, in fact."

"That's interesting. Very interesting. Anything else?"

"They traced the car to a rental outfit and lost the trail. The driver's license used for ID was stolen. They have a description of the major suspect—"

"I've got that. Nothing else?"

"Don't think so. Have fun spying, John. I'm leaving for a nice, peaceful evening at home."

Sanders hung up thoughtfully. "You guys know how far away Stittsville is?" he asked.

"Sure, about fifteen miles," said the sergeant. "Go out the Queensway to Richmond Road, old number seven. It's not far. Look, there's nothing much more we can do. Miss Jeffries can call us if she notices that there's anything missing. Oh, and tell her not to forget to call her insurance company. Here's my number," the sergeant added, dropping a piece of paper onto the table.

"Thanks," said Sanders. "You've been a real help. Almost as much help as last time," and pushed them out the door. As soon as their car pulled out of the parking lot, he bounded down the stairs and into Harriet's car. He found a map in her glove compartment, checked where he was going, and headed out for the Queensway and Stittsville.

The long spring evening was just beginning as Sanders pulled south off the expressway, grateful to get the low sun out of his eyes. A medium blue car pulled off after him; he slowed down perceptibly to get it off his tail. Instead of using the deserted road to pass, it too slowed down. He looked again. A fairly new Ford Escort, front license plates blurred with mud and rust. He picked up speed suddenly, found some traffic to put between them, and pulled far ahead before settling back down to the speed limit. The blue Ford appeared to be gone. He must be catching the prevailing local paranoia. He couldn't even let a perfectly ordinary car exit from the Queensway without being consumed by suspicion. He glanced at his watch. He'd be in Stittsville around seven-thirty.

At 7:30, Andy Cassidy put away the pile of surveillance reports he had been double checking. The casual complaints of bad and insufficient data that Ian MacMillan had passed on from Henri Deschenes—the ones he had dismissed so lightly on Monday evening—had rankled. Still, everything in front of him seemed normal; he shook his head and looked at his watch. The cleaning crew should be gone by now and he could get back to his fruitless search of Steve Collins's files. He walked down the familiar corridors to Steve's office in the gray half-light that found its way in from the long May evening. Steve's door was shut, his lights out. Cassidy pulled out the key he still carried with him and opened the office door.

Silhouetted against the darkening eastern sky, Betty's motionless form was perched on a table pushed against the window. She turned her head slowly in his direction in that unsettling way she had. "Don't turn the light on," she said.

"What's happening?" asked Andy. He had at least learned not to ask what she was doing there. It seemed to him that each time he'd asked that question, he'd lost the exchange.

She slipped down from the table and pointed over to the corner beside Steve's desk, where Andy had stacked boxes of files as he sorted them. It was empty. He looked around him. The whole office was empty. He ran over to the desk and began flinging open drawers. They were unlocked and rattled hollowly as he yanked at them. There wasn't even a pencil left behind. "What in hell happened to all Steve's things? Did you take them?"

Betty shook her head and moved closer. Now, even in the dusk, he could see scarlet patches in her cheeks and fury in her eyes. She raised a finger to her mouth and motioned him out of the room. He followed her down the hall toward her own cubbyhole of an office. "There," she said, as soon as she had closed the door. "Now we can talk."

"What happened?" he repeated.

"It was the RCMP," said Betty. "They arrived with authorization to seize his stuff. Because he was killed on their turf. Packed up everything and took it away, even his keys. You should have kept them."

"Who?"

"Ian MacMillan and a couple of constables," she said. "It was all legal, I think. Not that I had anything to do with it. I just wandered by to see what was going on. No one pays much attention to me."

"Bloody hell," muttered Cassidy. "Not that there was much there, as far as I could tell, anyway."

The scarlet patches in Betty's cheeks deepened and spread to her throat and forehead. "I just remembered this afternoon," she said, picking up a paper clip and beginning to untwist it viciously, "that Steve had left a few files in my small cabinet in here. He claimed he ran out of space in his own file drawers," she turned the paper clip into a triangle, "and could never find anything once the department had locked it away. I wrote you a letter about it this afternoon, but after those guys were in here, I decided I'd better wait and give it to you in person."

"Why didn't you come down to my office?" he asked, amazed.

"I wouldn't want to do that," she said. "It looks funny. Here," and she threw a letter at him before turning and fleeing. He closed the door behind her and bolted it before picking up the envelope. It was dated that day, and neatly typed:

Dear Andy,

I'm sure Steve would have wanted me to give you what he'd found. I don't know what's there, but he seemed to feel his case was complete. You'll find the key to the small black filing cabinet taped to the underside of the top section of the copier. Check the "clear paper path" instructions and open the section marked "B" and you'll find it. He was very concerned about that material—and I think you'll see why once you look at it. If it is what I think it is.

And thank you for doing this. I hope you catch the bastard who got him—no matter who he is.

With apologies,
Betty

The door leading from Betty's cubbyhole to the room containing the photocopy machine was locked. Cassidy looked around. Getting in couldn't be that difficult or she would have left him even more instructions on how to do it. He looked at the containers of paper clips and staples on her desk, and then flipped through the papers in her In tray. Nothing. He drew open the shallow top drawer and there it was. A key with a large and grubby tag marked "Photocopy Room." Not so difficult. He opened the door, turned on the light, and picked up the sheet of instructions. Sure enough. "To clear paper path," it said, with an arrow indicating the knob that had to be turned. The entire top of the machine slowly heaved itself up, and there in the corner, attached to the top, was a frizzled piece of electrical tape, which, when peeled away, proved to be hiding a small key. "Good girl," he muttered, and headed back to the small black filing cabinet. He looked at the array of material inside it, pulled out three folders, and settled down at Betty's desk to digest their contents.

Sanders looked at the big white clapboard house and thought for a moment. The most effective way to get somewhere with the landlady was probably to charge in, in his own person, waving his ID, and snow her with credentials. He reached into his pocket, fished out the fake leather case, and slipped it into his left hand, ready to be flashed open as soon as the landlady appeared. There was no doorbell that he could see. He picked up the large black knocker and let it fall. The sound reverberated on the other side of the door. There was no answering noise. He waited. Nothing. He shook his head impatiently, raised his hand to fling the heavy knocker against the door again, and was stopped by the faint sound of footsteps. A few seconds more and the door fell away in front of him.

He looked at the landlady and felt as if he had slipped into a time warp. She appeared to be a haggard thirty, or perhaps a youthful forty-five, perfectly preserved from the sixties. Her long brown hair was streaked with gray and worn in a single braid pulled forward over her left shoulder and falling over her chest. Her feet were bare and dirty, her legs encased in worn jeans, and her Indian embroidered shirt covered with strand after strand of beads. Not someone likely to support the maintainers of law and order? He hastily slipped his ID back into his pocket. "Hi," he said, leaning awkwardly against the door frame. "I'm a pal of Don's—Don Bartholomew. I read about, uh, what happened . . . in the paper. I didn't know what I should do. So, I came here. I'm John. John Sanders."

"What do you mean?" she asked suspiciously.

"Well, I'm not quite sure," he said, straightening up a little and running his hand over his hair. "I've never had this happen to me before—" He remembered his role and slouched again.

"Had what happen?" She broke in impatiently. "Look, if you've got something to say, say it. Otherwise I have things to do. Like there are flies on the back porch I haven't counted yet."

"Well," said Sanders, "I dunno. I left some, uh, stuff in Don's room, and I wondered if—"

"Stuff? You mean grass, dope?" she asked, with a grin. "Because if you did, pal, you're outta luck. Jesus, the place's been crawling with cops since Monday. One came to tell me what happened and he looked up in his room and then two more turned up a little later to search his room and then there was a third one. And he went up there, too. All in plain clothes, of course, but I can spot those bastards a mile away. Always could. I made them come up with identification all right. Anyway, they've walked off with everything but the bedposts from his room."

"Shit," said Sanders. "They took everything? But it wasn't anything like that. It was something I'd written. Did the fucking cops take all that away, too?"

"You're damned right they did," said the landlady. "Every piece of paper. Pigs, that's what they are. We were right back in the old days. They're still pigs." She leaned against the other side of the door frame and picked up the end of her braid, assessing him. Finally she seemed to come to some sort of conclusion. "They got everything but his notebooks."

"You mean . . ." Sanders paused before he could put a foot wrong.

"Yeah. The notes for his novel. And his journal. All great writers keep journals. Did you know that? Don told me. Anyway, I've got all that stuff. He didn't trust the other guys in the house."

"Maybe my stuff is in there, too," said Sanders, leaning closer to her. "When did he let you have it?"

"Four, five days ago," she said. "One of the other guys had been snooping in his room. What did you give him?"

"It's an outline, an outline for a story I was writing. My only copy, too, which was pretty stupid of me. I guess you wouldn't think to look at me that I wrote stories," he added modestly, "but then Don didn't exactly look like he did, either. Poor bastard."

She was still holding the end of her braid in one hand, twisting the tip around her second and third fingers. "What the hell," she said at last. "Come on in. I'm Miranda, Miranda Cruikshank. Let me see if I can find your stuff."

"Thanks, Mrs. Cruikshank," he murmured. "I really appreciate this."

"Miranda," she said. "You gotta call me Miranda," and took him by the hand to pull him into the house.

*   *   *

"Nice house you got here, Mrs., uh, Miranda," said Sanders. They were sitting in an enormous kitchen at a round wooden table. The scene was a parody of nineteenth-century rural nostalgia. Behind him a wood stove burned, enveloping the kitchen in stifling heat. On the painted pine boards in front of the stove, Mrs. Cruikshank had thrown a large and grubby braided rag rug. A fat golden retriever lay sleeping on a chintz-covered couch near the source of heat; in front of him, on the other side of the kitchen, was a stained, wooden drainboard with a shallow porcelain sink in it. The dog opened an eye, considered Sanders, thumped her tail on the cushion, and slept again.

Miranda looked around her critically, as if she hadn't noticed her surroundings in ten years. "Thanks," she said. "Not bad, I guess. I came up here with Wayne—my boyfriend—in seventy-one. Me and the baby. It seemed like a nice place, you know, to get away from the materialism and hypocrisy of the city and that sort of crap." She turned and stared out the window into the deepening shadows. "Except that a small town's got just as much hypocrisy. And materialism. Funny, isn't it? Anyway, the bastard took off one day and disappeared to somewhere. Vancouver, I think. He's probably living in the suburbs and working in a brokerage office or something like that now. And wearing suits and ties. So here I am. Amanda—that's the baby—she's gone to Toronto to get away from—what does she call it?—the stifling atmosphere of a dying small-town culture. So now I've got nobody and I live alone. What the hell, I'm used to the place. In fact, I kind of like it now and so I take in boarders. It's a living. Sort of. Keeps me from getting too lonely, if you know what I mean." She eyed him hungrily. "You'll have a beer? Come on," she added, coaxing, before he had a chance to accept or reject it.

"Sure," he said easily, and leaned back in his chair as if he had all the time in the world.

"There." She set a bottle in front of each place and opened both of them. Apparently there was something in her moral code that forbade the use of glasses. She turned to a set of cupboards, opened a bottom door, and pulled out a potato chip bag, unopened. She set it on the table between them. "Organic," she said. "They're wild. I'm thinking of opening a *real* health food store somewhere around here." Sanders's eye suddenly fell on the dirt ground into the floor, the work surfaces and piled up in the corners, and he shuddered at the thought of this woman running a food store. "Don't you think you could make a fortune out of it?" She ripped open the bag. "Have some chips."

Sanders gave another desperate look around. "You wouldn't have any idea where Don might have—"

"Oh, Jesus, I'm sorry," she said. "Your story. Well, if it's here, I know where it'll be." She got up with a rattle of beads and threw open a door at the back of the room. It led into a gloomy passageway. "The pantry," she said, her voice muffled. "I put it in here with the chili sauce and peach jam from last year. Figured nobody'd look there for that kind of stuff, would they?" Sanders shook his head. That would probably be the first place he'd look, but never mind. Maybe nobody had. She returned waving a large, rusty cookie tin. "Here it is."

She opened the tin with care and revealed a round shape wrapped in aluminum foil. "Last year's Christmas cake," she said, taking it out and putting it on the table. Under it was a round of cardboard, covered with waxed paper. "That's nothing," she added, and lifted it out, too. Underneath that, on a piece of greasy paper towel, lay a notebook, black, soft-covered, and slighty dog-eared. "Do you think it might be in here?" she asked.

Sanders reached into the cookie tin and picked up the notebook. The first page was headed "Dawn in Vienna" and was filled with apparently random jottings. "That's the name of his novel," said Miranda Cruikshank, pointing at the heading. "Neat, eh?" She sat back with a look of satisfaction. "And those are his notes for the first chapter. He showed me. I couldn't figure them out at all, but of course they made perfect sense to him." Her eyes filled with tears for a moment. "Such a damn stupid thing to happen to such a nice guy."

Sanders scanned the first three or four pages as casually as he could. He had to resist the temptation to whip out his pen and start copying, but Miranda, although she seemed more than willing to accept anyone at his own valuation, might get suspicious if he started taking notes on his old pal's writing notebook. "I'll bet this would've been a great novel," he said, injecting as much folksy sentimentality into his voice as he could dredge up. "I guess this must be his cast of characters, eh?—all these initials. Probably trying to think up names. It's hard to come up with good names, you know." Miranda Cruikshank nodded wisely. She had obviously had this sort of conversation before. "I wonder what he meant by that? Did he ever tell you?" He yawned and pointed at the bottom of the fifth page of the notebook, where Bartholomew had written "1700 Joe + 1" and drawn a box around it.

"It must've been important," said Miranda. She looked over at Sanders and picked up her braid again. She had done that while wondering whether to let him in the house and it made him nervous. "For him to do that to it."

"Naw," said Sanders lazily, hoping to head her off. "Just doodling, I'll bet." He began to flip idly through the pages.

"I guess my stuff isn't—" A piece of letter-size paper, folded in four, dropped out of the notebook onto the table. "Maybe this is it," he said, unfolding it and trying to hold it away from Miranda's prying eyes.

It was headed up "R.T./Hardy, F.F.T.M.C." and consisted of a meaningless series of numbers, some circled, arranged in what looked like paragraph form, filling the better part of the page. At the foot of the page Bartholomew had written, in what by now was familiar handwriting, "Party, May 18th, 720 Echo Drive."

"Is that yours?" asked Miranda, reaching out her hand for it.

Sanders shook his head and folded the piece of paper up again. He opened the notebook once more as if to replace it, palmed the sheet, and slipped it into his pocket. He went on staring at the fifth page, which, in spite of a jumble of initials, seemed to make some sense, and willed it into his memory. For a fleeting instant he had considered palming the entire book, but decided that even a trusting creature like Miranda would think its disappearance peculiar. Finally he looked up and answered her. "What's that?" he said, as if being dragged back from a reverie that had taken him thousands of miles away. "Mine?" He shook his head slowly. "No, this is all Don's stuff. Tragic, isn't it?" he added. "A great talent like that." Miranda Cruikshank nodded in solemn agreement. "I guess he must have mailed my outline back to me. And well, you know what that means. It could be weeks before it turns up."

"Probably," said the landlady. "After all, someone like Don wouldn't have lost anything you gave him. I mean, he was so, well, fussy about everything. Used to drive me crazy sometimes. Not like these other slobs I have living here."

"Unless he'd been drinking a bit," said Sanders, curious to see what her reaction would be.

"Drinking? Don? You gotta be kidding," she said. "You had to practically tie him down to get him to have a beer. Did he used to drink when you knew him?"

Sanders nodded. "A bit," he said cautiously.

"Must have gotten himself into trouble over it," she said. There was satisfaction in her voice. "I thought so. I mean, otherwise why be so careful about the stuff? And he never came in drunk like the rest of the guys. Never."

"Do those other guys who live here, your other boarders," he said, "do they work at that same construction job he was on?"

"Nope," she said. "The other guys he works with, they're staying at the hotel. He told me he had enough of them during the day, without having to live with them, too."

"That sounds like Don," said Sanders, standing up. He was beginning to tire of the deception, easy though it was. "Look, thanks a lot for the beer and the chips. And thanks for looking for my stuff. Don must have appreciated living in a place like this." At that he began to worry that he had gone too far, but Miranda Cruikshank smiled and held out her hand.

"Peace, brother," she said, solemnly.

"Uh, peace," gurgled Sanders, and fled.

Sanders climbed into Harriet's car as fast as he could get the key in the lock and headed through town for the nearest open garage to fill up her fast-depleting gas tank. As he pulled up in front of a lighted regular-unleaded pump and killed the engine, he thought that he caught a glimpse of a medium-blue Ford Escort through the corner of his eye.

Ridiculous, he murmured to himself. He was being swallowed up in some locally induced paranoia. He stretched, tried to look unconcerned, and then pulled out his notebook and began to jot down absolutely everything he could remember from those five or six pages. The more he wrote down, the uneasier he felt. On one of those pages hadn't Bartholomew mentioned a light blue Ford, license number 1 something something B something F—or E? Or had he made that up, remembering from that hot kitchen some fact that didn't exist, that had jumped backward into the book from his unconscious memory of the car that had just whipped by him. Then other words from those pages floated into his memory and began to tease and worry at him.

Who in bloody hell am I dealing with? he wondered. Who precisely, that is. He could always try the last refuge of confusion and ask. He looked at his watch. 8:30. He accepted his change and pulled back onto the highway again. Higgs had been complaining today about having to be at another concert tonight, he remembered, some chamber group playing with that violinist, sponsored again by the Austrian embassy. He headed north toward Ottawa.

The crowd was still milling around for the intermission when he arrived at the concert hall, but the ringing bell had started to herd them back to their seats. Higgs was standing near the main entrance door, facing inward, looking reluctant to commit himself to the second half of the program.

Sanders pulled open the door behind Higgs and spoke right into his ear. "Evening, Inspector," he said. Higgs jumped and whirled around.

"For God's sake, man," he said, seeing Sanders and stepping back in relief. "Don't do that. Not right now. I might have killed you."

"Probably not," said Sanders. "You're much too well trained to do something that stupid, I would say. But I apologize for startling you. How's the concert?"

"Who can tell?" asked Higgs, gloomily. "I'm just here to look around, that's all. No time to listen to the music. I suppose it's all right, and so far nobody's massacred anybody else, so it's a success from that point of view as well."

"You're really expecting something to happen, aren't you?" asked Sanders curiously. "I'm surprised. It just doesn't seem all that likely to me. Not here."

"Well . . ." said Higgs. "You hear a few rumors here and there and so you do something. You should know how it is. Most of them have no basis in fact at all and you look like a bloody fool tracking them down. One or two of them are the real stuff, and if you ignore those you end up administering local justice in some Arctic outpost." He shrugged. Right now, in the bright lights of the lobby, he looked tired and pretty human. Through the closed doors behind them came muted clapping, and then the muffled sounds of music. "What are you doing here? You come to this concert? You're missing the second half if you did."

Sanders shook his head. "I was just walking by on my way back from dinner," he said, "and I saw you through the glass. Thought I'd say hello is all."

Higgs made an indefinable snorting noise.

"Oh, there was one thing," said Sanders. "What in hell is 'Joe plus one'?" The RCMP inspector gave him a startled look. "I was over in headquarters talking to some people and this guy is staring straight at me and says it. Someone laughs and the guy next to him says, 'Sure, no problem.' I felt pretty stupid. What in hell was he talking about?"

Higgs laughed, and the taut lines disappeared from his face. "I haven't heard that for a while," he said. "Not for a couple of years." He shook his head. "One of the men in our detachment used to call the days of the week that."

"What?"

"The days of the week. I didn't know that anyone still remembered it. And the guy who did it is . . . never mind. Anyway, Joe was a bartender at someplace we used to go to, it doesn't matter where. He worked the bar in the evenings from Thursday through Sunday, so Joe plus one was—"

"Friday," said Sanders thoughtfully. "A neat system. He must have been a funny guy."

"He was," said Higgs, clipping off his words again. The mask of rigidity slipped over his face once more. "I must get back into the hall and keep an eye on things. Good night, Inspector."

Sanders stood at the door to the motel room and hesitated. There was a dim light glowing from behind the heavy curtains but no sound issuing from the room. He transferred the key to his left hand and let his right hand slip automatically inside his jacket. With a slightly awkward motion, he inserted the key and opened the door, keeping his body back from the opening. The area in front of him had been cleared of mess, but the portion of the bed that was visible from where he stood was still piled high with their jumbled possessions. He pushed the door open a little more. More chaos, but no sign of Harriet. And no sign of anyone else, either. He slammed the door back as far as it would go. It hit the wall with a satisfying thump of metal on drywall and he walked in.

Propped up against the lamp on the low chest was a terse note. "Couldn't stand this. In coffee shop. H."

She was sitting over the remains of a piece of apple pie and cheese. "Have some," she said calmly. "It's not bad."

He picked up the menu, ran his eye down it, and put it back down. "I wish you'd stop doing that to me," he said.

"Doing what?" She put down her fork and looked up.

"Scaring the life out of me. When I opened that door and you weren't there . . . All I could think was that it might have been nice to have more than one night. . . ." His voice trailed away and he picked up the menu again. The waitress took a couple of steps toward them and he called out, "A corned beef. And a beer, a Blue, I guess." Harriet raised two fingers. "Make that two corned beef and two Blues." He turned back to her. "Now, what happened?"

"Nothing happened to me, obviously," said Harriet. She could feel her cheeks burning under the steadiness of his gaze. "We lost him," she went on hastily. "It was pretty stupid of us, I guess. I was sure he hadn't seen me, and there was no reason why he would have recognized Scott, but we followed him out to the parking lot, got Scott's car, and followed his car right back into Ottawa and then up to the river and over into Vanier. Anyway, the car pulled into a motel parking lot, the driver got out, and—"

"It wasn't the same man?"

"How in hell did you know?"

"It happens," he said, grinning. "He probably spotted you, led you to the parking lot, and drifted off to his dormitory as soon as he found someone else for you to follow. Long before the person you were following got into his car."

"Well, I felt pretty idiotic. Harriet Jeffries, girl detective, screws up again."

He waited while the beer arrived, poured some, and raised his glass. "To Harriet Jeffries, girl detective. It's just as well you didn't find him, you know. At the risk of sounding repetitive, I have to say that these are probably not nice people. And I hate to think what stupid thing you might have done if you'd actually tracked him down to a motel room. Like charging up to him and asking for your pictures back."

She shrugged. "I wouldn't do something like that. I think. Not unless I was really furious." She raised her glass in return. "And where in hell have you been?" She was having trouble keeping her voice steady. "I was—"

"All over," he said, suddenly cheerful. The anxiety in her eyes and the catch in her throat as she spoke had ignited the fire in his belly once again, and he picked her hand up and held it in both of his. "I may have found out a lot. Then again, it might be absolutely nothing and totally irrelevant. I'll tell you as soon as I get something to eat. I'm suffering from having consumed nothing but organic junk food all evening."

"Organic junk food?" He surrendered her hand and shook his head as the sandwiches arrived.

"And that's what I've got so far," said Sanders, pushing his plate aside as he finished both his sandwich and his account of the evening. "This Bartholomew was keeping rather cryptic notes on some sort of activity when he was killed, but for whom I do not know. One thing is very clear, though. He sure as hell wasn't an ordinary construction worker, not even an ordinary snitch. I would have sworn he was roaring drunk when I saw him, and an hour later, when he died, there was no appreciable amount of alcohol in his system. So he was pretty good at blending in."

"This is all very interesting, but it doesn't tell us who stole my pictures, does it?" said Harriet, frowning.

"There is that party," said Sanders. "The one in his notes. It's tonight, isn't it?"

"Well, I'll be damned," said Harriet, "so it is." Her eyes began to glow. "What a coincidence. And here I am, dressed fit to kill, just itching to get to crash some glamorous affair. Come on, finish your beer, John Sanders. Let's go. In case everyone gets bored and goes home early. What time is it?"

"Ten-forty," he said. "But first we get ourselves another motel room."

"Check out at this time of night?"

"No, we don't check out at all. We leave everything here as it is. We can buy toothbrushes at an all-night drugstore. We'll leave my car here, drive up in yours, and leave it on the street somewhere. Any objections?"

Harriet shook her head. "Why should I have any objections? If I stick around with you long enough, I'll have fifteen different addresses. I've always wanted to live like the rich."

By now the data interpretation section of the Canadian Security Intelligence Service was dark and empty. Andy Cassidy sat alone in a small pool of light at Betty's desk and stared down at the file in front of him. He considered for a minute or two; tentative and potentially explosive as this might be, it was going to have to be passed along right away. Not hoarded, the way Steve Collins had obviously hoarded it for weeks and weeks. But passed along to whom? He pulled the telephone closer, lifted the receiver, and then put it down again. This was not the phone to use to talk about it. He extracted several pages from the file, picked up the folders, put them back in the black filing cabinet, and slammed the door shut. He locked it, went back into the photocopy room, hoisted up the top of the copier, restored the key to its odd resting place, and began locking up again. He gave one last look around Betty's office. The coffee maker was off, the note safe in his breast pocket, everything was as it had been. He headed for the telephone at the all-night diner near his apartment.

As he dialed the familiar number, it struck him that everything had changed now, that he had no business calling the unlisted number anymore, and that his reception might well be cool, even hostile. It was more likely, of course, that the number had been changed. But there was no interruption, no metallic message telling him the number was out of service. Henri Deschenes's familiar voice answered on the third ring, sounding alert and unhurried as usual.

"Henri? It's Andy Cassidy. Sorry to call so late and at home, but I've run across something that I think you ought to look at. No, no. Tomorrow will do fine. It's not that urgent, I think. Just let me give you a brief run-through. . . ." Five minutes later he hung up and wandered back to the counter to finish his lukewarm coffee, conscious of the blaze of burning bridges to his rear.

"The Mary Jo Motel doesn't seem to be quite as upscale as our last hovel," said Harriet as she settled herself back into the car. "But, as far as I can tell, it doesn't actually appear to have bugs."

"Come on," said Sanders. "It's not that bad. You just have some irrational prejudice against paper bath mats."

"And tin showers."

"And plastic bedspreads."

"And hourly rates," added Harriet, giggling.

"Be serious," said Sanders, looking out his window. "It's not that bad. You've never been in—"

"Now don't start with that worldly-wise, seen-it-all, scum-of-the-earth detective act," said Harriet. "I saw the expression of pure horror on your face when you opened the door. And there it is. Stop."

"What?"

"Seven-twenty Echo Drive. You just drove past it. The big house back there with all the lights. Back up."

"Why don't we just sit here and have a look?" said Sanders, pulling in to the curb and backing up a few feet.

"It's huge, isn't it?" said Harriet softly. "I love Georgian houses." She turned her head briskly back in Sanders's direction. "I wonder how hard it'll be to crash the party. Maybe I should try it alone. I might have better luck than you."

Sanders didn't reply. Instead, he slouched down in the seat, put his right arm around Harriet's shoulders, and pulled her toward him. He could feel a tremor run through her body as it touched his.

"What in hell are we doing out here?" she whispered huskily. The sting she was trying to inject into the words was lost in her rapid and irregular breathing.

"Sssh," he murmured, kissing her lightly on the temple and then the neck. She shivered. "Just sit and observe. Pretend you're bird-watching. For owls."

She reached her face up to his and kissed him, pulling him closer. For a second or two he succumbed to his own overwhelming need to respond, and then pulled away, placing a finger on her lips and shaking his head. She buried her face in his shoulder and encircled his chest with those surprisingly strong arms. After an age of silence, an age in which her warm body and agitated breathing infected him with a powerful restlessness he was beginning to have trouble resisting, a black limousine pulled up in the circular drive and stopped at the front steps. "Look," he whispered. Harriet raised her head and blinked in the light streaming in the window. A chauffeur got out, his cap and uniform clearly visible in the bright lights of the broad portico. The front door opened and Sanders pointed silently at the figure silhouetted in it. At the same time baroque music poured out over the neighborhood from the open door.

"Hey," said Harriet in a whisper. "It's Anna Maria Strelitsch. She's leaving. Can you see what time it is?"

Sanders held his watch up to the street light three houses away. "Twelve-fifteen. Maybe the party is winding down."

"I suppose it's possible. Who in hell lives there?"

Sanders shook his head. "I haven't the faintest idea. We can try the city directory tomorrow, and if that fails, I'll put Dubinsky on to finding out. My partner. It's wonderful what he can get done while sitting on his tail in Toronto."

"What now?" whispered Harriet. "Don't you think I should try to get in quick before everyone leaves? I can always say that someone asked me—it's been done before."

"No," murmured Sanders. "Let's wait here and see who else turns up on the doorstep." As he said that, half the lights in the front were turned off and the windows to the right of the front door were plunged in darkness. The door opened again and three people—men, probably—their bodies silhouetted and their faces shadowed by the lights, moved quickly down the steps and headed in the opposite direction. "Damn," said Sanders. "Did you see anyone you recognized?"

"No. They could have been the caterers for all I could tell." The lights in the other front room went out as she spoke.

"Why in hell," said Sanders, "does someone who looks like a lumberjack, who was some kind of informer for the RCMP, and who was doing a lousy job of pretending to be a novelist, want to go to a party where they play baroque music all night? It doesn't seem to be in character."

"Why worry about it?" said Harriet. "Nobody's consistent. And just how long are we going to sit here staring at a dark house? I'm getting sleepy."

"Sleepy?" said Sanders. "That's a funny way to describe it."

"Just trying to be delicate," said Harriet, and rubbed provocatively up against him in the tight confines between the steering wheel and his chest. "After all, we have a perfectly good bed to go to and this place is looking pretty uninteresting."

Sanders tried to hold her still. "Not more than a couple of hours or so," he said, grinning.

CHAPTER 9

Friday, May 19

Peter Rennsler slipped out of his bed in the Carleton University Residence. In the distance one early-waking bird was chirping; the sky was still almost black. He put on a dressing gown and padded softly down to the bathroom. He would have liked to shower, but didn't want to risk waking up any restless sleepers at the conference; instead, he washed and shaved quietly and with care. Minutes later he was dressed in corduroy trousers, a turtlenecked jersey, and a tweed jacket. Casual but elegant and very adaptable. He slipped a pair of leather gloves in his pocket. From the top drawer of his dresser he removed a thermos bottle and a jar of instant coffee. He spooned several teaspoonfuls of coffee into the thermos, added sugar, and plugged in the electric kettle that he had purloined from the communal kitchen the night before. He stared out the window as he waited for the water to boil, then poured it on the coffee and sealed it up. Last of all he removed a helmet, a folded tarpaulin, an attaché case, and a scarf from the closet, and left the room, locking the door carefully.

He walked rapidly out of the residence and headed for the most distant of the university's parking lots, where his motorcycle had been sitting since Wednesday. He fastened the tarp and his attaché case to the luggage carrier in back and put on his helmet; without a glance, he got on and drove off at a moderate speed north toward the deserted westbound Queensway and Highway 7.

He traveled without haste until he was well out of the city and the ring of suburban towns encircling it. Once on the two-lane highway he began counting intersections. At the third, he slowed and turned abruptly right. About a mile in from the highway, he stopped in front of a derelict barn and gently piloted his bike up the ruined laneway leading into it. The door was propped half-open. He halted his machine, pushed it inside, and waited for his eyes to adjust to the light. He undid the thermos and poured himself a small measure of coffee—he would want the rest later on. He finished the coffee, looked around, noted the existence of a large parcel wrapped in heavy plastic under the teeth of a broken-down cultivator, nodded in satisfaction, and checked his watch. Time to leave. He covered the bike with his tarp, left the barn, and headed briskly back to the highway on foot. Minutes after he arrived at the intersection, a car slowed down, allowing him to jump in. As it headed back to Ottawa, the morning sun was flooding the countryside with light.

The Mary Jo Motel didn't extend to the glamour of having its own coffee shop, and so at eight the next morning, Sanders was sitting in a dark booth in the nearest restaurant that claimed to serve breakfast, observing a sleepy-eyed Harriet. "I hope you're not expecting me to be bright and witty," she said, running her tongue lightly over her upper lip. "I feel as if someone just wrung me out and dropped me down here to mildew."

"What does that mean?" asked Sanders, surprised.

"I was afraid that you were looking at me like someone who expects conversation at breakfast. Can't you read a paper or something?"

"If I had one, I could," he said equably. "I hadn't realized you were dedicated to breakfast in silence."

"Not always," she moaned. "But this morning . . ." He pushed himself over to the end of the bench seat and stood up. "Where are you going?" she asked. There was an accusatory tone in her voice.

"I'll be right back. I'm going to buy us a paper."

"On your way out would you tell the waitress I'm going to expire if she doesn't bring the coffee right away? Please?"

"Will do." By the time he returned, an empty orange juice glass and half-filled cup of coffee sat in front of her place. He dropped the paper on the table between them and slipped back into the booth. "Which section?" he asked. "And then not another word until you've finished eating."

"Look," she said, paying no attention to him or the paper, "I've been thinking, and I want to know what you thought you were doing last night." Suddenly her pale cheeks colored and she grinned. "I mean before that. I know you're the professional, but what in hell were we supposed to get out of just sitting in that car and watching a dead house? And I don't see why you didn't want me to go in and look around. A party doesn't exist—short of a reception for the queen given by the governor-general—that I can't crash." She sat back and looked smug.

"I thought you didn't want to talk over breakfast."

"That's before I have coffee. And don't change the topic."

"I'm sure you could have got in there," said Sanders. "It's no trick for a single woman who looks like you to find space at a party. But what in hell were you supposed to do

once you got in?" he asked with sudden irritation. "Go
around asking everyone who stole your pictures? Ask the
host what his connection was with someone who might
have stolen your pictures? 'Excuse me, sir, but I was
wondering if you had happened to invite any of the unsavory
thieves and murderers that I'm looking for?' Be sensible,
Harriet, darling," he said, picking up her hand and trapping
it in both of his. "All I wanted to know was who was at
that thing, and we got there too late for that. Obviously
everyone interesting left just before we got there. Strelitsch
must have been the last guest to go. I can find out who lives
there today. I don't have to do it in the middle of the night."

"Ah, here comes breakfast," said Harriet. She looked
reflectively at him. "Maybe I'll drop around there this
afternoon with a camera or two and ask him if I can
photograph his house. Some people are pleased at the idea,
but even if they don't want to be photographed, they usually
don't mind chatting. Do you suppose Strelitsch is his
girlfriend?"

"Do you think all this could wait until we find out who
the owner is?"

"Certainly not," said Harriet, turning to her bacon and
eggs. "And Miss," she called to the waitress's retreating
back, "could you bring us another order of brown toast?
Thank you."

Harriet pushed her empty plate away after a silent meal.
"Now, the paper. Which section? No, don't answer. You
must be a sports fan," she said, grabbing off the first section
and pushing the rest toward him. "Men like you are all
sports fans, aren't they?" She gave him a wide-eyed look
and then winked.

Sanders, who hadn't looked at the sports pages for some
years, accepted defeat with good grace. He picked up the

paper, held out his coffee cup for a refill, and settled down to what he had. The choice was dismal: a pair of depressing articles graced the first page—one on violence in professional hockey, the other on cocaine use among baseball players. He rejected both, turned the page, and settled down to read a long article on the upcoming local high school track-and-field meet instead.

Just as he was getting to the last long list of prospects for the regional finals, he was interrupted by a slap as Harriet dropped her paper down. "John, look at this," she said. She had turned the paper half around and was pointing at a column headed FIRE IN STITTSVILLE CLAIMS LOCAL VICTIM. "Isn't that where you were last night? A boardinghouse in Stittsville?"

Sanders pulled the paper over in front of him and read the brief article. "Not very informative, is it?" he said.

"I don't know," said Harriet. "I haven't had a chance to read it yet."

" '. . . tragic fire in a rooming house . . .' " muttered Sanders in her direction. " 'Rescue workers made several unsuccessful attempts to enter the burning building. . . . No other bodies were found . . . house completely destroyed in the blaze, which raged for five hours. . . . After a preliminary investigation, Fire Chief Reginald K. Johnson estimated the damage . . . at $150,000. Cause unknown . . . neighbors expressed a belief to reporters that the owner of the house had been concerned about a faulty wood stove. The identity of the victim is being withheld pending notification of the next of kin.' "

"Is that the person you went to see?" asked Harriet.

"How in hell do I know?" Sanders snapped. He thought of poor, silly Miranda nibbling on the end of her long braid of hair, and a terrible weight descended onto his shoulders.

"There must be more than one boardinghouse in the town, it's not that small. And this article is worthless. It doesn't even give the sex of the owner. Jesus, what kind of garbage is this—'neighbors expressed a belief'!" Do they always write like this?" He pushed the paper back to her just as Harriet began to slide over to the edge of the bench she was sitting on. "And where are you going?" he demanded.

"To find out," she said innocently. "If it's the same person, that is. Not if they always write that way."

"How in hell are you going to do that?"

"You're going to give me her name, I'm going to try telephoning her and asking her if she has a room to rent, and if I do get through to her, then we know it was some other house that burned down, don't we? After all, if the house is totally demolished, the phone won't be working anymore, will it?"

"Not bad," said Sanders. "Especially for first thing in the morning."

"Thank you, sir," she said with exaggerated modesty. "You got any change?"

Several minutes elapsed before Harriet slipped back into the booth again. "Well?" asked Sanders. "What did you find out? Or are we booked into a room in Stittsville for the next week?"

Harriet shook her head. "I didn't exactly find anything out," she said. "But there's something funny going on."

"What happened?" asked Sanders. His voice was sharp. "Tell me exactly."

"Well, I got the number from the long-distance operator and dialed it. By the way, here's your money back. No one seemed to want it." She dropped a pile of coins on the table between them. "The phone was answered on the first ring by a man, which surprised me. I was expecting to get either the beautiful Miranda or the usual wait and then a little message about the number being out of service or something like that. Anyway, as I was saying, a man answered, and I asked for Mrs. Miranda Cruikshank, and *he* asked me who I was, and *I* said that all I wanted to do was talk to her, and *he* said could he tell her who was calling, and *I* asked him why he wanted to know. Then I decided that we could go on doing that forever, and meantime no one interrupted and asked me for money, and so I said that all I wanted was to ask if she had any rooms available and since when did you need a credit check to do that. I figured that if I really had been after a room I'd be getting mad by now. And he said that he wasn't sure and could I hang on while he found out? Anyway, still no one wanted my money, so I was getting suspicious—or, by now, *very* suspicious—and I hung up. They were tracing the call, weren't they? The line was clicking a bit."

"That doesn't mean much, but yes, probably. It sounds as if he was stalling."

"Does that mean we're going to be surrounded by hordes of gun-toting policemen any second now?"

Sanders shook his head. "Probably not. You weren't on the phone that long. On the other hand, there's no point in tempting fate and hanging around here. It can be very time-consuming to be suspected of torching a little old landlady."

"You think it was arson?"

He frowned. "They think so. Why the fuss if it wasn't? Of course, we're still not positive it was my landlady who went up in smoke, are we?"

"Aren't we?" said Harriet quietly.

Sanders shook his head, but whether in agreement or disagreement she couldn't tell. "Dammit. Why burn down that house?" he asked. "And if it was deliberate, why burn the landlady with it? As far as I could tell, she was insignificant, knew nothing. A bit crazy, maybe, but completely harmless." The memory of that blue Ford in his rearview mirror returned. Had he seen it outside Stittsville? Or had it followed him there and stayed behind to get rid of Miranda and her house?

"She knew about those papers under the Christmas cake," said Harriet. "And she can't have been killed just because you found out about them, can she?" she added. "How many people besides you do you suppose she showed them to? Or were you the only one whose charm she succumbed to?"

"You're a cruel woman, Harriet Jeffries," he said. "But absolutely right. If she showed them to me in all confidence, she probably showed them to a few other people in all confidence. After all, I just landed on her doorstep out of nowhere, didn't I?" He slipped out of the booth, grabbed his coat, and began to put it on. "Come on, lady. We'd better get the hell out of here."

They darted across the road through the morning rush hour traffic and landed, panting, in front of their new motel. "I'm going out to Stittsville again," said Sanders. "I have to find out what happened. Do you think you can stay out of trouble until I get back?"

"What do you mean by that?"

"Well, don't go off by yourself and try to break into the house on Echo Drive, for instance. Or stalk possible murderers. Stay in the motel room until I get back." Harriet grimaced. "Or at least leave a note with the manager telling me where I can find you. Under this name." He scribbled "Mr. E. Dubinsky" on a piece of paper torn from his address book.

"Who's that?" asked Harriet, with a puzzled shake of the head.

"Me, as far as they know. Actually it's my partner's name. I'm more likely to respond to it than I am to McTavish or Jones."

"On the other hand, it's pretty distinctive and obviously connected with you." Harriet frowned at the paper.

"Only by my colleagues, you fool," said Sanders, laughing. "And they're not the ones we're trying to sidestep. Are they?"

"I guess not," said Harriet. Her voice was creased with doubt.

Andy Cassidy closed the door to Deschenes's office and pulled a bundle of papers from his inside jacket pocket. "How secure is this room?" he asked.

"No more now than it ever was," said Henri Deschenes. "Why? Did you want to go somewhere secure?"

"It doesn't matter that much," Cassidy said briskly. "I just like to know. Here it is, and you'll find it interesting, I think. Before you look at it, though, I should tell you where I come in—in case you haven't heard." He looked over interrogatively in Deschenes's direction and got nothing but the same steady, courteous gaze he had been greeted with. "We're doing our own investigation at CSIS into any connection between Steve's death and the business at the secure site, of course—"

"What have you found out?" asked Deschenes.

Cassidy shook his head. "None of the workmen could have killed him. They're all clean and accounted for as far as we can tell. We're working on the assumption that he finally connected with the person he was looking for, the one Carpenter reported was nosing around, asking the workmen questions. Except that we can't make the descriptions fit with the guy in the bar who rented the car. The one who gave him a ride. Steve must have just drifted along with him to find out what he was up to. You remember how he worked, a great believer in giving people enough rope to hang themselves with."

"Entrapment," said Deschenes mildly.

"If you prefer," said Cassidy. "It works. Anyway, whoever he is, if that bastard took Steve Collins by surprise he must be one hell of an operator. So the answer to your question is nothing, I suppose. Nothing new, anyway. There's a fairly large contingent working on it because that's where the results are most likely to come in. And they do seem to have picked up a couple of interesting threads. But I was asked to nose around and see if there was anything else potentially explosive in his files, or if he was mixed up personally in anything else, and all that I can come up with is something he called Royal Twist. He had the craziest names for things, didn't he?"

"And that is?"

"It has to do with a lost heroin shipment and the murder of a dealer named Maurice Charbonneau. Steve was looking for someone connected in any way with drug enforcement near Montreal in the old days who seemed to have a bit too much money. This is the letter Betty Ferris wrote me about the material." He handed the slightly crumpled paper across the desk.

Deschenes read it and cleared his throat. "Interesting."

"We're all in it—anyone who was posted in the Montreal area five to ten years ago. I can't say I care much for what he says about me. In fact, I considered burning that page," Cassidy said with a self-conscious laugh, "but then I decided that on the whole it might be better to leave the material intact."

"Especially since Betty has probably read it all, you mean?"

"I mean," he answered, and grinned.

"Well, now," said Deschenes, picking up the first page. "What have we here? It starts with Superintendent H. Deschenes, as is only right and proper. I shall read out the salient facts and you can comment on errors and discrepancies, so don't fall asleep. It notes that I am forty-six, which is correct enough, and married to Marie-Claire, and have a house in Sandy Hill that is no longer mortgaged—God be praised—and that as far as he can tell, except for the purchase of a new car two years ago, have not indulged in any unusual pattern of expenditures."

'He seemed to think that you were as honest as cops go," said Cassidy.

"We'll see. Next is Charlie Higgs. Forty-four and a widower. Poor Charlie. He's taken that very hard, you know. He's gotten bitter. And it doesn't seem to be getting any better. He, too, has a house without a mortgage, and a cottage, two children, the boy a police cadet, the girl at Carleton. But we knew that, of course. He paid off his mortgage suddenly two years ago—"

"That was after Helen died, wasn't it? He must have used the insurance money."

"That's right. This list is garbage so far, Andy. How many years did Steve work on it? Never mind. Frank Carpenter, thirty-eight, married to Carmen, three kids—hellions, those kids are, and old enough to turn up in court one of these days—house, again no mortgage, cottage, new car, and holidays in Florida for the last three years. Sounds menacing until you look at the figures for bank accounts and credit cards."

"It still seemed to me to be a bit excessive."

"Maybe. But it's hardly yachts and weekends at Monte Carlo, Andy. Ah, here we go. Andrew Cassidy, thirty-five, single, no assets except for a registered pension with a trust company. New car, expensive vacations three out of the last four years, including trip to Ireland last summer. And a lot of comments about your private life as it relates to your expenditures. You know, Andy, you make the rest of us look like a dull lot. Who are these next people?"

"Drug Squad, Montreal. I'm not sure there's anything there, but look them over. There are some interesting people, but only one who merits investigation." He reached across the desk and pointed at one name on the list in front of Deschenes. "That's the only interesting one."

"I know him," said the superintendent. "Not a wonderful sort, but I think we have a pretty complete file on him already. Of course, we'll open it again." He turned to the last page, looked at it, and then went back to the first page again and ran his finger down the list of names on all the pages in front of him. "Where's Ian?"

"Ian MacMillan? He's on one of the sheets I didn't bring. I discounted him, I guess, because he wasn't anywhere near drugs at the time."

"But he was with us in Montreal."

"Sure, but he was on immigration, wasn't he? Doesn't matter. I'll bring it over tomorrow. There wasn't anything much. He seemed to be living pretty well for a while, but you know it was all his wife's property. And when they split up, he was left with his salary, that was all." Cassidy gave Deschenes a puzzled look. "What did you make of the last page?"

"Ah, that. We'll consider it later. Let me look at the figures again. Find yourself a magazine, Andy." Twenty minutes later, Deschenes pushed the pile of papers away. "I'm gratified to discover how rich the men I work with day by day seem to have become. You and I appear to be the poorest."

"True,' said Cassidy. "But then I have made two visits to the Caribbean, to islands where the banking laws would protect an illicit account from search and seizure. Lots of opportunity to stash away lots of profits."

"Which I have not," said Deschenes. "Although presumably I could have buried it all in my backyard until such time as it would be safe to dig it up again. It simply takes a little more patience." Deschenes went back to the beginning and began to run quickly through the file again. He looked up at last and shook his head. "There's nothing here, Andy. You must realize that. There's nothing here you couldn't find out by walking down the corridor and asking anyone you passed. Nothing you could build a case on. Certainly nothing that anyone would kill someone for." He slipped the material into an empty file folder. "Why did you bring it to me?" he asked at last. "Instead of someone at CSIS."

"I'm not sure," Cassidy replied slowly. "Because I assumed that the whole inquiry must have been instituted under you originally. Five years ago he was working for you. Didn't you give Steve his instructions?"

Deschenes shook his head. "Not on this one. If anything, he gave me my instructions. He didn't like what he thought was going on—not at all. And he wasn't going to allow it to happen."

"And so I figured you could decode the last page," Cassidy said simply. "Since I thought he had started the inquiry for you."

Deschenes shook his head and tapped the file with his forefinger. "He's using a simple book code here, as I suppose you've worked out already." Cassidy nodded gloomily. "And you were hoping that I had the key, weren't you? Because if Betty Ferris is telling the truth, Steve thought he had the goods on someone. But the material in clear is a matter of public record. If he had evidence enough to convict, it's on the last page."

"Maybe we can work around it, find out how many of that old Montreal-area detachment are in town right now—or were here on Monday," said Cassidy, shrugging aside the problem.

"I think you'd be better off finding out whether he left the key to the code around someplace else."

"Maybe it was in his diary," said Cassidy. "You guys have that along with all the rest of his stuff?"

"Not that I know of," said Deschenes. "Do we have all his things?"

Cassidy nodded. "If there was anything else, it might be in the place he was staying at, wherever that was," said Cassidy. "A boardinghouse near the secure site, I think. I have the address somewhere."

"The place he was staying at? Do you mean out in Stittsville?" Deschenes formed a pyramid of his fingers and rested his chin on it as he looked at Cassidy. "When did you get up this morning?" he asked suddenly.

"About half an hour ago," said Cassidy. "I was up late last night trying to work out that code. Why?"

"Do you think we're the right people to be looking for all this?" he said, dismissing Cassidy's question with an abrupt gesture.

"Who else would do it?" said Cassidy, startled.

"I'm not sure. An independent commission of inquiry of some sort, I suppose. After all, it's the RCMP and CSIS we're inquiring into. That's usually considered conflict of interest." Deschenes paused again, looking very tired, and for the first time that morning Cassidy remembered that he had been ill, very ill. "Don't look so worried, Andy. We'll give it a try. Perhaps you could go back to his files and see if you missed anything last night."

A knock sounded on the door. A heavy knock, like a harbinger of doom, or the hand of someone who has to knock on a lot of doors. Cassidy jumped. "Who in hell is that?" he asked.

"Ian MacMillan, I suppose," said Deschenes. "I asked him to drop by. If you want to leave before he charges in, may I suggest that you can always get out through the washroom. It still connects to the outer hall. I expect Higgs will be up as soon as that group of his takes a break." Cassidy uttered a squeak of protest and fled through the door that Deschenes was pointing toward.

MacMillan walked in, nodded briefly, and settled himself into a comfortable chair, crossing one long leg over the other knee. Before opening his mouth, he pulled out his notebook and flipped rapidly to a spot in the middle, slipped the book back into his pocket, and said, "Good morning. I trust I'm not late. Charlie not here yet?" Before the point could be scored, however, Sylvia flung open the door and ushered in Charlie Higgs. Deschenes looked at the two of them and frowned.

"Too many people are asking questions," he said abruptly. "I need to know exactly what you've got, beyond the worthless junk that has turned up in your reports."

"Questions?" MacMillan sat up slightly, as if astonished by the effrontery of people asking what they were doing.

"Yes. Steve Collins's death is getting harder and harder to keep in hand. The house he was living in out in Stittsville was torched last night and the landlady killed. There were people in and out, according to the neighbors. Constantly. Before the fire. The day before that. People who looked to them like police. Any of you go out there?" he snapped.

Higgs shook his head. "Are they sure it was arson?"

"That's what they say. Arson aside, was any one of us out there looking for what he might have turned up?"

"More likely to be his mates from CSIS," said MacMillan.

"Or whoever took him out," added Higgs gloomily. "You'd think someone would have had the sense to keep an eye on the house, wouldn't you?"

"I'm sure they did," said Deschenes, relaxing for a moment. "This is probably a *pro forma* inquiry."

"Any word on that picture?" asked MacMillan, yawning.

Higgs shook his head. "Bastard didn't turn up today. He's probably taken off back to Toronto with it as a souvenir."

"Either that or CSIS got it from him before we did. From what I can figure out, things are still pretty wild over there," said MacMillan. "My source tells me . . . well, let's say, he wouldn't be surprised if reports weren't getting through to us."

"What I can't understand," said Higgs doggedly, "is why we're not getting anything on what's going on with the Austrian delegation."

"Why don't you ask them? Talk to their security man. Or better still, I will," said Deschenes. "I'm curious about him."

MacMillan pulled himself to his feet. "Do you need me for this?" he asked. "I have a helluva lot to check on this morning, with the goddamn meetings starting this afternoon. Surely you and Charlie can deal with the Austrians, can't you? Especially since his little class of new security experts is going away at lunchtime." He picked up his coat and raised one hand in salute as he walked out of the office.

"I'd like to know what's going on," said Higgs. "The violinist seems to be moving closer and closer to the prime minister, as far as I can tell—"

"But aren't the Austrians keeping an eye on her?"

"You're damned right they are."

"Who's the businessman who gave the party?"

"Her boyfriend, maybe. But she might just have picked up with him to give her a door to the prime minister. I don't know. It's pretty difficult when you don't understand what's going on and no one's telling you anything and—"

"And they expect us to stop anything from happening. Maybe we'll send someone out to interview that businessman and have a chat with Austrian Security as well."

Sanders walked briskly to the parking garage where he had stashed his car. He had no desire to land in front of Miranda Cruikshank's house driving the same car he had been in last night. As he moved from street to street, and from sidewalk to garage, he kept glancing into windows and down alleyways. That vulnerable spot between his shoulder blades twitched, and he found himself watching for a light blue, new Ford Escort. He was going to start dreaming about that damned car.

Traffic was light once he got out of the city center, and all going in the opposite direction. He parked about two blocks away from Mrs. Cruikshank's house and began walking slowly toward it. The sun was bright, the sky a thin, clear, washed-out blue—the same color as that car, he thought, and shivered with guilt and apprehension—and the wind as cold as the nose on an Arctic fox. He turned up his coat collar and tried to look like someone drawn out for a stroll by the sunshine and his curiosity. It was difficult.

As he rounded the corner a gust of wind brought the smell. It was the stench of wet coal tar and old wood, of death and destruction. He hated that smell. He loathed being anywhere near a case where fire was involved, and was damned glad that most of them were handled with expertise and dispatch by the fire marshal. He moved ahead very slowly, sizing things up, and stopped before he got to any official bodies who might be posted to watch for late-arriving voyeurs.

There was a black gap, a rotten hole, in the long line of white clapboard houses that made up this section of the street. Whatever timbers had been left standing by the fire had been thrown down by the force of the hoses or the efforts of the firefighters to break apart the last, dangerous remnants of what was once a building. The house next door was streaked with black smoke; charring along the front corner post testified to the violence of the blaze at its worst.

A bored-looking man in the uniform of a fire department investigator was standing in the front yard and looking at the mess that opened up at his feet. Sanders opened the small gate in the picket fence and walked carefully up the concrete path he had been on the night before. The investigator barely flickered an eye in Sanders's direction before speaking. "Sorry, sir, can't come in here. The site is dangerous and under investigation." He sounded as bored as he looked.

Sanders extracted his identification and waved it in front of the man. "Sanders, John Sanders. I've been poking around on a case that seemed to involve the owner of this house in a marginal sort of way. Naturally, I was interested when I heard she had gone up with her house." The man looked impassive, but slightly less hostile. "Rooming house, wasn't it?"

"Mmm," said the man in front of him.

"Boarders, smoking in bed, I suppose," said Sanders. "These wooden houses are real firetraps."

"Not this one," replied the investigator with considerably more animation. "She was a bit odd, that woman, but she had a healthy respect for fire. House was fitted out with alarms and sprinklers everywhere. If it had been a slow-starting fire, trucks would have been there in plenty of time. Arson, this was. Someone waited until she was alone in the house, they did. Went up like a bonfire."

"Where were all the boarders?"

"Only two of them now, they say. Funny thing is, the third one died just this week. An accident at work or something. They were off at the pub boozing. Didn't turn up until it was pretty much all over."

"Do you think I could poke around a bit?" said Sanders casually. "We're looking for a piece of missing evidence. I was told it was in this house."

The investigator laughed. "Unless it was made of asbestos you're not going to find it now. Anyway, not a chance I can let anyone onto the site to look around. We're having enough trouble with people interfering with our investigation as it is. That's where my boss is, trying to get rid of a few nuisances right now."

"What do you mean, 'interfering with your investigation'?" asked Sanders.

The investigator shrugged. "Anyway," he went on, "there's nothing much left here to look for. It seems we're trying to find the person she was drinking with last night just before the fire started." He glanced at Sanders, fixing his look on him for a second or two, and then turned away to gaze back at the ruins of the house. "Well, I don't know," he said. "Maybe they won't mind if you just look around a bit.

Hang on a minute and I'll see if I can get permission to let you onto the site. Don't fall in the cellar while you're waiting or I'll be in deep trouble." He chuckled and headed off to an official-looking car parked in front of the neighbor's house.

It had taken Sanders a half-second to recognize that look and the fake casual friendliness that followed it. Before the investigator could reach for his radio, Sanders was striding around the corner toward his own car, blessing the prescience that had prompted him to leave it out of sight of the house.

He headed south, one eye on the rearview mirror, away from Ottawa, until he was sure that no one was interested in his movements. He pulled into a gravel side road and waited for five minutes. Nothing. A tractor pulling a wagon moved slowly by, a red sports car whipped past too fast to notice him; otherwise the highway was deserted. He flipped on the radio in time for the twelve o'clock news. The international situation got a minute—as much as it deserved, no doubt—and the current prime minister got another minute. The leader of the opposition was granted a mere forty-five seconds. Nicely calculated, that, thought Sanders, who was staring at his watch and looking at the road at more or less the same time. Then a minute for local news before the weather. There was still nothing along that road that could be looking for him. He put the car in gear and almost as quickly slammed his foot on the brake again. "Foul play," the boyish voice of the announcer was saying, "has not been ruled out. Police are currently looking for her drinking companion of the night before, believed to be a man representing himself as a police officer from the Toronto area. Anyone knowing the whereabouts—" Sanders turned off the radio with a vicious click that almost dislodged the knob from its stem. Dammit, he swore softly to himself. This was going to take a little bit of thought.

He backed up until he was parked on the other side of a small hill from the highway, no longer visible to anyone but a field of cows on his right. He pulled out his notes from the night before and began to study them with some concentration.

If he remembered correctly, and he thought he did, those pages had had a very familiar air. The last item on the page that he had been studying had been something about "ferret to O. r/v file #3 . . ." and some more numbers that he could almost see. "Advance payment given—amount not stated, but above $10,000?—on take-out target unspecified but specialized. 1700 Joe + 1." It was a style of note taking— not his own, but familiar. And it belonged to a professional. Not a snitch, but a sober, conscientious undercover officer with a gift for playing the stupid drunk, who had left something in semiclear because he was uncertain of getting through to his usual contact. The notes seemed to say that he had turned up a professional hit man after a big target for big bucks under one of the rocks he had turned over. And the hit was to be at 1700 hours on Joe + 1—Friday. Today? Next week? And Don Bartholomew had once worked—some time in the past—with Inspector Charlie Higgs, because Higgs had laughed with real affection for a moment over the memory of that strange phrase. And the next expression on his face had been sorrow, Sanders was positive about that.

As he thought, he penciled in notes against the paper in front of him until the thin point on his pencil broke. He sighed and reached into his pocket to see if he had another one stuffed in it. His fingers curled around a piece of stiff paper instead. He pulled it out. The bottom half of the bill from the restaurant in Brockville, and on it the telephone number that Scarface had been calling—maybe.

He took out his map and looked for the nearest town that might have a restaurant and yet not be too close to the beaten track. In fifteen minutes he was inside a suitably grubby one. He ordered a cheeseburger and headed back to the telephone.

When he got his partner on the line at last, Dubinsky sounded irritable. Sanders fed a pile of quarters into the machine and started talking, fast. "Look, Ed, I want you to check reverse listings for Ottawa and tell me what this number is." He read it carefully into the receiver. "Call me back as soon as you've got it. It's important."

"I don't have to check anywhere, John. That number is sitting on my desk right here in front of me. It's the number I'm supposed to call if I find out where you are, so be a pal and don't tell me, eh?"

"So, whose number is it, for chrissake?"

"It's the goddamn RCMP, that's who it is. And what in hell is going on? The whole world is looking for you. Did you really put a bullet through the head of some woman out in Stittsville? And shoot her dog, too? I told them you might have killed the woman, but not the dog, so if the same weapon got both of them they could forget it."

Sanders didn't laugh. "Which branch?"

"Security. Operations. And no, I don't have a name, just a department. Sorry. Look, sweetheart, I'm busy. But keep in touch if you can and let me know what's happening."

Since this was the first time his partner had ever called him sweetheart, Sanders deduced that someone had wandered, too close and too curious, in the direction of Dubinsky's telephone. More troubling than that, however, was the other question this telephone call had raised. What had

Scarface been doing calling the RCMP before heading off—presumably—to kill Don Bartholomew? Bartholomew, who had once worked for the RCMP. Unless, of course, someone else at the coffee shop had called that number often enough for the mynah bird to get attached to the melody.

He fished in his pocket for more change. The number at the Mary Jo Motel rang twice before he got a hesitant answer. "It's me," he said. "Anything going on there I should know about?"

"Some," said Harriet. "I don't know how critical it is, though. I've been rooting around about the Echo Drive house. It's owned by a Mrs. Muriel Smythe, according to the old City Directory. I called, got switched to another number, and got some female iceberg on the other end who said that Mrs. Smythe was unable to take telephone calls. I tried to find out where she lived—I mean, if she lived in the house—and the iceberg hung up on me."

"Where were you calling from?"

"Oh, I got myself a nice quiet pay phone at the library. Called Scott first and got him to get the stuff from the directory. I didn't feel like making a whole lot of phone calls from here, for some reason. Anyway, that's it. Did you get anything?"

"Lots," said Sanders, rather grimly. "Why don't we meet someplace quiet and unobtrusive?"

"Quiet and unobtrusive?" She paused for a moment to think. "How about the south end of Dow's Lake? That's nicely pastoral. Will that do? And do you want me to bring you a sandwich?"

He looked over at his table. On it reposed a cold, dried-out, greasy-looking cheeseburger. Anything but that. "Yes, bring me a sandwich and some coffee and we'll figure out what to do next."

As Sanders stepped out of the car, his ears were assailed by the combination of birds singing and the gentle lapping of water against the concrete barrier that hedged off the lake. Such bucolic sounds definitely belonged to another sort of day, not to the one he was having. He looked around in time to see Harriet making a razor-sharp left into a parking space, cutting off a modest line of traffic as she did so. There was a certain amount of horn honking that she appeared to ignore while waving cheerfully at him.

"Just one more left turn like that last one and off we go, lady," said Sanders as he jumped in her car.

"Hey, what about your car? You just going to leave it there? They'll probably tow it away. The law can be vicious up here."

"Good riddance," said Sanders. "I was getting tired of it. The floor mats are muddy and someone put cigarette butts in the ashtray. So, first priority: out of here, abandoning car. Second priority: where's my sandwich? I'm starved."

"You get stranger and stranger, John Sanders, and that's saying a hell of a lot. Because you were pretty odd to begin with," said Harriet. She put the car in gear and whipped into a small break in the traffic. "And it's on the backseat. There are napkins in the bottom of the bag. I think you'll need them."

"Thanks," he muttered as he reached into the large white paper bag and searched around for whatever it offered. "Did you think I was incredibly hungry, or are you eating as well?" he said, as his fingers encountered numerous paper packets inside the bag.

"I'm eating as well. Do I have to eat and drive at the same time?"

"War demands sacrifices from all of us, my love. Are they all the same?"

"Yes. Except that some of them are coffee. And where are we headed? Or do you want me to keep going south until I hit the border?"

Sanders put a pile of paper napkins in her lap, and then carefully handed her one half of a hot pastrami sandwich with mustard, left in its thermal wrapping for easier handling. "I'll decant the coffee later," he said, wrapping his own half-sandwich in a couple of napkins. "And back to Carleton. I was perhaps a little too casual about your friend the blond man in the picture. It's time to look him up again."

"But it's too late. Last night was the final banquet, wasn't it? Or am I going crazy?"

"No, you just don't see the logic of holding the final banquet the evening before the final lectures. That way everyone will come. Otherwise they all take off early and refuse to buy expensive tickets for a bad dinner and a lot of dull speeches. All conferences work that way."

"You mean the conference is still going on?"

"Of course. Otherwise I would have been much more concerned about our friend the blond man last night, wouldn't I? I, too, know how to use the telephone, my dear Harriet."

"Don't be insufferable." She brought the car to a sudden halt, waited briefly at a red light, and made an illegal turn in front of a wall of oncoming traffic before her signal had changed to green—quite. "Which parking lot?" she asked.

Sanders opened his eyes again. "The cheap one at the end. If he's been there for the whole conference, that's where he'll be leaving his car."

"I love all this intricate study of the human psyche," murmured Harriet. "One of these days someone's going to do something you haven't predicted, and then where will you be?"

"I'll be confused. It'd be nothing new," said Sanders. "People are always refusing to do the logical, sensible thing. But that's people like you, of course. People like our blond friend behave predictably. I knew before you left the room last night that he'd shake you and you'd end up somewhere miles away from him, following some perfectly innocent professor to his innocent bed. That was why I didn't really worry about you being left with that useless little what's-his-name."

"God, you're obnoxious. What if he hadn't succeeded?" Her voice was challenging. "If I'd been a little more careful and managed to follow him?"

"If he was that careless, we would have known he had nothing to do with anything. It's good to know that. Saves a lot of legwork."

Harriet handed some cash to the parking lot attendant and collected a yellow pasteboard ticket in exchange, which she dropped on the dash. "Now what?"

Sanders looked at his watch. "We'll sit here for a while. The last talk ended fifteen minutes ago. There's a lunch for members of the executive or whatever they call themselves. He won't be one of them. That means that he has to pick up his stuff from his room and put it in his car. I'm assuming that he was staying here for the conference."

"Why?"

"Because he led you straight into the parking lot and

melted off into the bushes. That is, he wandered off to his room, very conveniently, while convincing you that he was staying in a motel somewhere." Suddenly Sanders grabbed Harriet from behind the wheel and dragged her head down onto his chest. He bent himself awkwardly over her, as if they were embracing in some agonizingly intense manner. He heard a protesting grunt coming from somewhere near his tie. "Sorry, love," he murmured. "It's a pretty stale dodge, but it's the best I could think of in the time available. He's getting into his car."

Harriet's head popped up cautiously just beside the steering wheel. "That's him," she said. "I could pick out that profile in a million. What's he carrying?" she asked, diving back into Sanders's tie again.

"A suitcase and an attaché case. Very neat and professional-looking."

"John, what do we do if he turns out to be a member of the faculty at Harvard or something like that? Maybe he just gave a paper on Charlemagne. You know, now that I think about it, he doesn't look like a hood."

"He doesn't look like your conception of a hood, you mean. After all, what do hoods look like? Maybe he's a very high-class hood. In the big money." Sanders paused. "Okay, I want you to start the car now." Harriet turned the key in the ignition while her foot reached for the brake. "You'll be following him at a distance. I'll tell you when to drop back or speed up. And this isn't LeMans, remember. You are to pretend to be an ordinary, cautious, slightly nervous female driver, no matter how alien you might find that idea. All right?"

"All right," she sighed. "If that's what you want. When do I start?"

There was silence. Sanders had straightened up again, and

was looking idly out the window. "Now! And you'd better get to the exit fairly rapidly—he's speeding up. Not that rapidly, Harriet," he added, as the car leaped forward like a greyhound after a rabbit.

While Harriet was turning out of the parking lot and heading toward the main road, a pale blue Ford Escort pulled out of a space at the far end of the lot, where it had been out of sight behind a dark green van, and keeping well back, set out after them.

Harriet drove steadily and expertly, with a calmness Sanders didn't know she had at her command, keeping at least three cars between them and the blond man ahead. It was a simple enough task on the four-lane road, and she was beginning to enjoy herself. She glanced in the rearview mirror, changed lanes, switched, looked again, more sharply this time, switched back into the right-hand lane, and looked once more. "John," she said conversationally, "do you know anyone who drives a light blue Ford? Like your ex-wife, maybe? Or an old girlfriend? Someone like that?"

"Why do you ask?" he said cautiously.

"Well, it seems that whenever I get into a car and drive you anywhere, there's this Ford in my rearview mirror, unless I make a really determined effort to get rid of it. I didn't think it was worth mentioning at first—after all, a lot of people buy Fords, don't they? And blue is a very popular color. But I'm beginning to wonder who this is."

"Get rid of it," said Sanders.

"Really? What about Blue Eyes up there?"

"I'd rather you got rid of the Ford. It's been taking an unhealthy amount of interest in me these past few days." Sanders suddenly felt his spine being flattened into the back of the seat as Harriet accelerated, switched into the left-hand lane, and then executed a rapid U-turn in front of a sign forbidding that maneuver. Before he could orient himself, she had darted into the right lane, signaled, braked, turned, turned again, and was driving with due care and concern up a twisting road through a pleasant, well-grown subdivision.

"I think I lost it," she said. "And as far as I can tell, I haven't picked up a police car, either."

"Good. Pull over. I want to talk to you in peace·and quiet. Because there's something else I've got to tell you about what's been happening lately."

Sanders finished running through the events of the morning, or, at least, almost all the events. When it came to telling her about the telephone number he had fished from his pocket, the number from the coffee shop in Brockville, he fell silent. He could still see that man at the telephone, watch the relaxed movements, and hear that casual murmuring that spoke of a friendly call to an old pal. The implications, if true, were monstrous. He had a sudden vision of trying to explain the mynah bird and his conviction that he could decode the numbers from its whistle to a doubting Harriet. After all, what kind of nut would think a bird could imitate telephone numbers? And even if it could, would? And did he believe it himself? The absolute certainty he had felt when he called Dubinsky was dissolving rapidly into an uneasy sense of vague foolishness. If it had been any other number . . . He leaned back and stared out the window at the neat lawn they were parked beside.

"That certainly adds an interesting twist to the story, doesn't it?" said Harriet cheerfully. "How about some of this coffee?" She reached into the paper bag. "It might just still be warm."

"Thanks," said Sanders. "And I'm happy to see that you haven't let a little thing like my imminent arrest upset you."

"It's too deliciously ironic to be upsetting, you have to admit that. And I can hardly believe that your colleagues are going to hunt you down with slavering hounds and blazing guns. Really, John. Whatever has happened to the old masculine clubhouse atmosphere? Besides, I'm sure you're full of brilliant ideas about what we should do next. Aren't you?" She spoke in a voice rich with honeyed sweetness.

He glared at her. "This is no time to sit around being funny. But, yes, I do have a few ideas. They may not be brilliant, but at least they're better than nothing. The first one is to get rid of this car before we get picked up. It's known, and by now it'll be on the list of wanted vehicles. Assuming, of course, that they're really looking for me."

Harriet looked at him in alarm. "What do you mean, get rid of it?" she said. "This car is only eighteen months old. I like it, and I plan on driving it another ten years, at least. If you think I'm going to ditch it in the canal or something, think again."

"We're only getting rid of it temporarily. We'll park it somewhere and take a bus." He pulled out his notes. "Give me a minute to think first, though. These last few hours have been a little . . . startling. Okay," he said, adopting a lecturing tone, "Bartholomew was expecting something to happen today at seventeen hundred hours. That's five o'clock," he added kindly.

"I know. Believe it or not. What kind of something?" asked Harriet.

Sanders shook his head. "If I knew that, I wouldn't be sitting here asking myself stupid questions. Except, of course, that we're dealing with a professional, uh, exterminator," said Sanders, pointing at his notes. "And since the time is specified, this is not an ordinary hit."

"Why do you say that?"

"Because ordinarily if you hire a professional to get rid of a nuisance for you, you don't have to tell him exactly when and where to do it. This must be someone who is very hard to get at. Bartholomew found out about it and put it in his notebook. And he's dead. He gave the notebook to Mrs. Cruikshank."

"Who's dead, too," said Harriet flatly. "And the whole world thinks you killed her for some reason."

Sanders nodded. "But if I didn't kill her, then it seems pretty likely she's dead because of what's in the notebook. And I happen to be pretty certain that I didn't kill her."

"We'll accept that as a given," said Harriet gravely. "At least for the time being. So, since you didn't kill her, who did?"

"I don't know. The only people hanging around poor Miranda were the regional police and the Mounties. Except for that blue Ford, which was in town when I was there talking to her. And if the driver of the blue Ford was the person who killed Miranda," he added in sober tones, "then I led him out there." He turned his head and stared out the window.

Harriet reached out a hand to touch his shoulder and then drew it back. Sympathy wasn't going to help him right now, she realized. He needed answers. "Possibly," she said. "But not necessarily. What's the connection with the house on Echo Drive?"

Sanders shrugged his shoulders and turned back in her direction. "I don't know that, either. The address was in Bartholomew's notes and so I assume there must be a connection. But I can't pursue it any further because Dubinsky can't help me now. Not without someone finding out what he's up to. But the situation also seems to be connected with your pictures."

"What in hell is going to happen, then?"

The taut grimness of his expression was miraculously replaced by mock surprise. "Come on, Harriet. Surely even you can figure out what must be going on."

"Let's pretend I'm really stupid," she said, spacing out each phrase with exaggerated calm, "and you explain it to me, very carefully, in words of one syllable."

"With all these goddamn foreign potentates pouring into the city, for chrissake? You can't figure out what's likely to happen?"

"Oh, that. You mean one of them's going to get assassinated. Is that it?"

"What do you mean, is that it? That's enough to give every goddamn civil servant in the city nightmares for months."

"But they're always expecting these big shots to get blown up, or away, or whatever it is. Aren't they, whoever they are, ready for it?"

"Well, they are and they aren't," said Sanders. "They're prepared, but no one really expects it to happen, if you know what I mean."

"Ah, yes, not here. Things like that never happen here. We're too law-abiding."

He nodded. "I suppose."

"Then why don't you go to the RCMP with Bartholomew's notes and explain what we've found out to them?"

"Because, first of all, they might be the people who already know what's in Bartholomew's notebook. And next, whenever I run into those guys I get a strange itch between my shoulder blades. I don't want to end up resisting arrest and having something, uh, unfortunate happen to me."

"Come off it, John. A little paranoia now and then never hurt anyone, but this is ludicrous. Itches between the shoulder blades! You think you're psychic or something? I can't think of anything less likely. You're a cop, for God's sake. One of their buddies."

Sanders shook his head, still reluctant to bring up that blasted bird and risk looking like an even bigger idiot, and opened the car door. "Come on. Let's head for the nearest piece of public transportation."

"Where to?"

"The lab. Didn't you say the pictures were going to be ready? Maybe we should pick them up and arrange to put them somewhere safe."

She looked at her watch. "Sure. I asked them to do us a quality print, too. It'll be a bit pricey, but I'll just throw it on the account, and if I ever get my pictures back, I can bill it to Wheeler and Shogatu," she said cheerfully.

"That's fraud, you know," said Sanders. "Harriet Jeffries, did you realize that you are basically a dishonest person? Let's go." But before reaching for the ignition key, he pulled her toward him with sudden longing. She wound her arms tightly around his neck and shoulders and kissed him as though she were afraid they would never touch each other again.

"I'm not really," she said as she moved back and undid her seat belt.

Peter Rennsler pulled his car into the ruined laneway, turned off the ignition, and sat staring out the window. The dark-haired woman who had tried to follow him from the reception last night had been tailing him at least part of the way from the university. He frowned indecisively. She was neither police nor security—he was sure of that, although he could not have explained why—and he had lost her before he left the city. Therefore she was probably insignificant. If his employers had explained precisely what problems were cropping up, he would know what—and whom—to look out for. But they had merely assured him that the job was going as planned. In his experience, jobs never did. He removed the keys from the ignition, placed them carefully at the foot of the rickety gatepost, and covered them with a rock. Once inside the barn, he took out the parcel from under the cultivator, opened it, stripped down to his shorts and T-shirt, and put on the clothes he found in it. He folded his own things neatly and tightly, wrapped them in the same packaging, and stowed them under the cultivator again.

When he mounted his bike and moved off, he was dressed completely, from cap to boots, in the greenish uniform of the combined Canadian Military Forces.

He didn't stop again until he was about a mile from the target zone, where a pair of military vehicles formed an efficient roadblock. He left his bike by the side of the road and walked up to the bored-looking corporal in charge. "Hi," he said, unbuttoning the pocket of his tunic and taking out a set of papers. "Here you go," he added casually.

The corporal took the proffered documents and looked at them closely. "Right you are," he answered, apparently impressed by the signature in front of him. "Murphy, back that truck up."

"What the hell's going on?" asked Rennsler. "I was dragged back from leave an hour ago for some fucking colonel and told to get my ass out here with dispatches."

"Christ, didn't that happen to all of us?" said the corporal, yawning, as the driver backed one of the vehicles just enough to let the motorcycle through. "I haven't the faintest bloody idea what's going on. I just stand here out in the middle of nowhere and stop traffic. No relief, nothing. Fucking officers," he muttered, and stepped out of the way.

Rennsler carried on until he was out of sight of the roadblock party before stopping across from a farmer's field and wheeling the bike down into the ditch. He removed his attaché case and a pair of leather-and-metal objects hooked on to the edge of the carrier, laid the bike on the ground behind a small bush, and covered it with the tarp. He turned his attention next to the attaché case. First he removed another set of papers and buttoned them into his pocket; then he took out, one by one, the components of a Steyr AUG assault rifle, lightweight, reliable, and deadly, whose six parts had fit neatly into his elegant and workmanlike case. He assembled them with loving care and hoisted the rifle once, checking the scope. He smiled with pleasure. Even in the dimmer light of the woods, it would give him twice the range he needed for the assignment. He clipped his own webbed carrying strap to the assembled outfit and slung the weapon over his shoulder. He hooked the metal-and-leather apparatus over his belt, glanced down at the casually concealed bike, and suddenly remembered something. He flung back a corner of the tarp, reached into a bag under the seat, and took out his thermos of coffee. He flicked things into place again, crossed the road, and headed into the woods to wait until 2:00 P.M.

CHAPTER 10

"This is it," called out the bus driver as he pulled in to the curb.

"Thanks," said Harriet, and swung herself down onto the rear steps with one hand on the pole, landing with a thump as she did. Sanders followed her at a more decorous pace. The bus was filled with an early afternoon crowd of young mothers and retirees, and he could feel their curious eyes burning into the back of his neck as he hurried off the bus. "Come on," said Harriet. "It's just across the street."

Sanders laid a hand on her arm. "Wait," he said, and pointed. There, in front of Ace Colour Labs, was a pale blue Ford Escort, illegally parked.

"Looks familiar," said Harriet, and started briskly across the street. "Shall we go over and talk to him? Ask him what the hell he thinks he's been doing?"

"For chrissake, Harriet," said Sanders, exasperated, "hang on a minute." He grabbed her by the elbow and pulled her back. "If we just blend into the scenery over here we can get a good look at whoever it is. Why frighten him off? Or whatever."

"You're so goddamn cautious," she complained. "Don't you ever prefer the direct approach to life's little problems? But if you insist, I will defer to the superior knowledge that experience—I assume—has given you." She backed away from the curb and into the doorway of a wholesale office supply company. "I do, however, have a camera here with me," she patted the pocket of her jacket, "and I intend to get a shot of whoever it is. For posterity, or the police, whichever comes first."

The door to the processing plant was set at right angles to the front face of the building, up some four steps from street level. As they stood and chatted, apparently considering the merits of a set of brightly colored file cabinets, the lab door was flung wide open. Harriet raised her tiny camera in one hand, waiting for the profile to start down the steps and show full face. As he was turning, however, a huge truck belonging to one of the largest breweries in the province pulled in front of them and screeched to a halt. Sanders looked up the street in despair. A block away a red light glowered malevolently; a line of traffic had materialized out of nowhere to form an impenetrable barrier in front of them. That beer truck wasn't going to be able to budge until the light changed and the intersection cleared again.

Sanders swore loudly above the noise of the truck and started around it to the left. Harriet began to run to the right to get past the obstruction, her camera still ready in her right hand. He executed a shift in direction that would have looked impressive on a basketball court and pounded after her.

"Did you see him?" he asked, panting, as he caught up to her.

Harriet was staring at the disappearing rear bumper of the Ford Escort. She shook her head. "Not very well. I got an impression of tall and skinny. And pale. And fast as hell. It didn't take us that long to get around the truck." Her voice trailed off in disappointment. "I got a grab shot of him, but I'm not sure he'll even be in the negative. I was still running when I took it."

The traffic in front of them gradually began to move out of the way. In less than a minute the street was relatively deserted again. "What the hell," said Sanders. "Let's go see if your pictures are still there."

"They wouldn't give them to anyone else," said Harriet. She tried to inject confidence into her voice.

"Really?" said Sanders.

"Yes, really," said Harriet. Annoyed, she charged up the stairs two at a time ahead of him and stormed into the reception area. "Work ready for Parallax Productions yet?" she demanded as she walked through the door. "You were copying a slide and making a print of it for me."

"Yes, it is, Miss Jeffries," said the tiny, dark-haired girl behind the counter. "Came up half an hour ago." She reached into a space under the counter and extracted a brown envelope.

"Terrific," said Harriet, picking up the envelope. "Now you don't have to bother calling me." She peered inside to make sure there was something in there and then waved it triumphantly at John.

"Funny thing, though, Miss Jeffries," said the girl, frowning. "Someone was just in, said he was a friend of yours and wanted to pick up the negatives we'd been developing—that's exactly what he said. But I didn't know. When he didn't use your company name, and didn't know what kind of work we'd been doing and all that, I didn't think I should let him have them. Anyway, Suzie tried to call you," she nodded back at the office area,, "but you weren't in. Of course. You were on your way here, weren't you?" She laughed. "I hope I did the right thing. I mean, you usually pick up your own work, not like some people."

"You certainly did," said Harriet. "I never asked anyone to pick up any work for me. Must have been one of my clients trying to get out of paying for a print. Did he say anything else? Like who he was?"

The girl leaned forward with her elbows on the counter and shook her head. "Well," she said, "it was really strange. I said that we didn't have any work for Harriet Jeffries—and that's true, because our work was for Parallax Productions—and so he asked me for the name of another lab that might do color processing and stuff like that for professional photographers."

"What did you say?" asked Sanders.

The girl giggled. "I sent him over to Powell's Colour Labs. Right on the other side of town. I guess it was mean, but he wasn't very nice. The sort of customer that treats you like you're part of the furniture. You know—the part that needs to be replaced."

"What did he look like?" asked Sanders.

"Big guy. Real big. Like you," she said, looking up at him.

The door opened and a young man in jeans hurried in with an envelope, which he dropped on the counter. "As big as that?" asked Sanders.

The girl nodded energetically, picked up the package, and glanced at it. "Tomorrow morning?" she yelled at his retreating back.

"Fine," floated in to them from the closing door.

"Yeah," she said. "About the same size as Keith, I guess. Sure. With sort of light hair, I think, maybe blond or kind of red, like, and, uh, blue eyes. They might have been brown or hazel, but I think blue. And kind of ordinary looking. Nothing special about him. Actually, I didn't take to him much, to say the least, so I guess I wasn't looking very closely."

"Thanks, Liz," said Harriet, and turned to walk out. "That's terrific," she said as soon as they were outside. "Friend Keith, whoever he is, is at least four inches shorter than you are."

"I know," said Sanders gloomily. "It's because she's so small. Everyone over five foot six is a giant as far as she's concerned. Nice girl, but a lousy witness."

"At least she didn't give away my slide," said Harriet.

Once they were safely settled on the bus again, Harriet opened up the brown envelope and gently eased an eight-by-ten color print out of it. "Impressive, isn't it?" she said, handing it over to him. "They do very nice work there. A good, reliable lab. Pleasant, too."

Sanders stared at the print in disbelief. The small area in front of the west wing of the building had been blown up to fill the entire print surface, and the faces of the two men stared at him with the sharpness and clarity of a studio portrait. Scarface's dark eyes smoldered under their heavy brows; the blond was looking straight at the camera with a half-smile on his face, his hand raised as if in an attempt to cover it. He appeared to be waving mockingly at them. "How did you manage this?" he asked finally.

She grinned, a smug and self-satisfied grin. "I told you I was good. And the lab's no slouch, either. You ask for a hand-done print, you get quality. Of course, this is no four-dollar-and-ninety-five-cent special. They charge for this kind of work."

"How much?" asked Sanders curiously.

"They haven't billed me yet," said Harriet, "but it's Cibachrome. I expect it'll probably be around forty dollars or so. Worth it, though, isn't it? That's for the print, of course. The copy of the slide will be on top of that. I don't suppose the police—"

"Probably not," said Sanders. "Unless they're forced to."

"In that case," said Harriet. "It's back to looking for my pictures. I don't care how many cops are after you, we have to find those pictures or I can't afford all this charity."

"I think we'd better find someplace safe to stash these first," said Sanders. He slipped the print back into the envelope and handed it to Harriet.

"Damn!" she said, and stared down at the print in her hand as if the thought that she might lose this one had returned her to that state of awkward misery he had found her in. He shifted uneasily in the cramped space offered by the bus seat and tried to think of something reassuring to say. "I've got it!" she said. "Couldn't be better. Off we get. Quick."

Sanders scrambled off the bus after her, back onto Wellington Avenue, close to the spot where they first met. "Now what?" he murmured plaintively.

"In here," she said, dragging him into a stationery store. She scooted past the cards and into the writing paper section, scanned the various-size pads lined up in front of her, and picked up two of the cheapest ones. She checked them hastily for size against the envelope in her hand and nodded. "So far, so good," she muttered to Sanders, who had been stalking wordlessly after her. She dropped them on the counter, plucked a five-dollar bill from her pocket, and dropped it with them. "Don't bother to wrap them, please," she said hastily, as the woman behind the cash register took out a bag. "I'll use them here."

"Huh?" said the cashier, halting in mid-swoop. She was frozen in baffled immobility, holding the bag in her left hand and with her right reaching for the pads.

Harriet smiled brightly, ripped the stiff back cover off each pad, slipped one into the envelope behind the print, and then, with great care, worked the other in on top of the print. She picked up the pen sitting beside the cash register with another smile, this one apologetic, and began writing on the outside of the envelope. She pulled her notebook out from one of her top pockets, extracted two stamps from somewhere inside it, and pasted them down on the envelope. "Keep the paper, if you like," she called to the startled clerk, and flew out of the store. Sanders caught up with her as she was dropping the photographs into the nearest mailbox.

"You haven't sent them to yourself, have you?" he asked. "Because if you have, that is the oldest and stupidest dodge going. They'll just wait and grab them as they're going to your apartment in the mail."

"I'm not that dim-witted," said Harriet, looking too pleased with herself to be offended. She walked for some time in silence and then stopped and looked around her. "I sent them to my editor," she said softly. "In Toronto. She'll look at them, wonder what in hell they are, and then figure that sometime soon someone will explain why they were sent to her. In the interim, she'll put them on that huge shelf where she keeps piles and piles of manuscripts she hasn't finished working on yet. It must be the safest place in the world to hide something. I can't imagine anyone, no matter how clever he is, figuring that one out for a while."

"Not bad," said Sanders with a nod of genuine admiration, and raised an arm to hail a taxi.

"Where are we going?"

Sanders opened the door, nudged Harriet in, and jumped in after her. "Echo Drive," he said. "Somewhere in the five hundreds. I'll let you know where to stop."

The driver yawned and set the meter ticking.

"I thought you didn't want to go back there," said Harriet. There was a hostile edge to her voice now.

"I never said that, did I?" asked Sanders in surprise.

"No, it just seemed to me that you were avoiding it," she said irritably. "And me and my immediate problems. I mean, I've been trying to get in that house and find out what was going on, and you've been wandering off to hell and gone all over the place. Anywhere but there."

Sanders leaned back and looked at her, tempted to pick up the gauntlet. A sentence that pointed out her general selfishness and unreasonableness leaped into his mind, but framing it seemed too exhausting and futile an effort. "One thing at a time, sweetheart," he replied instead, and lapsed into silence. "That's it, just up ahead," he called out suddenly. The cab braked and slowed down.

"But we've gone way past it already," complained Harriet in a whisper.

"You need the exercise," he murmured back. The cabdriver yawned again, muttered an indistinct figure, and reached out for his money; as soon as Sanders told him to keep the change, he seemed to fall into one of those trances that are common to his profession. Sanders glanced to see if he was preparing to leave, and when it appeared that he wasn't in a hurry, grasped Harriet around the waist and propelled her toward the rear of the car. "Now," he whispered, "I want you to cross the street and walk up to any one of those houses, knock on the door, and when someone answers, ask for Charlie—no—Chuck MacTavish. I'll be right behind you."

"And when I'm told there is no such person?"

"Smile and apologize. If the cab is gone, just leave. If he's still there, string it out as long as possible."

"And what will you be doing?"

"Standing around looking awkward and embarrassed. I'm very good at it," he added bitterly, "Years of experience."

The cab finally took its departure while Harriet was explaining with great care what Chuck looked like to the tired-looking woman in the doorway. In the background a tiny baby wailed in misery. At last Sanders tapped her on the shoulder. "Look, I'm awfully sorry to have kept you out here so long," she said. "You've been so helpful. Thanks a lot. And the baby must be—"

"The baby's always crying," the woman replied dispiritedly. "But I'd better go have a look at her anyway. Sorry I couldn't have been more help."

"Now you've made me feel like an absolute bitch," said Harriet as she stormed down the steps. "That poor creature in there is obviously crazed with exhaustion and I kept her at the door trying to locate a nonexistent person living at a nonexistent address. What in hell are you up to?"

"Think of it as a change from listening to a baby cry. Now all we have to do is drift quietly back to the house and see what's going on. It looked pretty quiet as we went past it in the cab."

"What are we going to do when we get there?" asked Harriet, trying to drift as convincingly as she could.

"Ring the doorbell. If no one answers, we'll go around to the back and break in." Sanders began to drift more briskly.

"I don't believe this," said Harriet. "And you an officer of the law."

"When people are after you for murder," said Sanders. "I've noticed your outlook changes. The thought of a little B and E somehow doesn't seem so important."

"Anyway, what makes you think they'll be out?" she said skeptically. "You seem to be assuming that we'll have the place to ourselves," she added.

"Because it's three-thirty, and if something or other is going to happen at five, then they're probably running around doing whatever it is. If they are home, then we've probably screwed up completely and this place has nothing to do with anything—your pictures, Bartholomew's notes. Nothing."

By now they were around the slight bend in the road and in full view of the front of the Georgian house. Sanders stopped a couple of houses away and turned with his back to it. He was looking in apparent amazement at the beauty of a rock garden filled with tiny spring flowers, pointing at various specimens as he talked to Harriet. "Keep a little behind me," he said. "If anyone comes out, you won't be noticed. But tell me what you see."

She turned from contemplation of the rockery to looking at Sanders. "You were wrong, you know," she said conversationally. "Someone is home. He's coming out of the house right now. He's tall and big, as tall as you are and broader in the shoulders, I would guess. Sandy-haired, but I can't get a proper look at his face. There it is. Sort of north-of-England cheekbones, if you know what I mean."

Sanders glared down at her. "North-of-England cheekbones! What in hell are you talking about? Is he alone?"

"No," said Harriet, nodding her head in agreement. "You know, darling, my brother was right. I don't think we'd have any trouble turning that back section of the yard into a sweet little rock garden like this." Sanders stepped back, startled at her words, and saw a woman moving briskly toward them, trying to keep up with a young and energetic standard poodle on the end of a leash. "Now a medium-to-tall, dark-haired gentleman in a very conservative suit is coming out," said Harriet as soon as the dog walker had passed. "Ah, the black limousine that just went by is pulling up to collect him. And right behind him is a woman. It's Anna Maria Strelitsch again. What in hell is going on?"

"Have they all left yet?" asked Sanders. He began to move his head to the left.

"Wait. They're all in their cars now. Don't turn yet. There. They've rounded the corner. Now you can turn around."

"Let's go," said Sanders, and started walking quickly toward the house.

"Who in hell were all those people?" asked Harriet.

"How should I know," snapped Sanders, exasperated. "I couldn't even see them." He strode up the walk, took the steps two at a time, and rang the doorbell as if he were summoning a whole houseful of recalcitrant servants. They waited, listening to the bell peal through the empty rooms. "There's no one home."

"And now we just look and see if they accidentally left a door open around in back?" said Harriet innocently.

Sanders laughed for the first time in a while and began circling the house, heading left past the attached garage. He peered at the thin grass and dank weeds that grew in the narrow passage between the fence and the building—not so much as a tin can or piece of paper. He turned and shook his head. Harriet was crouched in front of the garage, working at the latch to the overhead doors with her fingers, growing visibly more and more frustrated. "They're locked," she said.

"Of course they're locked," said Sanders. "Here, let me try," he said, drawing out a bunch of keys and using one to pry at the lock. In less than a minute he was shoving the door up and back. "It's easier if you have something to force it with," he added apologetically. "My partner, now, he can pick locks with the best of them, but I have to rely on brute strength."

Harriet appeared not to hear him. She followed him into the garage and looked around briefly. It was empty of anything but a few garden implements. Sanders looked for the connecting door into the house—he preferred privacy when breaking into houses—but the original builders seemed to have forgotten to supply one. Undismayed, he followed Harriet out to the back garden and reassessed the situation. It could have been worse. Windows had been left open both downstairs and up. Fresh-air fiends, then. His eyes narrowed as he contemplated the problem. If he stood in the rose bed, then Harriet should be able to stand on his shoulders, push the downstairs window open a bit wider, and wriggle her narrow frame through. "Hey," he yelled, "come out of that bloody shed. I need you to crawl in this window here." He watched her walking across the garden and tried to calculate her weight. "And take your shoes off before you try it, too."

The two of them walked slowly through the ground floor, from the dining room where Harriet had just managed not to destroy a delicate walnut table as she went hurtling in, to a small sitting room in front, then into the massive hall and the formal living room on the other side of it. "Nice house," said Harriet at last. "You wouldn't think someone who lived like this would want to steal my pictures, would you?"

Sanders shook his head. "We don't know that he did. In fact, we don't know that he has anything to do with anything, do we? Maybe Bartholomew just got invited to a party here." Sanders punctuated his remark with a wave of the hand around him. The living room told them nothing. Like the other rooms they had been through, it seemed to be devoid of anything personal, even a magazine or a half-read book. They went up the sweeping staircase two steps at a time and paused in the equally large hallway on the second floor. They looked at the two closed doors leading into rooms at the front of the house and then at each other. "Split up?" said Harriet. Sanders shook his head. "This one, then," she said, and headed left. It took them only a minute to go through the bedroom. Every piece of clothing was in scrupulous order; each drawer and shelf was arranged so that one could find anything in seconds. Nothing was concealed. The small bathroom that the room shared with the one behind it also contained no secrets: towels, shaving things, soap, tissues and toilet paper, a bottle of aspirin, nothing else. Harriet tried the other door, glanced briefly into the room beyond, and backed away. "Empty," she said. They walked out the way they had come and into the room on the other side of the hall.

For a study it was profoundly disappointing. The desk drawers were empty, except for a small pile of brochures advertising clothing and sporting goods. Sitting on top of the desk was a much-thumbed mailing list, which Sanders automatically put in his pocket, but considering that it contained the names of several major department stores, he didn't have much hope for it.

The silence of the room was broken by an indignant cry. "My slides," said Harriet as he was finishing his brief survey of the desk. Her eye had gone past him and lit on the wastepaper basket. "All my goddamn slides are sitting in that basket. Find me a box or something to put them in."

"Wait," he said, his professional instincts surging to the fore. "Leave them."

"And look here," she said, paying no attention to him at all and walking over to the bookcase in the corner. On the top of it lay a pile of black-and-white prints of buildings in

Ottawa in a messy heap, and in front of it sat a carton whose stenciled label proclaimed that it had once held rum bottles. It was filled with strips of black-and-white negatives, curling in a wild and neglected mass, like worms in a bait can. "Christ almighty," she breathed. "If those negatives are scratched, so help me. Are there any envelopes or anything like that, sheets of paper, maybe, that I can put them in? For chrissake, John, give me a hand. I have to get them together."

Peter Rennsler finished the last quarter cup of coffee in his thermos, closed it tidily up again, and concealed it in the dead leaves in the hollow in the woods he had been occupying for the last two and a half hours. He rose cautiously to his feet. He was like a cat, steel-sprung and able to move from complete repose to total readiness in the gathering of a muscle, and now he slipped noiselessly and almost invisibly out between the trees to the roadway. He waited for a truck carrying new men to pass, and headed up the road a couple of hundred yards to the disembarkation area. At the checkpoint he handed his new set of papers to the irritated-looking sergeant who was attempting to position the influx.

"You didn't come with my lot," the sergeant said suspiciously, glancing from Peter to the paper in his hand.

"Uh-uh," Peter grunted, shaking his head. "Special transport."

"You're pretty late. The conference started a couple of hours ago. Do you know where you're supposed to be positioned?"

"That's right," he said, in a voice nicely calculated to be not quite insolent, the voice of a hard-to-replace specialist talking to a dime-a-dozen sergeant. Taking back his orders, he buttoned them into his pocket and trudged with an air of boredom into the secure area. He headed for a huge pine tree, bare for the first fifteen feet or so and thickly branched at the top. He bent down, buckled the lineman's spurs hanging from his belt onto his boots, and climbed the tree as casually as he would have ascended a set of stairs. He settled himself into the first solid branch facing the house and prepared, once again, to wait.

"Who's that?" asked a soldier standing nearby. He had been watching the ascent with mild curiosity as he swatted ineffectually at the black flies swarming around his head.

"Some hotshot sniper," muttered the man standing beside him.

"Some rifle, you mean," said the first enviously. "When did they start issuing those?"

"Jesus, how in hell should I know? They raided the museums to get the shit they handed out to us," he replied bitterly. "He probably knows somebody. Catch those bastards spending any money on us." He slapped the back of his neck. "Christ, these fucking black flies! Let's get the hell away from this patch of bog before they chew us to bits. Did you know you could die from black fly bites?"

"Weren't we supposed to stand here?' said his companion, looking around nervously—perhaps for signs of authority, perhaps for a murderous cloud of black flies.

"Who the hell knows where we were supposed to stand? They don't have bloody x's painted all over the ground, do they? Come on. The flies won't be as bad over there— it's not as swampy," he said in a voice that was almost kindly. "For chrissake, if you count the guy in the tree those assholes have put four of us covering the same god-damn ten square feet of bush. That bastard over there from the Mounties can cover our position. Can't you, mate?" he called. And Corporal Bill Fletcher lifted his rifle in response.

Corporal Fletcher felt a sense of relief at having some sort of semiofficial duty to carry out besides that of watching a sniper sit in a tree. His torment at having to cope with two contradictory sets of orders, one from Sergeant Carpenter, who would rip Fletcher's guts out when he found out the corporal wasn't carrying them out to the letter, and one from higher up, with its much more terrifying authority, was enough to make him oblivious to the damp, the chill, and the swarms of black flies in this swampy section of the woods. He rubbed his hand across his neck automatically and was surprised to notice that it came away covered with blood; nervously he leaned his rifle against a tree trunk and wiped the blood away from hand and neck with his handkerchief. If he'd had any brains, he reflected, he would have covered himself with insect repellent before coming out here.

He put the disgusting piece of cloth away and picked up his rifle again. He balanced it on his hand lovingly, and then checked the sight out against the sniper's back. It was a beauty. With this weapon, he could blast the soldier's rifle out of his hand as soon as he raised it to fire; there was no need to do anything so crude as kill him. For here, if truth must be told, lay the real source of his discomfort. Pride. Corporal Fletcher had case after case of medals—many bronze, several silver, and some treasured gold—hiding modestly in his drawer, medals that he had won for marksmanship. It offended him to kill a living target as if he were some two-bit hood with a shotgun dug into his victim's belly. That was a butcher's job; he considered himself an artist. But obedience was stronger than his pride, and if they wanted this man dead as soon as he fired on someone, he was certainly capable of carrying out the order. He sighed unhappily and wiped his bloody handkerchief across his neck once more.

Harriet had finished stacking the prints neatly so that their surfaces would not be damaged. "I can sort them later," she said, stepping back. "I wonder if that's all of them. It's hard to tell. Did you find me some envelopes for the negatives?" she asked in the same detached mutter, and it took Sanders a moment or two to figure out that the question had not been rhetorical.

"Envelopes? For chrissake, Harriet, we're committing half the crimes against property in the book, and you're worried about finding envelopes? Just dump everything in that box and we'll do something about it later. In the meantime, let's get the hell out of here." Suddenly a door slammed, and he stiffened. "What in hell is that?" he murmured unnecessarily.

"It sounds to me like someone coming home," said Harriet coolly, and picked up the box of negatives. She put them on the desk, inserted her fingers into the edge of the curling mass, and gently pushed it to one side. She gestured fiercely at Sanders to get her the stack of prints, which she slipped carefully into the space she had just created against the side of the box. "There."

"What do you mean, there?" said Sanders.

"We just take this box and slip down the back stairs—all these houses have back staircases—and out the kitchen door to the garden. We can climb over the fence into a neighbor's yard if we have to."

He took five seconds to find a flaw in the plan, failed, and nodded. "If you insist on bringing that stupid box, give it to me," he whispered. She shook her head. "Stay behind me, then," he added, and glided over to the door.

"Gladly," murmured Harriet, and picked up her box.

The broad upstairs hall was empty, although they could hear footsteps clearly enough on the polished wood floor beneath them. The main stairway was in front of them, taking up the center space to the right. To its right were the enormous bedrooms they had already explored; no staircases there. The most likely spot for such a thing would be down a narrow corridor to their left, across from the rear bedroom.

Sanders moved gently across the hall to the railing that protected them from pitching into the foyer; a board creaked and he silently cursed the owner of the house—what was her name? Mrs. Smythe?—for not falling prey to broadloom. He glimpsed the top of a head, surmounted by thick, dark, slightly graying hair, and ducked back to the relative obscurity of his place by the wall. This time he moved as rapidly as he could, sticking close to the wall to get away from creaking boards, until he made it into the narrow corridor. Harriet followed behind, her running shoes making slight squeaking noises as she tried to advance with silent haste. The cardboard box in her arms, although insignificant in weight, hampered her seriously by its clumsy bulk, and twice, unable to see the surface in front of her feet, she misjudged where she was and bumped noisily into something.

There was one closed door in the middle of the corridor and a pair of doors facing each other at the end of the hall. The stairs. One set to the third floor, one to the kitchen. Sanders cautiously turned the handle of the door to his right and opened it silently. He stopped so abruptly that Harriet slammed the box into his back and swore.

"What the hell?"

"Get back," he said tightly.

"Come on, John," she whispered, giving him a nudge with the carton, "let's get the hell out of here. I think I made a bit too much noise back there for comfort."

"That's easier said than done, I'm afraid," said a voice she did not recognize. "Inspector Sanders would have difficulty moving forward, Miss Jeffries. He would have to walk through me, I'm afraid. Just as you would have to walk through my friend here if you wanted to go back."

Harriet spun around and found herself staring into the barrel of a small pistol held in the hand of an elegantly dressed, handsome, middle-aged man with dark, slightly graying hair. He made a slight bow. "Fräulein," he murmured. The gun never strayed from her abdomen.

Peter Rennsler glanced at his watch and settled himself more firmly into his perch. His hold on his weapon was still light, his arms still relaxed and easy. The first session should be over in a few minutes, he reckoned, although there was a certain inexactitude about the hour when the talks were expected to finish for the day. From where he was sitting, he could fire straight into the window of the limousine as it moved up the slight rise past the guarded entrance gate. Behind him, the man who was to create the diversion that would let him slip away again had arrived and set up his position. He frowned. He didn't like plans that depended on the actions of others. For their completion or for their success. But he had allowed himself—foolishly—to be talked into this one. And he particularly didn't like plans that involved weapons at his back. He sighed lightly—it was too late now—and shifted position a hairsbreadth to relieve a slight tightness in his thigh.

*   *   *

The dark-haired man reached over to his right and opened the door beside him. "Please, Fräulein," he said with a grin of mocking courtesy. "You do not need to stand in the corridor. If you would go in there," he gestured sharply in the direction of the doorway, "and put down that ridiculous box, I am sure that we would all feel more at ease." Harriet glanced helplessly back at Sanders. His nod was almost imperceptible. She shook her head in confusion and walked into the room. "Sit down on the bed, please, Miss Jeffries. We are very pleased to see you; we had lost track of you temporarily. The person assigned to follow you is very impressed but frustrated by your driving skills. If we had realized that you were so reckless on the roads we would have hired a more professional driver." He smiled. "It was enterprising of you to find us. Perhaps in a while you will tell us just how you managed to do it. That would be most interesting." He stood by the door as she stalked into the room, put down her box, and perched on the edge of the bed. The room was starkly furnished: a small dresser made of drab, light-colored wood; a narrow, sagging bed, stripped down to its grubby mattress; a narrow, boxy, dark brown desk; and a couple of straight-backed chairs filled the available wall space. It reminded her of the cheap and smelly boardinghouse rooms she had lived in during those days when success and prosperity had seemed impossible dreams. The sense of unreality was sharpened by the heavy curtains that covered the one window, creating a dim twilight. Their captor reached over and turned on a bright overhead light; then with contemptuous impatience he kicked the box of prints under the bed. "Now, Inspector, I will relieve you of the weight of that—" He reached into Sanders's jacket and removed the pistol from its holster, slipping it into his own pocket. "And if you would be so kind as to follow her example—" A rough push in the diaphragm and Sanders found himself sitting, breathless, beside Harriet.

He pulled up a straight-backed chair and sat down facing them. "So," he said conversationally, "I am Karl Lang. This is my house that you have broken into, by the way. And behind me is my friend and business associate, uh, Mr. Green. Do come in, Mr. Green."

Sanders turned his attention to Green. Even without the scar it was a memorable face. Under the bare bulb in the ceiling the dark eyes and strong cheekbones stood out more strikingly than they had in the diffuse light of the restaurant in Brockville or in Harriet's picture. He smiled and Sanders could feel Harriet shiver beside him. Sanders had seen that kind of smile before. It used to appear with frequency on the face of a certain fellow officer, now edged out into Administration. It was the expression of someone who felt himself in control, powerful, untouchable, and who was confronting a member of a subhuman species without power or influence. It was a dangerous look, and it made him nervous. He wondered what particular reason Green had for feeling untouchable. Madness? Or something more pragmatic and real and therefore more menacing? Simple wealth, perhaps.

Green pulled a chair out from the desk in the corner and placed it backward in front of Sanders and Harriet. He straddled the chair comfortably, leaning his elbows on the back, and watched them for a minute or two with those bright, cold eyes before opening his mouth. "That picture," said Green at last. "I must insist that you produce that picture for us. You really should have stuck to photographing buildings, Miss Jeffries. Then you would never have bothered us."

"I don't know which picture you're talking about," said Harriet steadily. "I take a great many pictures."

"Come now, Miss Jeffries, or may I call you Harriet? Please don't try to irritate me. You know which picture. The picture I watched you take. The picture your friend told the police about, the picture you tried to say wasn't developed yet, the picture you are—for reasons unknown to me—hiding. Where is it?" There was a long silence. "I see," he said. He looked at the two of them side by side on the gray mattress and frowned. "Inspector, you will stand up—very slowly— and move over there to the corner. Now!" Sanders eased himself upright and walked sideways over to the east wall of the room. Mr. Lang followed his progress steadily with his pistol. "Stop. That will do," snapped Green, as Sanders neared the desk. "Karl," Green said softly. "Hold this for me, would you?" He handed his pistol to Mr. Lang, who pocketed it without taking his eyes off Sanders. "Just until I can get Miss Jeffries ready. There now," he said, grabbing her by the elbows and forcing her upright and very close to him, his knees pressing her thighs painfully against the bed frame. "You don't need that on." He reached around her to each shoulder, pulled off her jacket, dropped it on the floor beside her, and grabbed the waistband of her sweatshirt.

Surprise had slowed her reactions. Now she looked down in amazement at what was happening, and blinked. She jerked her arms up between them and pushed as hard as she could against his chest. "Get your filthy hands off me."

He grabbed her by the wrists, clamped them together, and encircled them with the long and very strong fingers of his left hand. Using her trapped arms as a lever, he pushed her backward until she thought her spine would snap, and then with his free hand slapped her on the cheek. She felt her jaw move sickeningly to the right and her head begin to spin under the force of the blow. "Shut up," he said, released her for a moment, and yanked the sweatshirt off. It caught her ears and her hair as he pulled it over her head, and she could feel involuntary tears of pain prickle her eyes. "Now sit down again." He yanked off his tie, grabbed her hands again, moved them around behind her, and knotted the tie around Harriet's wrists before fastening it also to the bedpost. "That's better," he said, and stood back. "Now. One of you is going to tell me where that picture is." He smiled. "Do you know why I know that? Because I am not stupid enough to try to force the answer out of you, Inspector. You look like one of those moral fools who prefers to die silent and noble in a pool of his own blood." He stared lazily at Sanders, who willed his body to stay motionless and relaxed. "Am I right? But perhaps after watching a little persuasion of Miss Jeffries, Inspector, you will change your mind. I fancy you are not very good at watching, are you?" Green turned his chair around, pulled it closer to Harriet, and sat down. "Herr Lang, on the other hand, enjoys such displays. They have a bizarre fascination about them that he appreciates. But I don't suppose you share his tastes, Inspector. I expect either you or Miss Jeffries will let us know where that picture is soon enough."

"I can't imagine that one or two little pictures could possibly be worth all this time and trouble," said Sanders. He paused to get his voice under control and then plunged on in an attempt to forestall whatever Green was planning to do. "And expense, of course."

"The fate of my country depends on that picture," said Lang suddenly. "If I am discredited, then who else will have the strength and determination to take over and cure the malaise she has fallen into?"

"But you're not even in the picture—"

"Ah," said Green, interrupting Sanders, "but I am. And I am glad to see that we are acknowledging the fact that the picture exists. Now it only remains to find out where." He reached over and placed one thin hand behind Harriet's head, grabbed her hair, and wrenched it back. She drew her breath in sharply. With his other hand he reached down and took a knife from a leg sheath. He balanced it in his palm as if trying to decide what to do with it before grasping it firmly and placing the point against her larynx. She could feel a tiny area of cold, sharp pressure in her throat, nothing more. "A twitch of the knife, Miss Jeffries, that's all it takes." Her mouth felt black, dry, and bitter-tasting with fear, and in spite of herself she swallowed. The pressure increased and the slight pain intensified. "But what would be the point?" he said, as he pulled back the knife and eased the pressure. "You would be incapable of answering me then, wouldn't you? But it is an action I would find very easy to do, Miss Jeffries, believe me."

Sanders had been watching intently as the knife pressed into and then moved back from her throat. When it was a safe distance away, he spoke, his voice friendly and casual. "It would be a very messy business, Mr. Green," Sanders said. "It's difficult to conceal that much blood, you know. Especially here, in the city, in a house."

"True, Inspector." Green's voice was as level and as casual as Sanders's; only a quick flicker of his tongue to the corner of his mouth seemed to betray any emotion at all. "But then, I wasn't planning anything quite so crude." He dropped the point down six inches and left it resting lightly on her breastbone. "The knife is remarkably sharp—too precise for mere butchery." Slowly and delicately he drew the point along the yellow cloth of her T-shirt, from her breastbone down and to the right along the outside of her breast. She screamed. The cloth separated, and a thin line of blood welled up from the tracery he had made. He moved the point back to her breastbone and waited. "Go ahead, scream," said Green. "Louder. No one can hear you but the inspector." The point began to move again, and Harriet made a gurgling sound in her throat. This time the cloth was not cut. "Do you believe me now?" said Green, his face suffused with heightened color, "or do you still think I'm bluffing? I think you still believe we're bluffing,'" he said in tones of mock amazement. "I don't suppose she knows what one can do to a girl and leave her capable of answering questions. You do, Inspector, don't you? Perhaps you've seen what's left when an interrogation like that is over. Not a very pleasant sight, is it?" He leaned back casually, his hands linked around his right knee, one eyebrow raised. "Well? The picture?"

Sanders rearranged himself against the wall in order to catch a surreptitious look at Lang. He was sitting forward in his chair, his legs crossed, one hand clutching his knee with sufficient force to whiten the knuckles. The other hand was gripping the pistol, pointing it toward Sanders, just inches from his gut. But Lang's attention was no longer fixed on Sanders. His eyes kept flickering over to Harriet; his breath had quickened and there was new color in his face. Sanders turned from his momentary study and looked back at Harriet. She was staring at the wall ahead of her, her face pale but impassive, whatever pain and terror she was feeling locked firmly within. With a little luck, the next thing Green did to Harriet, whatever it was, would so fascinate Mr. Lang, so quicken his breathing and loosen his fingers, that Sanders should be able to jump him.

A sudden peal of the doorbell shattered the tension that locked them all into silence. Lang raised a warning hand. "Not a sound," he whispered. "Not only will my associate be happy to kill you, but noise doesn't carry well from this room to the rest of the house." He removed his pistol from its position an inch from Sanders's belly, handed Green's pistol back to him, slipped his own weapon into his pocket, and walked out of the room, closing the door firmly behind him.

Green leaned back in his chair, his pistol aimed at Harriet, his eyes on Sanders. The three of them formed a frozen tableau, three points of a triangle. Harriet continued to stare intently at a spot on the wall just behind Green, her eyes never straying toward Sanders. Sanders lounged against the desk, calculating the force and the speed required to over-power Green without endangering Harriet. Too much, he was deciding reluctantly, unless there was some further outside distraction, when a tap at the door drew Green from his chair. As soon as he opened it, he was addressed in a stream of rapid German. It was Lang's voice, soft and very urgent. Green turned to Sanders. "If you two make any noise at all, I can assure you that Miss Jeffries will not live long enough to take another picture. I shall be right outside. Understand?" And he slipped out into the hall, leaving the door open behind him.

"How badly are you hurt?" whispered Sanders.

"It's nothing," she whispered back. "They're just trying to scare us. I'm sorry I screamed. He startled me."

Sanders looked silently at the bloody line on her breast and at the spreading stain on her T-shirt before edging himself very quietly along the wall over to the door to listen. "He's not here," he hissed back at Harriet. "I think he's over at the head of the stairs. I wonder what's going on," he muttered. "And how much time we have?"

"It's Anna Maria Strelitsch," said Harriet. "They didn't sound very pleased to see her."

"Jesus Christ!" said Sanders softly. "How do you know that?"

"Goddammit, John, don't you ever listen to me? I spent three years in Germany. I lived with a German, never spoke a word of English."

"Ssh," he whispered. "That means that Lang is occupied for the moment." He looked rapidly around the room, picked up one of the chairs, and hefted it, checking its value as an offensive weapon.

"Will they let us go if we tell them where the picture is?" asked Harriet. Her voice was faint and her composure seemed to be cracking slightly.

"No," he said flatly. "We know their faces, their names, and they don't give a damn. That means they don't figure we'll be telling anybody."

"In that case there's no point in saying anything," she whispered fiercely. "No matter what happens." Sanders put the chair over his knee in an attempt to break off the back leg. "Not that," whispered Harriet. "The sewing machine. Try the left side of the sewing machine."

"What sewing machine?" whispered Sanders.

"The one you were leaning on, you idiot."

Sanders ran his hand along the left side of the boxy-looking desk until his fingers touched the round end of a metal bar. He gave it a pull and it slid out about a foot. "Wiggle it," whispered Harriet. He moved it up and it glided free into his hand, a neatly shaped and heavy iron bar. He placed it behind him and leaned on the sewing machine table again.

"Untie me," Harriet hissed in exasperation.

"Not yet," murmured Sanders. "No time. We need him." He pointed at the open door. "Try to get him in here and distract him."

Harriet nodded. "Mr. Green," she called. There was no response. "'Mr. Green," she repeated with a new urgency.

"What in hell do you think you're doing?" snarled Sanders loudly.

Two heavy footfalls later a suspicious-looking Green was framed in the doorway, his pistol moving gently between the two of them. "What's going on?"

Harriet glanced nervously at Sanders. "If I tell you . . . what you want to know . . ." Her voice trailed off. "I mean, where it is," she added more firmly.

"For chrissake, Harriet, shut up," said Sanders.

She turned her head away from him with great deliberation. "Will you let me go? I won't tell anyone. I haven't any reason to. And it's just the one slide, you know. If you had that . . ." Her voice drifted off again in confusion. Green remained fixed in the doorway.

"Where is it?" he said at last.

She kept her eyes fixed on Green. "If you look in my jacket," she began, pointing with her chin in the direction of the heap of cloth on the floor.

"You mean the goddamn thing was in your jacket all the time?" said Green in a tone of near-admiration, moving a step into the room.

"Not the slide," said Harriet, "but if you look in the pocket of my jacket, you'll find—"

Green took another step and leaned over to pick up the jacket. The pistol wavered, pointing at the mattress, then at the wall as he bent down. Sanders grasped the bar in both hands and brought it down with as much force as he could exert on Green's head. The man crumpled, falling forward onto the bed, and then slid gently down onto the floor.

Sanders reached for the tie, cursing the recalcitrance of the knots, then grabbed the knife from Green's leg sheath and slashed them apart. He brought Harriet's wrists around and rubbed them for a few seconds to restore circulation. He threw her sweatshirt at her, and as she was slipping it on, picked up her jacket. "Let's get the hell out of here."

"But my pictures," said Harriet in tones of distress.

"To hell with your pictures," said Sanders. "Let's go."

CHAPTER 11

Voices trailed up the grand stairway, one huskily female, the other male and impatient-sounding. Sanders picked up the iron bar, grabbed Harriet by the hand, and headed once more for the narrow back stairs. This time they were empty. He tried to tiptoe down silently and swiftly, cursing every time his foot hit a squeaky board or kicked against the riser. Harriet, with her smaller feet and running shoes, drifted soundlessly behind him. He stopped at the closed door at the foot of the stairs, raised the bar in preparation to attack, and opened the door a crack. Still the voices wafted in from another room, the female one punctuated by throaty laughter, the male speaking in shorter and shorter bursts. Sanders located the rear door, and clutching Harriet even more firmly, ran for it, this time heedless of the hollow clump of his shoes on the elegant wood floor of the kitchen. It took him several agonizing seconds to undo the bolt and the latch, seconds in which Sanders was aware of an abrupt change in the sound of the voices. As heavy footsteps hurried in their direction, he yanked the door open and dragged Harriet out into the yard.

They flew across the damp grass to the six-foot-high wood fence at the back of the garden. Sanders let go of Harriet, put one foot on the lower framing two-by-four, his arm on the upper one, and heaved himself up. The fence lurched crazily under its unaccustomed burden. He reached down and grabbed Harriet by the forearm. "Jump," he said, speaking for the first time, and she threw herself up with a short cry of pain as he pulled, grasping the top of the fence with her other hand and getting her knee onto the crosspiece. The fence lurched again, and then began moving with ominous lack of speed toward the flower beds in the neighboring garden. "Off we go," said Sanders triumphantly, as they leaped down into the rich loam of a well-worked flower bed and sped across the lawn, leaving the collapsing fence listing in their direction at a forty-five-degree angle.

"Hey, what do you think you're doing?" A voice emerged from the back of the house as they passed through the garden gate, a voice filled with indignation and despair. "Come back here!"

They pounded between the houses onto the next street, paying no attention to the world behind them. "Which way?" said Sanders, looking up and down in some confusion.

"What are we looking for?" asked Harriet, who was panting, scratched, and muddy from their mad scramble through the gardens. And ominously pale.

"A telephone, of course," said Sanders in amazement.

"Right. Toward Bank Street, in that case," she replied breathlessly, turning in that direction. "And I wouldn't linger, if I were you. Whoever lives in that house seemed awfully unhappy about the fence."

"Right you are," said Sanders, striding as rapidly as his long legs would move, making Harriet trot to keep up to him.

"Look," gasped Harriet. "A milk store up there. They'll have—"

"There's one outside," said Sanders. "You got a quarter?"

"But aren't you calling the police? You don't need—"

"No." He yanked out the telephone book, still mercifully resting on its little shelf in this law-abiding neighborhood, and began rapidly flipping through the pages.

Harriet crammed herself in beside him, feeling about in the pocket of her jeans until her hand emerged triumphantly holding a quarter. "There," she said. "Who are you calling?"

The telephone at the Austrian embassy was answered with commendable promptness, given the emergency conditions engendered by the visit of a head of government, but the person who answered was adamant in refusing access to the ambassador or to the security officer, even by telephone. It mattered not to him who John Sanders was, or why he was calling. He was not on the ambassador's short list of preferential callers, and he could be dealt with by a minor flunky at his convenience. Friday was not a good day. "Next week, perhaps?" that discouraging voice suggested.

"No, I will not leave my number," snapped Sanders. "Would you take the time to ask the security officer, or his assistant, or his assistant's assistant, if he's heard of something called Dawn in Vienna? Now?"

There was a pause, a lengthy pause, and Sanders felt encouraged. He smiled down at Harriet, who was jammed in somewhere under his right elbow, and drummed his fingers in a thoughtful rhythm against the open pages of the directory. A couple of clicking noises later, and a new voice took over. "Carlo Hoffel here," said the voice with calm courtesy. "You have information on Dawn in Vienna, Inspector? You have my attention."

"There," said Sanders, five minutes later, as he hung up the telephone. "That's that. Now to deal—" He turned to Harriet and found her sitting hunched over in the corner of the booth, looking pale and very small. "Are you—"

"I'm afraid we won't have much of a chance to deal with anything," she said. She took a deep breath. "There are some people out there who seem to want to talk to us."

Sanders turned around and groaned. On the street outside the telephone booth, four Ottawa police cruisers were pulling up, red lights flashing, each one disgorging two uniformed officers of the law. "Dammit!" he said, and placed a hand, half helping, half warning, on Harriet's shoulder as she struggled to her feet. "Look, sweetheart," he murmured. "It might be best not to mention the fact that we broke into that house until things become a little clearer. Police officers get a little odd about breaking and entering. All right? Can you make it on your own?" She nodded in response to both questions, he opened the door and walked through, his hands spread peacefully out to each side.

A light blue Ford Escort was driving sedately down Echo Drive heading in the direction of the charming Georgian house that had been rented by Karl Lang for the year. The driver, an insignificant-looking man with pale red hair, of above-average height and more-than-average chinlessness, was whistling a faint and tuneless whistle as he drove. He checked his watch. 4:45. Precisely on time. The whistle became more energetic, although not more tuneful, as he rapidly calculated exactly how much he would be getting from Mr. Green. Although perhaps the bonus had gone up in smoke, since Mr. Green had been perturbed at his failure to recover the picture. Dammit. It hadn't been his fault that stupid bitch of a photographer drove like a maniac and he'd lost her. He couldn't afford to get stopped for speeding. Green knew that. Anyway, if he hadn't been sloping by at the right time, they never would have found out who was taking the damn picture. He had followed them on his own initiative and that deserved a bonus. And he'd been working sixteen-hour days, trying to keep track of the photographer and her boyfriend, the cop. His thoughts became aggrieved, as they often were. He followed the road around a bend cautiously—it would never do to get into an accident—and then pulled to a stop. The house seemed to be surrounded by police cars.

He stared at them, as though his halt had been occasioned by vulgar curiosity. A constable on the sidewalk waved him by with an impatient hand. He drove off, trying hard to remember if he had given either Lang or Green any real information that could identify him. On reflection he decided he hadn't. Except the capacity to pick out his face. There were those workmen, too, but they wouldn't remember him. Nobody did, usually. That was the advantage of looking the way he did. Still, perhaps he would take a nice spring vacation. Out west, say. He turned right at the next intersection and headed for the train station.

The prime minister of Austria was taking his leave of his counterpart in the Canadian government amidst a flurry of handshakes and mutually congratulatory remarks. The opening session of the conference had been an enormous success. This was no surprise to the organizers. All the difficult issues were being dealt with downtown, where the experts were meeting, and the agenda for the political heads had covered nothing up to this point that could not be handled by the vigorous application of platitudes. Surrounded by a minor bevy of soberly dressed, anonymous-looking aides and translators, the P.M. graciously readied himself to be wafted into his limousine for the ride back into town and preparations for a second state dinner. Suddenly the broad hallway was filled with a new group of soberly dressed, anonymous-looking men and women, these ones taller, on the whole, and broader in the shoulder, younger and more vigorous-looking than the original crowd. Security. A few words were whispered into the ear of the Canadian prime minister. A few more into the ear of the head of the government of Austria. Security men exchanged glances, nodded, and the Austrian contingent retired into the pleasant reception room off the hall, followed—after some further discussions with the security staff—by the Canadians. The press contingent waited impatiently outside, puzzled by the failure of the last two delegations to appear. A speculative buzz later they concluded that some sort of deal was being enacted under the table by the two countries. The press secretary assured them that no such deal was being contemplated and they left, confident that it must be so. A minor story, of course, involving two not-very-important powers, but lacking anything more interesting coming out of the first day of the conference, it would have to do. As the press were departing, a helicopter roared overhead, then a second, and a third. One gently lowered itself onto the broad lawns of the secure site. The Austrian prime minister, surrounded by a tightly knit phalanx of security officers, gave a cheerful wave to the Canadian delegation and climbed on board.

Peter Rennsler watched impassively as the limousine bearing the Austrian flag drove by empty of passengers and the procession of official cars unaccountably dried up. A hitch. He waited, just in case, for the last car, the Canadian one, to come by, on the slight chance that his man might be in it. Although if he were, Peter reflected philosophically, the chances were he wouldn't be able to get a shot at him. It would take a hand grenade into the backseat to achieve his end. And that wasn't his style. No matter. He heard the roar of helicopters and looked up. The first swept in his direction, hovered near his tree, and then settled delicately onto the lawn. A second flew in and wafted gently back and forth above the one on the ground. The third began a sweep across the woods. They represented a somewhat more serious hitch. He turned his attention to the doorway. But when it opened and his target emerged, he was completely surrounded by men half a head taller than he was. Rennsler waited until the prime minister disappeared into the helicopter, following the center of the group steadily in his sights, never getting a clear shot. He shrugged and swung his rifle over his shoulder. He wasn't responsible if his employers had screwed up their own security; he had done what he had been asked to do. Half of his exorbitant fee was already safely stowed away in a foreign bank account, and he considered himself well out of the whole operation. He hadn't cared for this assignment. His shoulders twitched as he thought of the man on the ground with the rifle at his back, and he climbed down the tree as rapidly and smoothly as he had climbed up.

"I guess you can go home now, eh, mate?" said the soldier keeping guard on the hill to his right. "Lucky bugger. We gotta stay and clear the woods again. Jesus. As if someone is going to fight his way into this fucking piece of bog just to get a shot at one of them assholes." He jerked his thumb in the direction of the house, now quiet and almost deserted. "See ya," he added gloomily as Rennsler walked lightly out of the woods and headed toward his motorcycle.

* * *

Corporal Bill Fletcher stood, puzzled, with his rifle pointing toward the ground. His instructions had been clear enough, as far as they went, but no one had told him what he was supposed to do if the putative assassin didn't shoot anybody. Should he have tried to arrest him? Jesus. Maybe he should have. If he really moved, he could still catch him. But what for? Being one of the bad guys? As far as he, William R. Fletcher, could tell, the man hadn't done anything. Fletcher was willing enough to risk censure for killing someone in the commission of a crime—under orders, of course—even though in the circumstances and with the weapon he had in his hand, the inquiry board was going to be as suspicious as hell. He wasn't willing, however, to make a fool of himself by arresting a soldier on duty for the crime of sitting in a tree and holding a rifle. He shrugged, and headed back to base.

Sanders sat in the interview room and glowered at the officer interrogating him. His identification sat on the table in front of him, while the Ottawa Police Department awaited confirmation that he was who he claimed to be. Otherwise they had reached an impasse. Sanders was willing to admit to being in Stittsville, and to trespassing, including incidental damage to a fence and flower bed—although it probably had not been Mrs. Henryson's fence, he pointed out to the insufferable sergeant, since the construction framework had not been on her side. He was not willing to discuss the question of arson, nor what had happened to the weapon that should have been in his shoulder holster, nor what he had been doing dragging a young woman across the backyards of Ottawa. And there they sat, for the moment, in silence.

The door opened. A constable stuck his head in the door, shoved some paper at the sergeant, and said cheerfully, "He's the genuine article, Sergeant. Or so they say in Toronto. And they would like to know what in hell is going on."

"*They* would!" sputtered the harassed sergeant. "What about me? Look, Inspector, just tell me what in hell you thought you were up to, okay?" There was a hint of regret in his voice as he mentally scratched the charge of "personating a peace officer (119, sec. a)" off his little checklist.

"Would you do something for me?" said Sanders. He got a glare in response. "What time is it?"

"Five-thirty-seven. That was what you wanted?"

Sanders shook his head. "Would you contact Inspector Charlie Higgs at RCMP headquarters? He's in Security somewhere, shouldn't be too hard to find." Sanders leaned back. He had a sinking sensation in his gut, as though he had just made some sort of decision that might not be very clever.

The sergeant looked at him with a new wariness. "Security. Inspector Higgs." He pushed his chair back and yelled for the constable, who poked his head in the door with suspicious speed. "Look, Coleman. Call RCMP and see if you can locate an Inspector Higgs in Security. Ask him if—don't bother." He sighed, watching the confused and panic-stricken look on Coleman's face. "Sit in here and watch this guy. I'll call the RCMP."

Sanders and Harriet were sitting tranquilly in the backseat of a patrol car, being sped toward the grim fastnesses of Mountie headquarters. Sanders had made mild objections to their riding as prisoners in the rear, considering who he was and where he was accustomed to sitting. "Look, buddy," said the uniformed constable, unimpressed with Sanders's rank or his power. "I was told to come and pick you two up and to make damned sure that you actually got to head-quarters. Those were the words. So I am. Making sure." Sanders gave up gracefully and climbed in after Harriet.

"How are you?" he asked anxiously. "They weren't very forthcoming about you back in there."

"I'm fine," said Harriet. The gray of her cheeks and lips belied her confident assertion. "Really. Just a bit battered-feeling. What did you tell them?"

"Absolutely nothing. What did you tell them?"

"I said we were out running and we just felt like cutting through that backyard. I don't think they believed me," she added. "But it seemed friendlier to tell them that than just to sit there and say nothing. I thought they looked a little annoyed." She dropped her head back and closed her eyes. "What do they want us at headquarters for?"

"I don't know, ma'am," said the constable, whose ears were apparently sharper than either one of them had realized. "I was just told to pick you up and bring you here. Nobody told me what for," he said as he turned into the drive and pulled up in front of the building. "I expect the superintendent will let you know." He stopped, unlocked the doors, and came around to escort them into the building.

By the time they reached Henri Deschenes's office, Harriet was leaning heavily on Sanders's supporting arm. Several others were already milling about there. A tired-looking Sylvia neatly snaffled Harriet as she went by her desk. "I expect they'll want to see you later," Sylvia said, "but for the moment, perhaps you wouldn't mind sitting out here with me. I'm about to call down for sandwiches and coffee. Would you like some?"

"No thanks," said Harriet faintly, suddenly sickened by the thought of eating.

"The egg salad is pretty bland," Sylvia continued, paying no attention to Harriet's reply, "the cheese is inedible, but they do a nice turkey and a really good hot corned beef and mustard." She glanced sharply at Harriet's white face. "Let me take your jacket," she said, and reached for one edge of the collar as she began to move behind her.

"I think I'd rather keep it on," said Harriet. "I'm awfully cold." But the peacefully mundane quality of the exchange seemed to signal that her ordeal was over for the time being and, overcome by a wave of exhaustion, she sat down abruptly in a large, comfortable chair that had appeared out of nowhere.

Sylvia stood looking at her for one indecisive moment and then turned toward an alcove in the corner. "I'll get you a coffee." Harriet heard her feet brush over the carpeting, then the sound of her voice murmuring in the distance. In a minute she returned with two mugs of coffee. "Here," she said, "I put the sugar in already. And the doctor will be up in a minute."

"What doctor?" said Harriet, looking doubtfully at the mug. She hated sugar in her coffee, but she was suddenly hideously thirsty.

"You're bleeding over that sweatshirt of yours," said Sylvia. "And I just had the carpet replaced in here. We wouldn't want to ruin it, would we? Drink your coffee."

Sanders was seated at another table on the other side of the door, in an atmosphere noticeably less hostile than the one he had just left. Charlie Higgs had come down to the elevator to meet them, presumably to erase the negative impression caused by their mode of transport, and Superintendent Deschenes seemed tranquil enough in humor as he stepped around his desk to shake hands. There were three others sitting quietly in the room. One of them, a dark, squarely built, powerful-looking man, rose to his feet as Sanders entered the room. He stepped forward and grasped Sanders's hand firmly.

"Carlo Hoffel, Inspector Sanders. I was talking to you earlier on the telephone. I would like to offer you the thanks of the Austrian government for helping to avert a most unpleasant situation."

"You mean the tip was good?" asked Sanders with a pleased smile. "You never know about these things. I didn't have much to go on, and for all I knew, it could have been next Friday, or any Friday next month."

"Ah," said Higgs. "Joe plus one. I wondered what you were on to. Remember Steve Collins's system?" he said, turning to Deschenes, and then walking over to the conference table and sitting down, apparently willing to wait for elucidation. The others got up automatically and followed him.

"Actually," said Deschenes, "we don't really *know* that the tip was good, although we are piecing together some interesting things."

"Yes," said Hoffel. "There were some interesting things at the house on Echo Drive—"

"The hell there were!" said Sanders, nettled. "I went over that house and found nothing—except Miss Jeffries's pictures, which were what I was looking for all along."

"You didn't go far enough, Inspector," said Hoffel. "There were things up on the third floor. Weapons, ammunition, files. It's wonderful."

"We had to leave you people something to do," said

Sanders. "Besides, we were otherwise occupied. And I would be extremely grateful if you could somehow extract those pictures from the house. They have no evidentiary importance. The only one you might want is in the mail on its way to Toronto. The box should be in a small back bedroom on the second floor, under the bed," he added.

"Indeed," said Deschenes, opening the file in front of him. "Charlie, could you call down and see about rescuing that box of pictures?" Higgs nodded and moved over to the telephone on the conference table.

There was a short rap on the door. Sylvia swept in, dropped a note in front of Deschenes and swept out again before anyone could register her entrance. Deschenes picked up the note and turned back to Sanders. "Would that be the same small back bedroom that also contained an armed man, unconscious, concussed, and bleeding, when we arrived?"

"Mmm," said Sanders. "Is he badly hurt?"

"Adequately," said Hoffel. "But we got Karl Lang, and that was what was important. Groenwald is merely a, uh, lackey, a dangerous one, a Canadian citizen with a criminal record and Austrian connections; but we wanted Lang. He's one of ours. And not only that, but you have supplied what we never had before—and that is a clear-cut reason for someone to hold him while we seize his records and investigate him without interference from his well-meaning friends in the government."

"What's that?" answered Sanders, startled.

"Come now, Inspector," said Deschenes. "Surely you are not that deficient in your knowledge of the criminal code. Forcible confinement, assault causing bodily harm." He picked up Sylvia's note again. "It seems that Miss Jeffries's injuries are serious enough to fall within the meaning of the act. By the way, Miss Jeffries is being looked after. My secretary has obtained medical attention for her. She will be fine. We have Lang on charges that could bring in a good ten or fifteen years, maybe. Long enough before he comes to trial, at any rate, for the Austrians to carry out their investigations."

"I hope you're investigating the violinist as well," said Sanders. "Do you realize that every time we went near Lang's house she was there, in the middle of things?"

"Precisely," said Higgs, nodding in a pleased sort of way at Sanders, as though he had invented him. "But you were obviously aware of her complicity," he added, turning to Hoffel.

Hoffel shook his head and grinned. "She's good, isn't she? Although I think Lang was getting a little suspicious of her in the last couple of days. I told her she would have to stop, uh, hanging around his house so frequently. You see, we hadn't been able to get anywhere near Lang on our own. But he can't resist these glamorous, artistic types, though, and so—when he seemed to become, uh, well, infatuated with her—we used it."

"Well, I'll be damned," said Higgs. "You mean she's one of your people? No wonder . . ." He turned toward Hoffel and shook his head. "Let me give you a piece of advice. The next time you have someone under cover, don't hang around staring at them all the time. I picked her out right away, only I figured her for a psycho with a Beretta in her handbag and you knew about it. No wonder Lang was getting suspicious."

Hoffel reddened and raised his hands in a gesture of acknowledgment. *"Mea culpa,"* he said. "I found it difficult to let her operate on her own."

"You have world-class musicians in your organization? That's very impressive," said Sanders.

Hoffel laughed. "No. That was the problem. She's not really in the organization. She's my friend, uh, girlfriend? Is that what you call it?"

"Only if you mean that you and she are ..." Higgs paused, looking for a precise term to cover the situation.

"Right. My girlfriend from the old days. We come from the same small town. When we both moved away, we ..." Hoffel paused as if baffled how to explain the situation. "But we hadn't seen each other for several years," he said simply, "until we met again in Vienna, and Herr Lang never discovered that I was in her background."

"Weren't you worried that he would?" asked Higgs curiously.

"Worried? At times," Hoffel answered with a suddenly grim and tight-lipped countenance.

"What was Lang up to?" asked Sanders, partly to change the subject and partly because everyone else appeared to take his mission for granted.

"Oh, to assassinate the prime minister, of course, and take over, if possible, in the ensuing chaos. He belongs to a group of maniacs in the right wing of our politics. Very difficult to deal with, because he has many friends who are reasonable people and who believe him to be a good man, conservative in nature, but loyal. We had information, from Anna Maria, of course, that his organization was going to try something here. They have, it appears," Hoffel said, turning to Deschenes, "some sort of contact of an official nature helping them in this country. You might wish to investigate that, Superintendent. Perhaps later in the evening, Miss Strelitsch and I could discuss what she has discovered with you."

"Contact?" said Deschenes in the ensuing silence.

"Yes. If you would excuse me, Superintendent, gentlemen,

I must report to my ambassador. I will return, if you wish, with Miss Strelitsch." Hoffel rose, and nodded gravely to the assembled company. Henri Deschenes rose as well and followed him out into the secretary's office.

Charlie Higgs and Ian MacMillan got to their feet as soon as the two men were out of the room. Higgs looked around him vaguely and reached for his briefcase, which was lying on a chair. "I think I ought to be going now," he said. "You people don't need me anymore."

"And I think you never needed me," said Ian MacMillan genially. "Good night, Andy."

"I really don't think you guys had better go," said Andrew Cassidy with a slightly worried frown. "I think the old man has a lot more he wanted to go into."

"So, tell him I'll call in," said MacMillan. "Look, I haven't had supper. I have to go over today's reports for any snags and revise our plans for tomorrow. I don't have time to sit around and mumble about spies and Austrian terrorist organizations. If you ask me, nothing happened today because nothing was supposed to happen. That prime minister could have walked back to Ottawa and no one would have touched him. Coming, Charlie?" And the two men walked out of the office by the rear door.

"Have Ian and Charlie left?" asked Deschenes as he came back in. He seemed neither surprised nor disturbed. "We have a few other things to ask you about, Inspector. That's why I invited Andy Cassidy to be here. He's been looking into the death of Steve Collins."

"Steve Collins?"

"Don Bartholomew to you, probably," said Cassidy. "He was under cover, for us. CSIS."

"And the regional police seem to feel that they have been stumbling across you everywhere they go. Some of it we can understand—we have heard about the business of the picture—"

"Just one thing," said Sanders. "Unofficially, off the record, no lawsuits, nothing, was it you guys who trashed my motel room? Obviously it was Lang and Green, or whatever it was that Hoffel called him, who broke into Miss Jeffries's apartment, because they had the pictures. Do you know how she is, by the way?" he asked, suddenly conscious that some time had passed since they had whisked her off.

"The doctor has been in to see her. She's fine. My secretary and the staff nurse have her tucked away in some warm corner lying down. And no, we didn't do that. At least it was not authorized from here," Deschenes added cautiously. "But when you turned up in Stittsville . . . What were you doing?"

"Trying to get Miss Jeffries's pictures back. Since we didn't have much hope of finding the man in the picture on our own, I thought I'd nose around the victim's end of things, on the assumption that Green hadn't just picked him out at random. And actually, we did find the other man in the picture, but we lost him again."

"Indeed?" said Deschenes. "And who was this man?"

"Don't know," said Sanders. "Average to tall, just under six feet, I would guess. About thirty, blond hair, tanned, slender build, very fit-looking, maybe one-hundred-fifty-five to one-hundred-sixty pounds. No obvious distinguishing marks. He was attending a conference at Carleton University and we spotted him there. He lost us very smoothly and professionally."

"Andy, could you collar someone out there to do something about it?" Cassidy got up and left the room. "It would have been very helpful, Inspector Sanders," said Deschenes, the ironic edge to his voice getting sharper and sharper, "if you had let us in on these secrets a little earlier."

"I realize that," said Sanders. "But I had a certain problem about it all." He paused. Deschenes regarded him steadily. "The local police seemed to regard me as a dangerous maniac addicted to arson. I wasn't really excited about letting anyone here know, either, because I wasn't sure what was going on. You see, when I was in Brockville, Green made a telephone call." He reached into his pocket and found the piece of heavy paper still sitting there. "To this number."

Deschenes looked at it, impassive. "Interesting. Did you recognize the number?"

Sanders shook his head. "Not at that point."

"Odd that you should write it down, then."

Sanders was about to describe the mynah bird and checked himself. No need to develop a reputation for insanity at this point. "I don't know. I'd been driving for hours on no sleep and I suppose I wasn't being very rational. I heard him punch in the numbers and jotted them down. He dialed twice, you see," added Sanders, trying to give an air of possibility to his tale. "It was the second time around that I caught the numbers."

Deschenes didn't react. "It's fortunate you were sitting close enough to the phone to hear."

"By the time he called, the place was deserted," said Sanders.

"What did he say?" asked Deschenes.

Sanders saw the trap and hedged. "He was muttering. I could hear him, but I couldn't make out the words clearly enough to get a sense of the conversation. Besides, I had no reason to try to listen in. So you see, I really didn't know what was happening."

"What in hell were you doing out in Stittsville?" asked Cassidy, who had come back in and was listening again.

"I went out to see Bartholomew's landlady," said Sanders uneasily. "An odd type. You know, beads, long hair, bare feet, and organic food. She let me see some of his stuff."

"The devil she did!" said Cassidy. "There wasn't a cracker crumb that belonged to Steve Collins in that place after Tuesday night. We cleaned out everything."

"Then you didn't look in Miranda's Christmas cake tin," said Sanders. "She was hiding stuff for him in there."

"You mean she managed to hold out on us?" said Cassidy. "Jesus! Why?"

"You turned up as the heavies, the forces of law and order," said Sanders. "And she didn't trust you. Now I turned up pretending to be an unsuccessful writer, and she thought I was pretty great." There was a certain bitterness in his tone. "Of course, since I was probably followed out there, trusting me wasn't the best thing she ever did."

"I wouldn't worry about that," said Cassidy dismissively. "Anyone who was after Steve knew he was staying at Miranda's. He never tried to hide that. What did she have?" he asked, and leaned forward across the table, his arms stiff with tension, his eyes bright with nerves.

"A notebook," said Sanders. "Entitled 'Dawn in Vienna.' It was filled with jottings in his own sort of shorthand, semiclear, most of which I can't remember because they meant nothing to me. What I could remember, I wrote down after I left the place." He reached into his inside breast pocket and took out his own notebook, opened it, and placed it in front of Cassidy. "Inside the notebook," he said, drawing out his words and conscious of an almost sadistic quality in his enjoyment of their suspense, "was a slip of paper headed up 'R.T.' " He paused again and fished into his breast pocket once more. "Here. I palmed it. Which is just as well, since you guys seem to have burned the place down along with the landlady and the notebook."

"Hey, we didn't burn the place down. We thought you did." Cassidy took the paper and opened it up very carefully. He looked at it for a while before placing it neatly in front of Deschenes. "That's it," he said. "And I suppose that's how you turned up at the Echo Drive address, too."

"Sure," said Sanders. "Does that help?" he asked innocently.

"It's our key, Inspector." Cassidy's voice danced in triumph. "The key I've been turning Ottawa upside down for."

"Clearly a simple book code," said Deschenes. "Do you know what the book is?"

"Doesn't he say?" asked Cassidy, leaning over. "Sure, there. Hardy, F.F.T.M.C."

"You have the advantage over me," said Deschenes. "I wasn't educated in English. Is this a common book?"

"Well," said Sanders, "it'll likely be Thomas Hardy." He thought for a moment. "Ah, *Far from the Madding Crowd.* It doesn't say which edition, though. There'll be a lot of them, you know."

"The one in his apartment, I imagine," said Cassidy. "He had a hell of a lot of books."

"Then take the file and get over there and see what you come up with," said Deschenes. "Just a minute," he added, raising a hand. He went over to his desk, picked up the telephone, and spoke briefly into it. "I'm sending you with an escort, Andy, in an official car. Just as well to have witnesses, I think." He sat down again at his desk. His face was gray with fatigue and he was beginning to breathe shallowly. "I think we might take a break, Inspector," he said after a minute. "The constable out there will locate Miss Jeffries for you and you might want to get some dinner if she is feeling recovered." He waved his hand in a gesture of dismissal.

The hotel corridor was quiet and deserted. Most guests were at dinner or out for the evening, many to the official events of varying levels of prestige lavishly scheduled for the end of the first day of the trade conference. The elevator stopping at the floor below made a distinctive pinging sound that could be heard in the silence of the floor. It would have taken excellent ears, though, to hear the soft footsteps on the staircase, or the door being gently opened. A tall man stepped into the carpeted hallway, glanced around to check the sequencing of the room numbers, and padded noiselessly toward the other end. When he reached Room 507, he pulled a key on a heavy tag out of his pocket and slipped it into the lock. It turned without a sound, and he opened the door a fraction of an inch. No reaction from inside the darkened room. He pushed it open a little farther. He was assuming that she would be at dinner, but he was a cautious man, and quite prepared to back discreetly out of the room again if she was in there. He stepped inside, gently pushed the door closed behind him, and blinked to accustom himself to the dim twilight created by the tightly drawn curtains.

Hands grasped him from each side at his next step, two pairs of hands. They drew his arms behind his back and snapped handcuffs around his wrists. Another hand reached out and turned on the overhead light. "Sergeant, what in hell do you think you're doing?" said the man as soon as he saw his captor.

"Sorry, Inspector Higgs, sir. Orders from the superintendent. He would like you back at headquarters."

"Like this?" said Charlie Higgs, moving his arms slightly.

"Sorry, sir." And the three men headed out toward the elevator.

An hour and a half later, Harriet Jeffries and John Sanders were sitting once more in the outer office, waiting for Superintendent Deschenes. He had come out of his office a few minutes before, this time looking not merely tired, but stricken with a hideous illness. "I'll be with you soon," he said curtly. "Something has come up."

Whatever further he might have considered saying was interrupted by the sound of rapid footsteps in the corridor outside the office. A fist was raised and banged on the glass once and then the door was flung open. It was Sergeant Carpenter, red-faced and furious-looking. "Excuse me, Superintendent," he said. "They told me downstairs that you were still in."

"What's the problem, Sergeant?" said Deschenes, pushing aside the In tray and sitting down on Sylvia's desk. "And who is that cowering behind you in the corridor?"

"It's Corporal Fletcher, sir," said Carpenter, looking even more ruffled. "And it's about him that I came in."

"Yes?"

"I was going over the reports on this afternoon's activities, sir, and I discovered that according to at least two different people, Corporal Fletcher wasn't at his station this afternoon."

"Look, Frank, I know things are tough out there. You've had a lot of problems, but so have we. More than you can imagine right now. Write it up and we'll deal with it after the conference. We can't even afford to suspend someone right now. We need every man we've got out there."

"No, sir. It's not that. I wouldn't have bothered you for a simple breach of discipline. I hope you realize that, sir. It was what he said when I called him up on it."

"And?"

"He said that he had been posted in Sector LG by a senior officer, with orders to shoot an army sniper as soon as the man fired his weapon."

"What?" said Deschenes, sitting up erect again.

"And I called Lieutenant-Colonel Williamson—he was in charge of that group of men the army lent us—and he said they didn't send a sniper. Got real mad at me, sir, said that no one had asked for army snipers, thought we did that sort of thing on our own, and on and on, like I was criticizing him for not having a sniper there. But Fletcher saw the man, said he was in army uniform and carrying a rifle. Sat in a tree, Fletcher said, facing the house. Then Fletcher said he was really bothered about it because he was supposed to shoot to kill. Fletcher's a crack shot, sir, and felt that he was capable of disabling the man temporarily without killing him. So he didn't like to kill him. Isn't that so, Corporal?"

A mutter from behind him could have been taken for assent.

"Did he say who the senior officer was?" asked Deschenes.

"No, sir, he refused to say. He said that he had been told that there would be the severest consequences if he said anything about it. So I brought him down here."

"Come into my office, Fletcher," said Deschenes, standing up again. Sanders watched the superintendent walking to his door, erect, but like a man going to the gallows.

* * *

Charlie Higgs was standing at the window, looking out at the dark outlines of the trees against the night sky, thinking of nothing of all, when the door opened to admit the two men. "Hello, Corporal," he said wearily. "What are you doing here?" Two shadowy figures lounged by the boardroom table, watching and taking notes.

"Reporting to the superintendent, sir. We had some excitement out at the secure site this afternoon."

"So I heard, Fletcher, so I heard."

"Now, Fletcher," said Deschenes sharply, "tell me who it was gave you those extraordinary orders. Right now. This needs to be sorted out tonight."

Fletcher looked around in panic. "Excuse me, sir, but I can't say, especially in front of three people who don't know anything about it, sir. I mean, I was told it was top secret, sir. That no one was to be told without authorization. I told Sergeant Carpenter too much already. And he told everyone in the outer office—"

"You mean there is no one in this room who, to your knowledge, had anything to do with those orders you were given?"

"No, sir," Fletcher said firmly, gathering up the shreds of his self-respect. "No one here."

"Once again, Inspector Higgs," said Deschenes suddenly. "What were you doing in Miss Strelitsch's hotel room?"

"I told you, Superintendent. I was afraid, sir, when I heard that Lang's organization had a contact in Ottawa, that it might be one of us, an RCMP officer," he said miserably. "And if it was one of us, she might have been in some danger, sir. With Hoffel off seeing the ambassador, I didn't want her ambushed before she could tell us what she knew. I figured she was probably safe in the hotel dining room, and so I was going to wait in her room. No one seemed to have been detailed to watch her, as far as I knew."

Deschenes pulled the telephone toward him and began to dial. He was biting his lip with impatience as he waited for the call to connect. When it was answered and he heard the voice, a brief smile flickered across his face. "Ah, Miss Strelitsch. Superintendent Deschenes. Are you all right? Good. And are you alone? Excellent. Who is with you? Good, put him on, will you? Mr. Hoffel, we may have been premature. Perhaps you could keep an eye on Miss Strelitsch until we get some more people over there. Thank you."

As he put down the phone, he looked thoughtfully at Charlie Higgs. "Charlie—" he began slowly. He was interrupted by a hurried knock on the door. He turned to see a grim-faced Andrew Cassidy looming in the doorway.

"Excuse me, Henri. Here it is." He was waving a file folder slowly in front of his face.

Deschenes looked at his watch. "You drove over to tell me this? Why didn't you call it in?"

"It only took me five minutes to get here and I didn't think it was a really terrific idea to use the phone. I didn't know who would be answering it." Cassidy placed a piece of paper on the desk. Deschenes walked over, sat down, and pulled the paper toward him.

"So it's him," he said.

"Yes, if it checks out, and I suppose it will. It's all there. Location of banks, account numbers, size and dates of deposits—two of them correlated with a couple of big drug deals. It goes back over ten years."

"Charlie, come here," Deschenes said, his finger pointing at the page. "I want him found. Check that hotel, his apartment, the train station, bus station, the airport here and at Mirabel as well," he added, looking at his watch. "He'd have just about enough time to get to Montreal by now. Take Sergeant Carpenter and get moving."

"Shall I call from here?" Higgs asked. "It'll be faster."

"No," said Deschenes. "I don't want to listen to it."

"When you find Steve's diaries, Charlie, could you let me have them? As a favor? I don't think there's anything in them you'd be interested in." Andy Cassidy turned and began to walk out of the room after Higgs. "Good night, Henri," he said.

"You reporting in?" asked Deschenes.

Cassidy shook his head. "Nothing to report, really. It was your pigeon. I just took a couple of hours out of a boring evening to pay a debt to an old friend."

"Have you eaten?" asked Deschenes.

"No, but thanks, anyway. Actually I'm going off to report to Betty Ferris. I made a promise to her—about Steve's death. I have to tell her I didn't do much, but it got done, anyway." He paused for a moment. "How long does it take a woman like Betty to get over someone's death? Do you know?"

Deschenes shook his head. "I don't know. A year, maybe? Two? If she ever does."

"Don't say that. Good night."

Inspector Ian MacMillan made his way through the labyrinthine twists of the Mirabel parking garage toward the ranks and ranks of ticket counters. He casually dropped his keys and ID in a waste container as he strode along. He had reckoned with fair accuracy the length of time it would take Deschenes to piece together anything the Strelitsch woman could tell him. He figured that gave him until 10:30 or 11:00. He had allowed himself the few minutes required to book a flight before he picked up his packed suitcase, new passport, and ticket and walked out of his Ottawa apartment for good. The crowds around the corner for boarding passes were horrendous, except at the modest first-class counter on the end. This was no moment for economy. He headed for the ticket counter, frowned when he saw the line, mentally calculated how many of the people there were merely part of each traveler's support system, and elbowed his way ruthlessly past the throng. He reached into his pocket for a handful of fifties to upgrade his ticket. His cold glare caught him the attention of a free ticket agent; for minutes that felt like hours she labored over the flimsy document. He snatched it up with his change and thrust his way back through the waiting hordes, slapped it down on the first-class counter, and found himself suddenly enveloped in the aura of privilege that accompanies the expenditure of cash.

He sat down in the first-class lounge, rejected, then accepted, a drink, stretched his long legs out in front of him, and relaxed for the first time in months, for the first time since he got wind that Steve's bulldog tenaciousness of purpose might be getting him somewhere. He had thought that once Steve shifted over to CSIS he might forget about this investigation. After all, no one else believed that there was anything to it, or at least anything anyone wanted to tangle with. Except bloody goddamn righteous Steve Collins, who couldn't let anything lie. It had been sheer bad luck that someone had decided to get rid of Maury Charbonneau. Stupid creep. Especially since the bastards who did it had been bunglers who let him live those few hours and let Collins get onto him. And he should never have trusted a fucking dealer like Green and his friend Karl Lang to clean up his mess for him. Even if they did work with Teutonic efficiency. Shit! Here's to the end of making mistakes, he said to himself, and raised his glass of Glenfiddich in a silent toast.

As he put the empty glass down, he was suddenly aware that three men were surrounding him. Three men who hadn't come in the main door to the lounge. He reached automatically into his jacket before realizing that, as a quiet and peaceable businessman, he wasn't carrying a weapon anymore.

"Inspector MacMillan?" said one of the men. He stood up without a word and walked docilely with them toward the exit.

CHAPTER 12

Saturday, May 20

Sanders stepped out of his car—rescued the night before from its resting place near Dow's Lake, two tickets neatly stuffed under the windshield wipers—and looked around him. RCMP headquarters loomed ahead, as formidable as ever, but the sun was shining benignly, and the trees and shrubs were perceptibly greener than they had been six days before. Harriet's car pulled up behind him; she honked and waved him firmly out of the parking space he was standing in. He hadn't seen her since last night, when she had pleaded exhaustion and allowed herself to be chauffeured home by a bouncy little Mountie, neatly avoiding Sanders's silent entreaty to stay with him. And here they were again. One last confrontation and that was it. One more statement and he could head off wherever he wanted to go—home to Toronto, anywhere for a week of leave. His head reeled with indecision as they walked in tense silence up to the entrance.

By the time they had recounted—separately, to two separate and patient interviewers—everything that should have been said last night, and hadn't been, it was well past noon. Sanders stepped into the corridor and found Harriet standing there, looking uncomfortable. He made an awkward gesture toward her and seized her hand abruptly.

"Wait," said Harriet. "Let's not say good-bye in a place like this." She waved her other hand around and winced. "It smells of law enforcement."

"Thanks," said Sanders. "What's that supposed to mean?"

"Nothing much," she said coolly. "I'm starved. How about lunch before you leave Ottawa? On me. In gratitude for getting my pictures back."

"Lunch sounds like a wonderful idea," said a voice behind them. "And I have another picture for you, Miss Jeffries." Henri Deschenes was walking toward them, trailing Anna Maria Strelitsch and Carlo Hoffel behind him. "Why don't you join us? And I will make a formal presentation of it to you. The original slide. We have taken the copy and the print. You see, we can tell the difference." Harriet glared at Sanders.

"I'm glad it wasn't Higgs," said Sanders, putting his knife and fork down on his empty plate and reaching for his wineglass. "Although I would willingly have locked him in a dungeon for putting us through all those dreary lectures."

"They weren't his idea," said Deschenes dryly. "He was as irritable about them as you people were." He leaned back in his chair and pushed away his glass. "Anyway, I'm glad it wasn't Charlie, too. I had a few bad moments when it seemed to be pointing in his direction. But I couldn't imagine him on the take. Drunk, maybe, or violent, overstepping the line with someone, but not on the take."

"Is Inspector MacMillan a big man?" asked Harriet. "With sandy hair and north-of-England cheekbones?"

"Not those again!" groaned Sanders. "What in hell do you mean by that, Harriet?"

"A bony face, very strong, with forehead and cheekbones that stand out like this." As she spoke her hands flashed over her face, creating a brilliantly clear picture.

"Un visage Normand," said Deschenes quietly. "A Norman face. Yes. That's him."

"I saw him coming out of Lang's house yesterday afternoon, but of course I didn't know who he was."

"Everyone connected with the affair seemed to know something crucial," said Deschenes, "and no one put it all together. Except Steve. And he didn't have a chance to tell anyone."

"But why did your Mr. Green kill Steve?" asked Harriet. "He had nothing to do with him, did he?

"He's *not* my Mr. Green," protested Sanders.

"That's simple," said Anna Maria Strelitsch, suddenly looking up from her chocolate and Grand Marnier sundae and waving her spoon in Harriet's direction. "He did it for Inspector MacMillan. As a favor, I think you would say."

"They seem like pretty strange buddies to me," said Sanders. "Was MacMillan on counterespionage?"

"I don't know," said Anna Maria, scraping the last of the chocolate sauce from the dish. "But that's not how they met. Or at least I don't think it is. Karl recruited Groenwald—that is, Green—because he had useful connections with the criminal world. Drugs, mainly, I believe. He was into"—she waved her spoon again—"the import-export trade."

Deschenes nodded gloomily. "When Ian was on immigration detail in Montreal."

Anna Maria shook her head vigorously in agreement. "And Green and MacMillan already knew each other when

Green joined the movement. Anyway, there was a trade. Your Inspector MacMillan arranged things so that the sniper Lang hired could kill our prime minister, and in return Groenwald—Green—killed your Mr. Collins. Of course, it was—was it not?—to Green's advantage to have Collins dead. Because he was also investigating Dawn in Vienna. Lang's organization. But I am not sure if Green realized that. There were things that they did not discuss in front of me. I believe they thought that no one really threatened them. Except you, Fräulein, and your picture."

"I still don't understand why the picture was so important," said Harriet. "Perhaps I'm being stupid, but really. John and endless other people had seen Mr. Green, hadn't they? And people had seen him with Lang, too."

"Ah, but your picture was the only thing we know about that connected Green, and therefore Lang, with the sniper," said Deschenes. "It seems that he wasn't supposed to leave the secure site alive. Dead, they were planning to blame him for the deaths of Steve Collins *and* the prime minister. The perfect villain to wrap up our case for us, nice and neat. That picture would give the game away."

"How could they be sure that he wouldn't get away?" asked Sanders.

"Very easily. Our local sharpshooter had been ordered to finish him off as soon as the prime minister was shot at. MacMillan fed him some wild romance about the prime minister being in a bulletproof vehicle and perfectly safe. He was a great talker, Ian MacMillan was. And he certainly baffled poor Bill Fletcher."

"I would not give much for this Fletcher's chances for survival if the assassination plan had worked," said Hoffel. "Surely he would have identified MacMillan."

Deschenes shook his head. "I don't know whether MacMillan was planning to leave anyway, or if he had something else ready to silence Bill Fletcher. Of course, you know, he baffled all of us—screwing up the intelligence reports from time to time just enough to confuse what was going on, and sitting back laughing as I tried to make head or tail out of them. It must have given him great joy to watch me," Deschenes added with a sigh. "He never quite got used to the idea of working for a frog."

Anna Maria Strelitsch frowned in lack of comprehension. "A frog?" she whispered to Harriet. "*Einen Frosch?* Why was he working for a frog?"

"A Frenchman," said Harriet, trying not to laugh. "From Quebec. M. Deschenes. They don't usually call themselves that, though," she added in sudden alarm. "It's not exactly—"

"I understand," said the violinist, "I think."

"Did you get the sniper?" asked Sanders.

"We should have," said Deschenes. "That photograph is magnificent. But I think he probably was out of the country before dinnertime yesterday. We've been able to use it to confirm that he wasn't the person who broke into your motel room. Nor was he the person who was hanging around Mrs. Cruikshank's house just before the fire."

"That was MacMillan? Both times?" asked Hoffel. "The other man with light-colored hair?"

"Without a doubt," said Deschenes. "When we find his weapon, we'll be able to check it against the bullets in Mrs. Cruikshank and her dog."

"Why did he have to kill the dog?" said Harriet fiercely. "That seems—"

"It's better than leaving it to die in the fire," said Sanders. "It shows a certain elementary humanity in the man. But there's one more thing. Can anyone tell me who in hell was following us all over the countryside? Everywhere we went, there was this car—"

"Karl was paying an exorbitant sum of money to some unimportant sort of person to find out where you were and get those pictures back," said Anna Maria. "He used to call Karl every two or three hours to explain where he was and why he didn't have the pictures yet and leave him in a terrible rage. I am very glad that it is over," she said. "I'm glad it is all over." She shook her blond hair out of her eyes, and looked sideways at Hoffel. "It is time we left, Carlo," she murmured. "There is another reception tonight and I must practice." Whereupon the burly head of security for the Austrian delegation leaped to his feet and began making their excuses. "He is well trained, is he not?" she whispered to Harriet, and winked.

"It's time we left as well," said Harriet. She stood up and laid a hand on Sanders's shoulder. "You have a long drive ahead of you." And amid a flurry of meaningless phrases and exclamations, the party scattered into the parking lot.

Sanders walked over to Harriet's car. "I could," he said, leaning down and looking in her window, "postpone my return for a day or so."

"You look exactly as though you're about to give me a ticket," said Harriet, laughing. She caught the look on his face and resumed her usual expression of grave sobriety. "I don't know," she said uncertainly. "There is always the possibility of stone architecture in the Ottawa Valley for a couple of days. Once I get my equipment together again. There are some very pretty towns. Very quiet," she added.

"Why don't I meet you in the parking garage and we'll talk about it over a pint?"

"I'll buy if you can get there ahead of me," said Harriet and winked. She eased the car into gear and left him standing in a shower of dust and gravel.